Scorch

Scorch

Marc Paoletti

FIVE STAR
A part of Gale, Cengage Learning

Detroit • New York • San Francisco • New Haven, Conn • Waterville, Maine • London

Five Star Publishing, a part of Gale, Cengage Learning.

Set in 11 pt. Plantin

Printed on permanent paper.

LIBRARY OF CONGRESS CATALOGING-IN-PUBLICATION DATA

Paoletti, Marc.
Scorch / Marc Paoletti. — 1st ed.
p. cm.
ISBN-13: 978-1-59414-657-2 (alk. paper)
ISBN-10: 1-59414-657-8 (alk. paper)
1. Pyrotechnists—Fiction. I. Title.
PS3616.A54S35 2008
813'.6—dc22 2007047786

First Edition. First Printing: May 2008.

Published in 2008 in conjunction with Tekno Books and Ed Gorman.

Printed in the United States of America
1 2 3 4 5 6 7 12 11 10 09 08

To Mom and Dad for the love you've given and continue to give.

ACKNOWLEDGMENTS

Hordes of cool people helped make this book a reality.

Sincerest thanks to the staff of the Grossman Burn Center at Sherman Oaks Hospital for the walk-through and for being tireless angels of mercy; Paul Staples, senior pyrotechnician and founder of Hollywood Special Effects, for giving me the coolest job I've ever had; Tom Chesney and Image Engineering, Inc., for giving a young punk a chance (and letting him on-set during that shower scene); Don McNichols, senior pyrotechnician, for notes on the cool contraptions; Joseph Viskocil, Academy Award–winning pyrotechnician, for making movies fun to watch; Mike Black for generous help with the submission; Donald C. Lacher, Police Captain Retired, and Jerry Robinson, Arson Investigator Retired, for sharing what they know, and they know plenty.

Big wet kisses to Kimberly Goldstein and Milo the cow-eyed Chihuahua for letting me hide out any time I need for as long as I need; Amy Hammond for impeccable pirate-counting; Nathan Walpow for kind words and the Succulent Queen; Bret Battles for sharing first drafts; Graham McDougal for boundless friendship and fine scotch; Tom O'Leary for being my way-back partner-in-crime; the Chicago Writers Group for constant inspiration; the Los Angeles Writers Group for making It possible; and the MFA Fiction Department at Columbia College in Chicago for teaching me a few things.

Heartfelt grins to Jeff Mikos at Slushpile.com for answering my dumb computer questions and creating a landing pad for writers; Scott Miles for walking the path; and Chauncey Hollingsworth at Zephyr Syndicate for creating the Web site for this book. Check it out at www.scorchthenovel.com and visit the Syndicate at www.zephyrsyndicate.com.

Jittery, caffeinated nods to Candice C. Ziol and Donald D. Ziol and the staff at Bean Addiction Coffee in Chicago for letting me write there all day for the modest price of one delicious iced coffee.

Also, thanks to the kind, consummate professionals at Tekno Books and Five Star, especially Martin H. Greenberg, John Helfers, Hugh Abramson, Tiffany Schofield, and Alja Collar, and to the jacket designer, Chris Wait.

Finally, infinite love and thanks to those who went far beyond the call: Chris Lacher, my brother in spirit, for getting me started; Jim Paine for being a great friend and royal pain in the ass; William Relling, Jr., for friendship and unflagging support—we miss you, pal; Mort Castle, one of the finest people I know, for teaching me the value of telling a Story; Patricia Pinianski/Rosemoor for friendship, professional know-how, and bottomless margaritas; and Tracy McGowan for too much to go into here. . . . I'd be lost without you, angel.

Needless to say, any mistakes in this book are my fault, though I should mention that I tweaked and/or omitted certain details about the explosives so people with a Jackass bent will be less likely to hurt themselves. This book is for entertainment purposes only, okay?

“Battle not with monsters lest you become one.”

—Friedrich Nietzsche

Chapter 1

David Cole couldn't let the man get to him. Not when he had only ten minutes to get the shot. The morning sun was rising fast over the Santa Susana Mountains, and soon it would be obvious that this part of the scene had been filmed during a different time of day.

"I repeat, don't touch anything, Brandenburg, and wait for my cue," he said into the walkie-talkie.

"This is bullshit!" came the crackling reply.

Wiping his brow in the July heat, Cole surveyed the arid movie set, which was dressed like a battle zone in the first Iraq War. Scorched sand, trenches lined with concertina wire, a shattered concrete bunker, machine-gun nests . . . his stomach twisted.

The scene was accurate enough to bring back memories of that terrible night, the worst of his life, but he pushed the thoughts away and concentrated instead on the order of pyrotechnic gags: bullet-hits in the sand, grenade effect in the bunker, missile effect near the wire, landmine effect around the nests. And then the distant ranch house, renovated to look like an Iraqi stronghold, blows up. Big.

It was all about ready to go.

But even though the scene was make-believe, thankfully, the danger to cast and crew was very fucking real.

The pyrotechnics he'd rigged were no joke—blends of gasoline, black powder, and high-grain explosive, they'd detonate huge with scorching, concussive fury.

Ned Brandenburg's voice crackled over the walkie-talkie. "You're hidin' us away in here! I'm gonna tell my uncle to fire your ass!"

Cole ignored the call. As special effects supervisor, he considered safety his top priority, and therefore critical that he keep the idiots on the other end of the walkie-talkie in line.

Brandenburg and his partner Levar Watkins were sloppy, no-talent pyros, making them as dangerous as the explosives themselves. A crossed wire. A mishandled connection. It didn't take much to cause horrific bodily injury, or worse. Lives were literally at risk when shooting a scene like this.

Even so, Cole couldn't bounce the men from set. Not when they'd been hired by Gary Stanford, the film studio's president, who also happened to be Brandenburg's uncle. All he could do was give them out-of-the-way, idiot-proof tasks.

He'd indeed stuck the men away in the detonator's shed, and given them responsibility for the stronghold. Constructed of solid steel, the shed would protect them while providing a close and unobstructed view to safely trigger the explosives. Brandenburg and Watkins had only to push one button. One. They couldn't possibly screw that up.

Cole raked back his steel-gray hair, then checked his watch. Shit. In fifteen years as a pyro, he'd never missed a cue. He wasn't about to start now.

He jogged toward his son who wore a blue-and-white Dodger cap, and was rigging bullet hits on an extra playing a doomed Iraqi soldier. Yep, this was nepotism, too. But this worked. "How's it coming?"

Ronny pulled out his earbuds, and Cole could hear the faint strains of "Master of Puppets" by Metallica, the kid's favorite album to work by. "Just about finished, Dad."

Cole peered over Ronny's shoulder to examine his progress.

The soldier wore a sleeveless mesh vest covered with tiny pockets, each of which contained a dime-sized explosive squib that would mimic a bullet strike when covered by a uniform and detonated. Also in the pockets were thin metal plates to protect the actor and condoms filled with Karo syrup, condensed milk and red food coloring—the perfect blood mix. Each squib had its own wire, which Ronny had bundled together and taped along the inside of the soldier's right arm. He was now attaching the bundle to a handheld trigger so the soldier could detonate the squibs when shot by the hero. It was good, tight work. At twenty-one, Ronny was equal to a powder-man years his senior.

"Five minutes," Cole said.

Ronny nodded, kept working.

Cole jogged away into the special effects staging area. Cordoned off with orange cones, it was located a safe fifty yards from the machine-gun nests and bunker, and one hundred yards from the stronghold. He stood behind a long table, which held a shoebox-sized wireless triggering device called a hellbox. Across the top were four red buttons, each corresponding to an explosion that would be detonated during the scene. After triple-checking the hellbox, he triple-checked the nailboard next to it—a six-foot plank bristling with nails that had wires coiled around them that led to squibs on set. The car battery at his feet had a striker wire attached to the positive lead which, when run across the nails, would close the electrical circuits and detonate the squibs. The nailboard was old-school, but Cole believed Ronny should be skilled at fundamentals, too.

Soon after, Ronny appeared beside him without the earbuds now. He'd need to hear Jennifer's cues. "Good-to-go, Dad."

Cole nodded as Jennifer Shrager, the film's director, called to him from behind the staging area. "How are we doing, David?"

He turned. Jennifer sat behind a Panavision Digital camera—

one of six positioned around set to get full coverage of the dramatic scene—looking at him with apprehension in her green eyes. Though harried, her chiseled, elegant features maintained a sort of regal calm. Cole noticed that even her long brown hair seemed to move with grace.

"One second, Jen," he called back, then said into his walkie-talkie, "You ready, Brandenburg?"

"Uh, yeah," came the muddled reply.

The man's voice sounded strained. "You okay in there?"

"Just fuckin' relax, willya? Let's do this thing."

Cole shook his head. Asshole. "We're ready when you are, Jen!" he said, and then told Ronny, "Remember to stay focused until the director says cut."

Ronny nodded and took his position at the nailboard.

"Camera!" Jennifer yelled.

"Speed!" the director of photography yelled when all the cameras were running.

"Annnnnnd action!"

The movie was called *Bringing Them Back,* the story of Marine Corps Sergeant Rocky Slaughter who single-handedly assaults an Iraqi stronghold to save a pair of downed airmen. Heavy on flash, light on substance, Cole knew. But these types of movies kept him in business.

A moment later, he watched Rocky Slaughter run onto set shirtless, muscles oiled and bulging as he hefted an M-60 machine gun. An Iraqi soldier in front of him raised his AK-47 assault rifle to open fire. Too late! Slaughter's M-60, loaded with blank ammunition, thundered and spouted flame.

Taking the cue, Ronny dragged the striker wire across the nails, triggering squibs buried in the dirt in front of the soldier, imitating near-miss bullet strikes. A split-second later, the Iraqi soldier triggered his handheld device and convulsed as blood sprayed from the blood packs that Ronny had wired on him.

Ronny pumped his fist in excitement as the effect went off flawlessly. Cole clapped him on the shoulder, sharing his triumph.

Slaughter yanked a grenade from his belt, pulled the pin with his teeth and lobbed it at two more Iraqi soldiers who ran at him from within the shattered concrete bunker.

Cole pushed the first button on the hellbox, setting off a black powder "hard-pack" charge—a plastic freezer baggie filled with four ounces of fine-grain powder and bound tight with duct tape—which threw up a fountain of dirt and smoke. At that same moment, the soldiers stepped onto hidden nitrogen-powered air rams that catapulted them eight feet into the air, making it look like they'd been pitched forward by the concussion.

Slaughter ran another few feet, prompting Cole to push the second button, which ignited a three-gallon plastic jug mounted on a metal plate that was filled with gasoline and wrapped with detonation cord. The jug exploded into a fifteen-foot fireball that mimicked an anti-tank missile strike.

"Keep an eye on the machine-gun nests," Cole whispered to Ronny. "That's where I put the shotgun mortars you loaded."

Slaughter vaulted a roll of concertina wire, and then broke a tripwire stretched between two machine gun nests piled high with sandbags. As soon as the tripwire snapped, Cole pressed the third and fourth button on the hellbox to trigger the shotgun mortar hidden in each nest. The narrow, three-foot-long metal cylinders were sealed on one end and loaded with gasoline, sawdust to give the fire shape and weight, chunks of harmless fiberboard to act as shrapnel with a black powder hard-pack "kicker" to propel the mix. With a hollow cough, the mortars belched jets of flaming debris that crossed dramatically behind Slaughter to simulate the detonation of claymore mines.

"Perfect!" Ronny exclaimed, smiling, but quickly returned his focus to set. He knew which cue was coming next: The stronghold.

Slaughter kept running, gripping the M-60 with both hands, face strained with exertion. When he was a few feet away from the stronghold, he tugged another grenade from his belt and lobbed it through the open door. Then he turned and ran like hell.

A few steps more, Cole thought as Slaughter cleared the machine gun nests and vaulted the concertina wire. He plucked the walkie-talkie from his belt and pushed the key button as Slaughter cleared the blown-out bunker . . .

"Now, Brandenburg!" he said into his walkie-talkie, preparing for the massive explosion that would tear the stronghold apart. But nothing happened.

He heard Jennifer behind him, "Where's the explosion? Cue the explosion!"

"Brandenburg!" he tried again, but got only static.

He turned and faced the small army of filmmakers arrayed behind him, who stared at him questioningly. Jennifer had an expression of horror and apology on her face.

He held up both hands to make sure the crew stayed away from the stronghold as his mind swarmed with the stronghold's wiring schematics, unable to conjure his mistake. What could have gone wrong? And then a thought chilled him.

Misfire.

Inside the stronghold, he'd rigged eight "V-pan" mortars in a tight cluster with the open ends facing up and out at thirty-degree angles. Set twenty-four inches off the ground on sandbags, each quarter-inch steel mortar was three feet long, two feet wide and deep, and was loaded with a twenty-gallon trash bag filled with gasoline that sat on a ten-ounce, black-powder kicker. The wide-mouthed V-pans would expand the blast, making an already huge explosion even bigger, and the

100-grain det cord he'd laced the ceiling with would go off a split second earlier, incinerating the roof and allowing the explosion to roll free. It was a fireball they'd see from space—and now it could detonate without warning.

He shouted into his walkie-talkie, "Brandenburg? Watkins? If you can hear me, stay where you are! Do not leave the shed, do you copy? DO NOT LEAVE THE SHED!"

"What's going on, Dad?" Ronny asked.

"I want you to keep everyone away from the stronghold."

"Where are you going?"

"Just do as I say!" he said, and bolted onto the set.

After sending Slaughter and the Iraqi soldiers scurrying back toward Ronny, he kept running, trying not to think about how the stronghold could detonate at any moment. Reaching the shed, he burst through the door, ready to usher Brandenburg and Watkins to safety. But what he saw stopped him cold. The hellbox was on the ground, cracked open with wires exposed, and the two men were working desperately to put it back together.

The problem wasn't a misfire, Cole realized. But negligence. And with the hellbox wires exposed, an errant radio wave or bit of static electricity could have set off the stronghold explosion prematurely. "What the hell is going on here?"

Brandenburg and Watkins looked up in surprise, and then stood and backed away. Cole dropped to one knee and twisted together the exposed wires, shunting them.

"Get off my set," he said. "Now."

Brandenburg stepped close. He was six-five to Watkins' six-two, with greasy red hair drawn back into a long ponytail. Watkins was bald with skin the color of pitch. Each was clad in a white T-shirt and soiled blue jeans, and reminded Cole of dinosaurs: lumbering, loud, brains the size of walnuts.

"Read the fine print, asshole," Brandenburg said. "I'm a lifer on this project."

Cole stood. "I don't give a shit whose nephew you are."

Scowling, Brandenburg snapped open a buck knife and lunged. Cole grabbed Brandenburg's knife-hand, twisted, then smashed an elbow into his chin. Brandenburg dropped to his knees, the knife tumbling from his slack fingers. Cole stooped to grab it, and on his way up, Watkins took a swing at him. Cole ducked and countered with a blow to the solar plexus, his fist punching into the man's soft gut. Watkins doubled over, wheezing.

"Pack up your shit and get out," Cole said. He folded the knife closed, stuck it in his pocket, and stalked back into the staging area where Ronny was pulling the spent wires from the nailboard. "I'm sorry about snapping at you before, son."

Ronny continued to work on the wires. "No problem, Dad. I know you were trying to keep everybody safe."

Cole continued to where Jennifer was standing at the camera. "Brandenburg and Watkins broke open the hellbox somehow."

"Oh my God," she gasped, realizing the danger.

"I told them to get the hell out."

"David, you're aware that Ned is Gary Stanford's—"

"I don't care who he is," Cole interrupted, beyond compromising now. "This could have ended in disaster."

She nodded. "You're absolutely right."

"I shouldn't have let them on set in the first place."

"We're all safe, that's all that matters." She paused and looked around. "Well, we can shoot the stronghold explosion separately and splice it in later. Not as good as a single shot, but it'll do."

"I'm afraid it's not that simple," he said. "Brandenburg and Watkins were in and out of the stronghold all day. Who knows what else they could have screwed up? I need to double-check every wire. Every connection."

"David, we can't afford the time."

"I'm not asking."

"I agree with you, believe me, but I can't make a decision that would compromise the schedule."

"I'm not asking you to," he said, walking away.

"Where are you going?" she called after him.

"To talk with Gary Stanford."

Gary Stanford sped between cars on Santa Monica Boulevard en route to his Century City office. He preferred a late morning commute, after rush hour, so he could enjoy what his BMW Z8 Alpina was designed to do. He casually gripped the leather-covered steering wheel with both hands, nudging the wheel left, then right, to whisk past a blue minivan going the forty mile-per-hour speed limit.

Were the morning like most others, he would be enjoying this little exercise of power. But due to factors outside his control, he most decidedly was not.

"Maybe you didn't make the urgency of our situation clear," he said.

"We're already borrowing against the future earnings of *Bringing Them Back,*" replied Janet Skinner, his Head of Development. The woman's voice issued from the car's Bose speakers in digital clarity. He heard the rustling of paper—spreadsheets no doubt—before Skinner followed up with, "We may be able to renegotiate our production contracts and free up some capital."

"Time is a luxury we don't have, Janet," said Steven Huxley, his chief financial officer. "We needed that money *yesterday.*"

"I'm telling you, Steven, the bank won't budge."

Stanford jammed the car into fourth gear and punched the accelerator, watching as the traffic outside his windshield transformed into a multicolored blur.

"If we fail to front Anne Devereaux the two million, we'll lose credibility," said Huxley. "We'll never be able to attract the type of talent it takes to get a major project like *Mothers and Daughters* off the ground again."

"Believe me, I'm doing everything I can," Janet said.

Stanford frowned. For whatever reason, slasher films and erotic thrillers were no longer in vogue. As a result, Loki Productions was hemorrhaging money. *Bringing Them Back* was his appeal to patriotism, always a solid bet. But his ace-in-the-hole was *Mothers and Daughters,* a story about survivors of incest that promised to connect with a more sophisticated audience. With Anne Devereaux on board, the film would garner mainstream press coverage and save his company from bankruptcy. It would also catapult him from B-list to A-list producer.

"No more excuses, Janet," Stanford said. "Get it done."

Before Janet could respond, Tammi Cross, his executive secretary, came on the line. "Gary," she said. "There's a problem on set."

He sighed. "What kind?"

"Ned was fired by the special effects supervisor."

"I'm the only one who can hire and fire members of the crew. Fire the supervisor and tell Ned to go back to work."

"You'll have the chance to tell him yourself."

"Who? Ned?"

"No, David Cole, the special effects supervisor. He's on his way over to see you now."

"The ex-SEAL? For God's sake, stop him in the lobby. The last thing I need is some raving veteran in my office," he said. There was a beep as Tammi disconnected. "Steven?"

"I'm still here, Gary," Huxley said.

"Be in my office in fifteen minutes."

Stanford pushed a button on his steering wheel to hang up. As he continued to weave in and out of traffic, his thoughts settled momentarily on Brandenburg. So his nephew had gotten himself into trouble. Hardly a surprise.

If he hadn't promised his sister before she died that he would look after her son, he would have cut the boy loose long ago. At thirty, Brandenburg was still more or less an adolescent. Yes, his father had abandoned the family when he was eleven, but to Stanford, that was no excuse. His own father had been murdered when he was eight years old, yet here he was, ruler of his own empire, which included a Hollywood production company. And he was on the verge of accomplishing much more.

A minute later, he was pulling into the vast underground garage of Excelsior Tower. He left his car with the valet, and then took the garage elevator to the thirty-fifth floor—the top floor of the building. The doors opened onto a marble lobby with large, brass letters mounted on the opposite mirrored wall that read: LOKI PRODUCTIONS.

Exiting the elevator, he took a moment to examine his reflection. At fifty, he was holding up well. His black hair was free of all but the subtlest hint of gray at the temples, his eyes were a clear, piercing blue, and his skin was still smooth. As always, he wore a tailored suit—today's choice was charcoal with a red patterned tie—and he required the same level of dress from his staff. Although he'd spent most of his life in L.A., he eschewed the relaxed look so prevalent in the city. A sloppy wardrobe could send the wrong signal, and he would not risk the outcome of a business deal on a variable so easily controlled.

He smoothed his tie, and then pushed through a pair of glass doors into a thickly carpeted reception area. He noticed that the buxom receptionist smiled uncomfortably as he walked by. Fine, he thought. The entire staff should know that he was unsatisfied with their performance on the Devereaux project.

He continued down the hall and into his corner office. It was his home away from home: a white leather sofa, marble bar, bookcases filled with gold-embossed volumes, antique paintings, plush white carpeting. Nearly half the size of a football field, three walls were made of glass, providing a spectacular view of Century City and beyond. The fourth wall was covered with photos of him shaking hands with such Hollywood luminaries as David Geffen and Michael Eisner.

Steven Huxley was there, seated on the couch, wearing a dark blue suit and black tie. As Stanford walked to his desk, he thought, not for the first time, how robust the man looked for seventy years old. His posture was strong, his hazel eyes were focused, and his snowy hair was full, not showing the least hint of thinning. Stanford would consider himself very lucky if he looked so good in twenty years.

Stanford sat behind his desk, uncapped a bottle of water, took a sip, and said, "What the hell is going on, Steven?"

Huxley shook his head. "It'll be a miracle if we can come up with Devereaux's retainer. I thought we might have more leverage with the banks, but the box office returns from our last few films didn't help."

"I authorized squeezing funds from other assets."

"Yes, and we may still come up short. You know how the game is played."

Stanford knew. Organized crime was a brutal art, but it was also a subtle one. If you didn't squeeze hard enough, you could lose your territories to competing syndicates. But if you squeezed too hard, you risked insubordination and attracting the attention of law enforcement. They could extort only so much from drugs and prostitution in the short term.

The irony was that Stanford had founded Loki Productions to launder money from his other businesses. But after he'd sampled Hollywood glamour, he'd worked like hell to make it their biggest asset.

He cursed under his breath. The very quality about Devereaux that made her marketable was causing the problem. Were she a lesser-known actress, they might be able to stall the retainer. But she was a recent Academy Award winner. If they didn't commit to her now, she would move on to another project, and the damage to Loki would be done.

"Can we get anyone else in time?" he asked.

"Incest is risky material, Gary. Since Devereaux cut her teeth in independent films, she thrives on risk. It's what makes her marketable. But I wouldn't hold my breath for Julia Roberts to come calling."

Stanford slammed a fist on the desk with such force that the Evian bottle fell onto its side and spilled water across the desk. Making no move to clean up the mess, he swiveled his chair and peered out the window at the late morning sun rising over the city. With this deal, he could produce films with real budgets and real star power. With real earnings. He could rise to the level of Hollywood luminaries hanging on his wall.

Huxley said, "You've already accomplished more than most."

"It's not enough. Not yet."

For Stanford, succeeding in Hollywood was not a matter of ego. It was a matter of legacy. He would not compromise his father's sacrifices by failing when success was so very close.

"It's not enough," he repeated. "Not for the man my father wanted me to be. Not for the man my father was."

Huxley took a breath. "There's also the matter of our silent partners, Gary. We've already lost a considerable amount of money these last couple years. Losing this deal on top of that will not go over well with them. Not well at all. Forgive me for saying so, but aspirations aside, we could be in real trouble."

Stanford nodded. He knew the danger.

As a boy, he'd seen the way in which his father had conducted business—an approach that used legitimate means when necessary, but one built fundamentally on manipulation, intimidation and violence. His father, wanting an heir to his criminal throne, made no effort to insulate him from it. But as smart and successful as his father had been, he hadn't been smart enough to cheat death when his partners had taken out a contract on him. Stanford didn't know what mistakes his father had made, he only knew that Huxley, his uncle, had subsequently taken him from New York—and from his mother—to start anew in Los Angeles. And now, after decades of following in his family's successful footsteps, he was perilously close to suffering his father's fate.

"My father . . ." Stanford's voice trailed off as he turned to face Huxley.

"Your father was a great man. You are truly his son."

"He seemed unafraid, even toward the end."

"He took solace in his conviction. He was unafraid to do what it took get the job done." Huxley looked at him evenly. "Unafraid to use bold, ruthless action for bold gain—as are you, Gary. Never forget that. Your father raised you to be a survivor. A warlord. *A conqueror.*"

"He gave me everything I need."

"Seeing all that you possess, he would be proud."

But survival itself was not enough. It hadn't been for his father, nor could it be for him. "You're right, of course," Stanford said, snapping out of the fugue. "Though we had better find this opportunity for bold action soon, Steven. For both our sakes."

As Cole ascended in the elevator, he felt his anger build. By hiring Brandenburg and Watkins, Stanford had disregarded the film crew's safety. Most importantly, Ronny's safety.

Watching his son on set had filled him with pride, as it always did. But more than work, he felt extraordinarily lucky at how close they'd become. Cole had lost a wife to ovarian cancer, but Ronny had lost his mother. It had been devastating for both of them, and the trauma could have torn them apart. But instead, they'd helped each other cope, which had cemented their bond. They trusted each other implicitly, which was important for any relationship—especially one that involved such a dangerous profession.

Cole scowled. He'd be damned if he'd let Stanford put his son at risk. He'd known military officers like that: so engrossed in their own goals that they compromised the well-being of those around them. To Cole, the attitude was, and always had been, unacceptable. This was not a time for tact, he knew. Men like this responded only to confrontation. He exited on the thirty-fifth floor, entered the lobby.

"Sir," the receptionist said firmly, attempting to stop him. So someone had warned Stanford that he was coming. "I've been told not to—"

Without waiting for her to finish, Cole blew past and continued down a hallway lined with publicity posters for films with titles like *Coed Killer, Beauty and the Beach, Spring Break Bonanza,* and *Some Babe to Watch Over Me.*

A class act all the way, Cole thought, winding through a multitude of cubicles until he spotted the corner office. He stormed past a pretty blonde woman who had the tight, professional posture of an executive secretary, then burst through a lacquered mahogany door.

Stanford was there, seated behind a large desk while an older man sat on a white leather couch. The older man rose to intercede, but Stanford waved him off. "We'll continue our discussion later, Steven. Thank you."

The older man looked hard at Cole for several moments before walking out of the office and closing the door behind him.

"Your nephew screwed up today," Cole told him.

"I heard."

"He also pulled a knife on me." Cole placed the buck knife

on the edge of the desk. Stanford's eyes flashed toward it and back without a change in his expression. Like a big reptile watching birds in the swamp. "You don't seem too bothered."

"I'm not. There's no use dwelling on it. We have a schedule to keep."

"Look, people could have been hurt." He moved in front of the desk. "My *son* could have been hurt."

"Was he?"

"Fortunately, no."

"Fine," Stanford said, "then let's make one thing clear. By firing Ned, you overstepped your bounds."

Unbelievable, Cole thought. The man was dismissing the issue. "I had no choice. I wanted to keep the crew safe."

"That is no longer your concern. As I said, I do not tolerate insubordination. My production manager is searching for your replacement as we speak."

Cole shook his head. The guy was some piece of work. "Good luck. As special effects supervisor, only I know the wiring schematics. No effects guy in the city would be foolish enough to tinker with explosives he hasn't wired himself."

Cole felt a measure of satisfaction when a look of defeat briefly darkened the producer's face. His assessment had been right. Men like Stanford had to be cornered into compromise.

"What do you want, Mr. Cole?"

"I want those two yo-yos to keep the hell away from set. We're lucky nobody got hurt, and I want to keep it that way."

Stanford let out a measured breath. "Ned assured me that he and his partner were up to the job. Consider them gone."

"We're not through yet. I need at least two days to double-check every wire, every charge, and every connection in the stronghold. God only knows what else your nephew may have screwed up."

"Out of the question. I'll lose my location."

"Buy it back."

"New permits, contracts and labor will cost close to a quarter million dollars."

"The demand is nonnegotiable."

"I agreed to remove Ned from set. With this matter, you will make do."

Cole placed both hands on the desk and leaned forward, still unable to believe that Stanford was arguing. "No, *you'll* make do, or I'll report your unsafe practices to the deputy fire marshal and have the production shut down."

Stanford's face clouded. "If we lose this location, I might as well shut down the production myself."

"You should have thought of that before hiring your nephew."

Cole could see the man weighing his options like the politicians who'd sent his SEAL Team on missions. Everything was a matter of "justifiable" body count—as long as the body count didn't include them. He'd once been blind to the terrible irony. Now it made him sick.

"Tell me what you want," Stanford said finally.

"I just did."

"An additional ten thousand dollars, payable before the end of post-production?"

"You've got to be kidding," Cole said. "We're talking about the safety of your crew."

"Have you ever produced a film, Mr. Cole?" Stanford said. "There's more at stake than you realize. Much more."

"I realize exactly," he said. "People like you never think about the consequences of your actions."

"I warn you to reconsider."

"I'll be waiting for your decision," Cole said, and then left the office. Let the bastard try to come after him.

Chapter 2

"You're not wearing that inside, are you?" Ronny asked.

Cole put the truck in park, and then looked down at the long-sleeved green shirt he was wearing. "What's wrong with it? Should I have worn something else?"

Ronny laughed. "Relax, Dad, you look fine."

Cole shook his head. "I should have flushed you down the toilet as a baby."

"Don't worry, she likes you," Ronny said, still chuckling. "She's always giving you eyes on set. Besides, she invited you to dinner, didn't she?"

"She wants to discuss my meeting with Gary Stanford."

"Please tell me you aren't this naive, Dad."

He smiled. The truth was, the mere thought of Jennifer Shrager caused warmth to flood his face and body. *Bringing Them Back* was their third project together. Since meeting her on an action film called *Under the Radar* a couple of years ago, he'd grown to respect her professionalism and enjoy the pleasure of her company. She always had a smile on her face, always looked on the bright side of life. She also made sure her crew was well taken care of, both financially and emotionally. If she called you a friend, she stuck by you, no matter what. She was a true joy to be around. This time on set, the chemistry between them had been undeniable. He hadn't felt this way about a woman in a long time.

"I don't have women lined up around the block like some

people," he said, reaching between the seats for the cabernet they'd picked up on the way over. "I'm out of practice."

"Things will take care of themselves," Ronny assured him. "I wouldn't be surprised if you got some action tonight."

"Ronny!" he exclaimed, and then smiled again. The possibility brought all sorts of images to mind. Some romantic, some quite a bit more than that. The intensity of the feelings, too, was the strongest they'd been in a long time.

"Just don't drop the wine, smart guy," he said, handing Ronny the bottle.

They climbed from the truck. The house was a desert-red Spanish-style, built on a lot that commanded an impressive view of the Valley. A warm, gentle breeze rustled through jade bushes and played with wind chimes hanging from the porch. Cole led the way up a concrete path lined by tiny cactuses with pink and white blooms.

"Are you okay with this?" Cole asked his son.

"With what?"

"This," Cole said, indicating the house with a gentle sweep of his hand. He'd been so caught up in the day's hectic events that he'd forgotten to ask his son's opinion that he was dating another woman. What if Ronny was putting on a good face for his benefit? What if being here was bringing back painful memories? Or maybe Ronny thought that Cole was committing some sort of betrayal by pursuing Jennifer?

"Dad, both of us went through a lot after Mom died," Ronny said. "I'm just happy you've found someone you like."

"You know that I loved your mother."

"You don't have to explain. You did everything you could for her," Ronny said with conviction, then smiled. "Now let's make sure you don't screw up this date."

Cole put an arm around his shoulders. He was lucky to have a son like Ronny, and it filled him with fury that Gary Stanford could have put his boy at risk. The producer was arrogant, cavalier. And, as such, dangerous. He made a mental note to keep an eye on the man before pushing the thoughts away, refusing to let them ruin the evening.

When they stepped onto the front porch, he took a deep breath and pushed the bell. As he heard twin, melodious chimes from within the house, he suddenly lamented that his chest and biceps were no longer as big as they once had been. At forty-five years old, he still had his hair, for the most part, but it was definitely thinner in spots. And his stomach, though flat, wasn't exactly rippling with muscle.

I'm a mess, he thought.

And then Jennifer opened the door, smiling, and Cole felt his insecurities melt away. Her kind, green eyes shone and her brown hair hung loosely about her shoulders. She wore a simple but elegant plum embroidered top with snug-fitting jeans and high-heeled boots. Metal Mexican-cuff bracelets adorned her wrists and a large, intricately engraved silver medallion hung around her neck.

"Hi, you two," she said. "Were my directions okay? Mulholland Drive can be a bit confusing."

"They were perfect," he said.

"Great, then come on in," Jennifer said, stepping back and opening the door wide.

Ronny stepped inside first, and Cole followed.

"This is for you," Ronny said, handing her the wine.

"How thoughtful," she said. "It'll go perfectly with what we're having."

Jennifer closed the door and then continued ahead, leading them into the house. She said, "I hope you're hungry because dinner is ready."

"Starving!" Ronny said.

"Good, then you'll be easy to please!"

They walked down a short, arched hallway that led to a sunken living room bordered by large windows that gave a magnificent view of the Valley. The southwestern theme had been tastefully continued with orange overstuffed chairs, a green overstuffed couch and a terra-cotta tiled floor that were complemented by brightly colored tapestries and paintings that hung on pale-yellow walls. Several shelves of a floor-to-ceiling bookcase were dedicated to hammered metal sculptures that had the same look and feel as the medallion that Jennifer was wearing. The late afternoon sun beamed through the windows and gave the space a luminescent, almost ethereal quality.

Everything in the house was organized, put in its place, perfect, Cole thought. The room smelled nice, too. Not overly feminine as he might have expected, but an earthy blend of sage and lilac that helped him feel at ease and at home.

"Dad," Ronny whispered. "Compliment something she has on."

"That's a beautiful medallion you're wearing," he told her.

"Thank you, David," Jennifer said, glancing over her shoulder. "It's one of a kind. I bought it from an art dealer friend of mine in Mazatlan. Every year she puts aside her Aztec inventory so I can have first pick."

They turned a corner and stepped into the dining room, which held a long, heavy wooden table accented by wrought-iron brackets. Overhead there was a matching wrought-iron candelabra. At the end of the table, near the kitchen doorway, were three place settings. He found himself impressed with the simple beauty of the settings when he normally wouldn't give a second thought to such things. Three flickering orange candles softly illuminated the room. The china was off-white with a modest floral pattern, and placed on pale-green woven mats. Orange cloth napkins had been rolled and bound with sculptured metal rings that matched heavy, solid-looking flatware.

And absent were the usual thin, crystal wine glasses—there were goblets instead, made of thick emerald art glass.

"Have a seat wherever you like, I'll be right out," Jennifer said, and disappeared through the kitchen doorway. Cole and Ronny sat opposite each other, saving the head of the table for her.

"Remember to tell her how delicious everything is even if she cooks like you," Ronny whispered.

"Very funny," Cole whispered back.

Jennifer reappeared carrying three small plates heaped with salad, three dinner plates, and the bottle of wine. She set down the plates in front of them with measured efficiency, then opened the wine with a corkscrew and filled their goblets. As she put the half-empty bottle to one side, he noticed that she'd neglected to fill her own glass. He knew that recovering addicts often chose not to drink.

He focused on the wonderful meal: Salads tossed with pistachios, Gorgonzola cheese and sliced pears all drizzled with vinaigrette dressing, and a main course consisting of grilled fillet of salmon with a light mustard sauce and brown rice on the side.

"Everything looks delicious," he said.

"Thank you," Jennifer replied. "So tell me, David, how did Gary Stanford take to you firing his nephew?"

"About as well as you might expect."

"Did he acknowledge the danger of them being on set?"

Cole was about to answer when he was struck suddenly by the way the candlelight brought out the green in her eyes. He realized that he could easily lose himself in those eyes. Lose himself, and forget to eat, forget to breathe . . . and forget that Ronny was kicking his leg under the table to make him stop staring and answer the question.

"The man refused to admit there was a problem," he said,

snapping out of his trance. "Since no one was actually hurt, he thought he could blow me off."

"How do things stand now?"

"I told him I needed a few days to double-check the wiring before restarting production."

"That'll be expensive."

"I won't compromise the safety of the crew no matter how much it costs."

"I don't blame you," she said, taking a bite of salad. "But Gary Stanford doesn't like to be cornered."

Cole knew that much about Stanford, but precious little else. A man could react in unexpected ways when his back was against the wall. He wondered if storming into Loki Productions had been the right tactic, and if the bribe that Stanford had offered was only the beginning. "He doesn't have a choice. Otherwise, I'll have the fire marshal shut him down."

"Who would you like to take up the slack now that Brandenburg and Watkins are gone?" Jennifer asked.

"That'd be Lawrence Fuchs," Ronny said.

"I don't think I've met Lawrence."

"He was on another production the last time we worked together," Cole explained. "He's one of the best."

"And he's an ex-cop," Ronny added.

"I plan to visit him tomorrow to see if he's available," Cole said.

"He'll be first on the list, then, as soon as we get the go-ahead," Jennifer said. "Would either of you like more wine?"

"That'd be nice," Cole said. "Tell me where the other bottle is and I'll be happy to—"

"Don't be silly," she interrupted. "You're a guest. I'll be right back."

She got up again and disappeared into the kitchen. This time, he watched her go and couldn't help but appreciate the way her jeans hugged her body. At first he felt guilty for ogling her, but then enjoyed that fact he was in the presence of an intelligent, beautiful woman. What's more, he was enjoying the evening with his son.

Cole turned to give Ronny a paternal wink and found that Ronny was staring directly at him with a smirk on his face.

"You were checking out Jennifer's butt," Ronny whispered.

"I don't know what you're talking about," he said lamely.

"C'mon, Dad, I'm sitting right here. I can see exactly what you're doing," Ronny said. "I don't blame you. She's hot for an older chick."

An older chick? "She sure is," he said, and then added, "And smart, too. And talented."

Ronny grinned. "Sounds to me like somebody's in looove."

Before he could respond, Jennifer returned with an open bottle of red wine and refilled their glasses. "What are you two whispering about out here?"

"We were talking about how you could teach Dad a thing or two about cooking a great meal," Ronny said. "If he ever tricks you into trying his meatloaf, you'll find out what I mean."

Nice cover, Cole thought, rolling his eyes at his son. Ronny rolled his eyes back.

Jennifer laughed and sat back down. As the conversation turned to more pleasant topics that had nothing to do with the day's events, Cole thought again about how good a kid Ronny was. Always taking care of his old man.

He looked at Ronny and Jennifer and appreciated, too, the way they bantered easily and treated one another with respect. It wasn't difficult to imagine this sort of exchange happening again. Or on a more permanent basis, he thought with conviction that both surprised and pleased him. He felt happy in Jennifer's presence and realized now, more than ever, that she was a woman he'd best hold on to if he could.

A short time later, after he and Ronny helped Jennifer clear the dishes from the table, they moved into the living room and sat together on the couch. As they ate dessert—a delicious lemon tart from a bakery in Los Feliz—Ronny asked Jennifer about what she'd done before becoming a film director. In reply, Jennifer retrieved a thick, blue photo album from a bookcase, and shared production stills from straight-to-cable and B-grade horror movies that she'd acted in. She was delightfully self-effacing about the work, but obviously proud of it, too—a rare combination in Hollywood, and one that Cole found refreshing. And attractive.

As Ronny continued to flip through the album, he said, "Hey, Dad, we should invite Jennifer to the barbeque."

"What barbeque is that?" she asked.

"Fourth of July at a friend's house," Ronny explained. "Dad and I were thinking about going."

"Would your friend mind if I tagged along?" Jennifer asked. "I make a mean potato salad."

"I haven't decided to go just yet," he replied quietly, afraid that the perfect evening might be ruined. He felt a pang of frustration at Ronny, but knew the kid meant no harm. He was simply trying to help his old man set up another date.

"Why not go?" she asked.

"The barbeque is at the house of a friend of mine named Ted Roberts . . . we served in the Navy SEALs together . . ." he began, at a loss of how to explain the relationship. "After we left the service in 1991, I became an F/X man and referred him to the LA fire department, where he eventually became an arson investigator. But we haven't kept in close touch."

"Why not?"

"I happened to save his life during our last mission together in the Gulf War. Ever since he's been trying to prove how worthy he is. I've tried telling him that he doesn't need to prove anything." He frowned as thoughts of that fateful night began to unfurl, and forced them away. "I guess we bring back too many memories for each other."

"You may be over-thinking this, David," she offered. "I don't think Ted is trying to pin you down. It sounds like he just needs a friend."

He looked at Jennifer and saw an expression similar to the one he'd noticed after she'd passed on the wine. This time he could sense something deep within her that understood pain—real pain. But her eyes were tempered with softness that said she'd made peace with that pain and moved on.

"Hey, Dad, I need to get something out of the truck," Ronny said suddenly, breaking the serious mood.

Cole nodded and tossed him the keys.

"Great, I'll be right back."

After Ronny left the room, Cole looked away from Jennifer shyly. He wasn't good at this sort of thing. Not good at all.

"So what are you going to do about the barbeque?" Jennifer asked.

Cole felt her voice gently tug his focus back towards her. "Of course, you're right. Ted only has the best intentions at heart."

"So you'll go?"

"I'll go."

"Well, then I'll have to come along to make sure you keep your word," she said, and then leaned over and kissed him. She brushed his lips with her own, and then gently pushed her tongue into his mouth. He pulled her closer and cradled her face gently with both hands as if it were a precious jewel. The kiss lasted a few, wonderful moments. Not too long to become uncomfortable or too brief to leave him wanting. It was just right.

"I have a confession to make," she said, eyes sparkling. "I've been waiting all night to kiss you. Well, that's not entirely true.

I've been waiting six weeks, ever since we started work on *Bringing Them Back.* I just didn't have the courage to invite you over until now."

"I'm glad you found the courage," he said and kissed her again. This time the kiss lasted a few moments, and became more insistent.

After what seemed like a blissful eternity, she pulled away. "Ronny will be back any second. I don't want to make him uncomfortable."

Cole looked toward the front door. "It's been twenty minutes since he went out."

Jennifer nodded. "I wonder what's keeping him."

Cole stood and walked to the front door. Jennifer followed. When he opened it and looked out onto the dark street, the truck was gone.

"He took the truck," Cole said, turning to her. "I'm sorry about this. I don't know what he was thinking."

She laughed. "I know exactly what he was thinking, and there's no need to apologize."

"He's the one who'll be sorry, believe me."

"Oh, don't be mad," she said, placing a warm hand on his forearm. As soon as she touched him, he felt his anger subside to a low grumble.

"I'll call a taxi," he said.

"You can stay a while longer if you like," she said.

Still holding his arm, she led him back into the living room. They sat on the couch.

"I can't believe my son did that," he said.

And then he felt her slide closer and thought that maybe Ronny had the right idea after all.

"It's okay, really," she said, smiling. "Not everything has to be under your control, David. You have to learn to roll with the punches."

"Look who's talking, Miss Control Freak."

"Mmm-hmm," she agreed, leaning in. "We both have a lot to learn."

"You fired Brandenburg and Watkins, and now you want me to take their place. Am I right? Shit, man, I knew that would happen. No fucking way. You got me? Stanford is a turd. A *turd.* I ain't doing it." Lawrence led Cole through the kitchen, and then out a door that led to a browning yard cluttered with rusted engine parts, old tires and stacks of firewood. "I ain't gonna do it. Nuh-uh. We ain't even gonna *talk* about it." He stopped, turned. "Let's talk about you instead. How'd your date go last night? What, you think I wouldn't remember?"

"Ronny reminded you, didn't he?"

Lawrence smirked. "And if he did? Let's have it, Dave."

"The date went well, big man," Cole said, squinting as the early afternoon sun made its appearance from behind the Santa Susana Mountains. He inhaled, relishing the scent of split trees in the warm air. The area, spillover from the Los Padres National Forest, was as beautiful as it was remote. After leaving the NYPD, Lawrence had purchased the property at state tax auction and built the cabin himself. A Lincoln-log type, with narrow windows, a wide front porch and a gray stone fireplace that canted to the left. The place wouldn't win an award in *Architectural Digest,* but it was sturdy enough, watertight, and blended nicely into the landscape. Cole could imagine building his own cabin, someday. Maybe with Jennifer, if he played his cards right.

"Quit stalling and gimme the story," Lawrence said.

"That is the story. We had dinner, then spent a little time on the couch."

His friend glared like he was back in the interrogation room. "What do you take me for, Dave? Those bags under your eyes say different."

Cole shrugged. Although he found Jennifer attractive, he hadn't been ready to consummate the relationship last night. Call it nerves or vestiges of loyalty to Caroline or whatever else. Jennifer, to her infinite credit, took it all in stride. In fact, she'd smiled sweetly, and told him to take as much time as he needed.

"I've never lied to you before," Cole said. "And I'm not lying now."

Lawrence grunted. "Yeah, well, I still can't believe you're asking me to work for Stanford. Okay, tell me what happened on set. No, I don't wanna know. *Christ.*"

The man stormed across a tract of brown grass, then down a twisting path crowded with Jeffrey Pine and chaparral. As an ex-cop, Lawrence was dead-set against working for a guy like Stanford, whose business ethics were less than admirable. But Cole knew the man better than he knew himself. He had to yell, get used to the idea. Then he'd calm and come around.

Cole hurried to keep up. Even at two-hundred-fifty pounds, the man moved quickly and smoothly, like a shark. Lawrence attributed his speed to genetics; his great-grandfather had been a buffalo soldier. Whatever the reason, the man was fast.

They eventually emerged at a clearing that Lawrence had transformed into a seventy-yard shooting range built to police specifications. Ventura County would fine you $1,000 for littering, but if you wanted to build a shooting range in your backyard, fine. Perfect for Lawrence, a man who made his living as a weapons handler, supplying real and prop guns for the movies.

Cole peered downrange at a dozen tall stakes planted in a row with paper targets mounted on them. Today, Lawrence had opted for the bad-guy-pointing-a-pistol-at-you design.

Ronny, having run ahead, emerged from a metal shed, wearing plastic safety goggles and holding a Tech-9 automatic pistol with both hands, barrel pointed at the ground.

Although Cole made a living with mock explosions and gunfire, he shunned actual firearms. Too many memories. But he did admire Lawrence's dedication to the job. The shed was the size of a three-car garage and stored hundreds of pieces of ordnance. The collection included pistols, assault rifles, heavy caliber machine guns. Lawrence had even bought crates of Vietnam-era landmines from some collector in Fresno. Cole would have preferred that his son and friend bonded over another activity, but the bond was the most important thing.

"You loaded up?" Lawrence asked Ronny.

Ronny nodded.

"Safety on?"

He nodded again.

"Alright, go cap some bad guy's ass."

Cole watched as Ronny walked to the range, planted his feet shoulder-width apart, and then aimed the Tech-9 with both hands as he released the safety switch with his thumb. He squeezed the trigger. The pistol coughed three rounds. Downrange, dirt on either side of the middle target jumped in angry tufts as the shots flew wide.

Satisfied that Ronny was handling the pistol correctly, Lawrence turned back to him and sighed deeply. "Okay, spill it. What happened with Tweedledee and Tweedledum?"

"Remember the stronghold explosion I told you about?"

"The big one at the end of the movie, yeah."

"They tore the wires from the hellbox."

"Jesus, are you kidding me?" He shook his head, already swept into the situation. "Shit, what if the explosives went off when the crew was standing around it?" His expression darkened. "Or if Ronny was nearby?"

Watching Lawrence react caused Cole's earlier feelings of anger to return. He pushed them away. Losing his cool would only make things worse. Lawrence would feed off his anger, and become more difficult to convince. What's done was done, and he needed his friend's help to fix the situation on set. "I paid Stanford a visit and gave him a choice," Cole continued. "Give me the time and manpower to recheck every connection, or kiss the production goodbye."

"And?"

"He said he'll get back to me."

"You went to the guy's office to keep his crew safe and he's fucking with you?"

"That's right."

Lawrence shook his head. "And you're not walking away because . . . ?"

"Big man, you know as well as I do that the industry is in a slump right now. I don't have the luxury to be choosy, especially when Ronny doesn't have enough industry contacts to make it on his own."

"I say again: *The guy's a turd.* Why can't you see that? He's power-tripping you."

"A paycheck's a paycheck, which is how you should be looking at it, too."

"The guy is bad news, Dave. I know his type. Hell, I've *arrested* his type. Do yourself a favor and walk away."

Cole felt another twinge of unease. He trusted Lawrence's cop instincts—in some cases, more than his own. If his friend tagged Stanford as a threat, he'd do well to listen. But the die had already been cast. The best he could do now was watch his back. "Enough with the speeches, big man," he said. "Are you in or out?"

"How much you say it was?"

"Twenty-four hundred for three days."

"Man . . ." Lawrence pulled a banana clip from his back pocket, slapped it into the AK-47, and then held it out to him.

Cole shook his head. "I'm still on the wagon. Seen too much of the real thing."

Lawrence glared, always the cop. "Just so we're clear. I'm working for you. Not that shithead Stanford."

His friend was loyal, if not a little intense. But he always meant well. Your fight immediately became his fight, too. "You'll be working for me. Have I ever lied to you?"

"You so fucking owe me for this."

After Ronny emptied another clip from the Tech-9, Lawrence walked to the range and tapped him on the shoulder. Ronny stepped dutifully aside. Lawrence sighted the rifle and fired a sweeping, thundering burst. Every target bucked as bullets perforated them.

"Nice shooting!" Ronny said.

"How can you be sure Stanford will cave to your ultimatum?" Lawrence said, still looking downrange.

"Simple," Cole said. "He can't afford not to."

After dropping off Ronny at his apartment in Sun Valley, Cole steered his truck into the driveway of his Sylmar home at 11 p.m. Keying open the front door, he crossed the dark living room and checked the answering machine on the kitchen counter. The red digital readout indicated one message.

He pressed the play button, and Ronny's voice crackled through the speaker. The kid apologized again for stealing the truck, and offered to buy dinner that weekend as penance. As embarrassing as the stunt had been at the time—Jennifer handled it more graciously than he had any right to expect—he had to admit that he was glad that Ronny had done it. The three of them at dinner had been good. Spending time alone with Jennifer had been just as good, if not better.

A single message on the machine meant something else too, of course. Stanford hadn't called. For a man obsessed with schedule and budget, he was certainly dragging his feet. *Go ahead and waste time, pal. It's your pocketbook.*

As he padded through the dark living room and down the bedroom hallway, Cole felt a swell of anger. Guys like Stanford failed to understand that poor working relationships compromised trust. And lack of trust meant lack of respect in a dangerous field that demanded clear communication among everyone involved.

But that's not the only reason you lost your cool. Cole knew that his reaction to Stanford had roots that stemmed back to when he was a SEAL. He'd let the producer's casual arrogance get under his skin—a trait that so many politicians and military brass had displayed at the cost of so many lives. However justified his behavior may have been, he was bothered at how the war continuously found a way to creep into his life. Shaking his head, he pushed away the concern. The ball was in Stanford's court now.

Cole walked into the bedroom. A breeze played with white curtains as dim light from a streetlamp cast the room an eerie yellow. The window was open.

It was not an oversight, he realized. But a diversion.

He started to turn.

"Too late," a man whispered.

Cole had time to register only one thought: *I* know *that voice.*

Chapter 3

Cole opened his eyes.

His head throbbed and his vision was blurred, like he was looking through an out-of-focus camera lens.

He was sitting on a chair in a room without furnishings. He could determine that much. A bright light from somewhere cast a pallid glow on faded hardwood floors and stark plaster walls.

And then memory returned in a stubborn trickle: Jennifer. Stanford. A voice he'd once known, but from where?

He tried to stand, but something pinned his arms around the back of the chair, preventing him from doing so. Glancing over his shoulder to see what held him, he noticed an oddly familiar shape.

What the hell?

It was the cluster of V-pan mortars he'd rigged that morning, loaded with huge amounts of black powder and tens of gallons of gasoline. The sharp scents of the volatile substances assailed his nostrils. He was in the Iraqi stronghold on the set of *Bringing Them Back.*

"Dickhead's awake," came a voice from behind him. *Ned Brandenburg.*

"Hold the fucker!" came a deep second voice, also behind him. *Levar Watkins.*

Brandenburg walked into view, his massive frame eclipsing the light, and clapped his hands on Cole's shoulders, pressing him into the chair.

"He ain't going nowhere," Brandenburg said.

The set was secluded, Cole realized. A perfect location to "persuade" him to change his mind about the safety check he'd imposed on Stanford.

He wondered how the idiots could have gotten the drop on him. But more, he felt profound disgust at the cheap tactic. He took a breath, anger thrumming in his chest. If they wanted to test his mettle, they were welcome to try.

Loops of coarse rope slipped around his wrists. In another few seconds, he'd be at their mercy. *I don't think so . . .*

He shot his knee up between Brandenburg's legs. The man grunted and spun away. Then Cole jerked his wrists from the tightening loops of rope, leaped to his feet and whirled to face Watkins who was crouched behind the chair. With a roar, Watkins lunged. Cole met the attack with a vicious right cross, which sent Watkins reeling.

"Funny how the training never leaves you."

It was the same voice he'd heard before losing consciousness. A voice from another time. Another life. He turned.

Frank Ruger stood underneath a naked bulb, the harsh glare washing out his face and turning his eyes into sockets. Even so, the man's features were nearly as Cole remembered them: dark hair, once cropped, was now shoulder-length, hawk nose, weighty shovel jaw. He wore a black suit and white shirt that did little to hide his muscled bulk. On his feet were combat boots. In his right hand was a silenced SIG Sauer 9mm pistol.

Cole's mind swam as past and present worlds collided. The man didn't belong here. This was the life he'd built after the SEALs, one filled with joy and family and peace.

"How?" was all he could manage.

"Gary Stanford isn't as big a dipshit as you thought. He did his homework on you. On *us,*" Ruger said. "As you can imagine,

I jumped at the chance to see my good friend Commander David Cole again. The man saved me the search." He motioned with the gun. "Sit the fuck down."

Seeing no alternative, Cole did. Brandenburg and Watkins picked themselves off the floor and cautiously tied him to the chair.

Clearly, Ruger had been the one who'd grabbed him. Brandenburg and Watkins couldn't have even gotten close. That being the case, why were the two men here?

"Tell Stanford I won't compromise the safety of the crew," he said.

"This isn't about Stanford," Ruger said. "Not anymore. Now tell me: How much time?"

Cole frowned. Did Ruger mean the time they'd served together on the SEAL Team? Or since they'd last seen one another? He wanted to answer—to learn what was going on—but was at a loss. "I don't understand the question."

Ruger nodded at Brandenburg. In reply, Brandenburg slipped the fingers of his right hand into a set of gleaming brass knuckles.

Cole took a breath . . . detached himself from the coming pain. He'd been trained as a SEAL to withstand torture, and those methods came back now. Too easily, he noted with alarm. Like the cold-blooded soldier inside him had never left.

"Remember how you dissed me on set? It's payback time, motherfucker," Brandenburg said, and punched him in the face.

Cole's face exploded with pain. But thanks to his training, the pain was muted, like a rotten tooth injected with Novocain. *Stay conscious,* he told himself. *You can't get out of here if you go under.*

"Still with us?" Ruger said.

He looked up. *Still here, asshole.*

Ruger met the glare with dark intensity. "Let's try again:

How much fucking time?"

Suddenly, he understood. Only one thing could provoke such fury in the man. "The disciplinary board recommended two years."

Ruger nodded again, and Brandenburg delivered a second blow to Cole's jaw. Cole gritted his teeth against the slamming pain as the chair flipped backward and landed on the floor with a thud.

"Fifteen years," Ruger said. "They let me rot for fifteen years!"

Cole shook his head to keep from blacking out as Brandenburg righted the chair. Yes, he'd recommended Ruger for psychological care—but fifteen years?

"I lost everything," Ruger continued. "My freedom. My family. My medals. All of it." He closed his eyes, and his anger seemed to abate beneath memory and sorrow.

"The disciplinary board wanted to help you, and so did I," Cole said carefully. "Please believe that."

"I did what needed to be done, Commander, and you fucking betrayed me."

Commander. He winced as Ruger used the term again. He hadn't been called that since the service, and it threatened to bring back memories of Iraq, which he forced away. He could not let Ruger dishonor the memory of the Team with this charade. "You want regrets, Frank? I thought you could handle yourself that night. I was wrong."

Ruger took a menacing step forward, face knotted with rage. "You have no fucking idea what it takes to get the job done."

Cole braced for another punch, but Ruger didn't give Brandenburg the go-ahead. Instead, the man settled into an icy calm, which filled Cole with dread.

"I told you this was no longer about Stanford," Ruger said. "Now I'll show you what I mean." He walked away, disappearing into the shadows of an adjacent room.

Cole slumped in the chair. He was tired of fighting. Tired of justifying his actions those many years ago.

He flexed his wrists against the coarse rope. There was no give. Given enough time, he might be able to work free, but for now he was at the mercy of the idiots before him. He looked at Brandenburg who stood nearby, and then at Watkins lurking farther back in the shadows.

If Ruger had ambushed him, there was no reason for the two men to be there.

Unless they had their own task to perform.

Ruger walked back through the doorway holding Ronny by the arm. "Dad?" the boy asked with a trembling voice.

Cole's heart pounded. *Oh my God . . .*

"It'll be alright, son," he whispered, fighting the tremble in his own voice. And then to Ruger, "Let him go, Frank. He has nothing to do with this."

"On the contrary, he has everything to do with this."

Brandenburg placed another chair about fifteen feet across from Cole, and then pushed Ronny onto it and slapped a strip of gaffer's tape over his mouth as Watkins tied the boy's hands behind his back.

Straining against his own ropes, Cole noticed that Ruger's eyes were no longer cloaked by shadow. He saw deranged hatred there. The soul-reflection of a man who'd made an ally of violence. Cole fought the urge to scream as panic blossomed in his chest.

Ruger handed his pistol to Brandenburg, then opened his jacket and removed a ten-inch K-bar knife from a sheathe hanging underneath his left arm. Ronny, although obviously afraid, stared defiantly. "We both know SEALs have a high threshold to pain. I doubt your son can say the same."

The whimper he heard next was his own. "Frank! I'm sorry

for everything. That night in Iraq was my fault. Mine!"

"I want you to learn what it means to lose everything, Commander."

"FRANK!"

Ruger slashed the blade across Ronny's face, missing it, seemingly, until blood welled from a cleft in the muscles above his left cheek.

Cole blinked. Couldn't move. This couldn't be happening. God, this couldn't be happening.

With the second strike, Ruger released a jet of blood from Ronny's other cheek.

And then Cole screamed. His howling echoed off the walls as he kicked in the chair, but the ropes were too tight. He screamed so loud it felt like the inside of his throat was peeling away, felt like his lungs were about to explode . . .

. . . *My boy! Get away from my baby boy!* . . .

Ruger inserted the tip of the blade into each of Ronny's nostrils and slit them open. The boy panted through his ruined, bubbling nose, but refused to utter a sound. Still refused when Ruger severed his right ear and tossed it at Brandenburg who yelped and jumped away.

Cole screamed, head thrown back, mind washed blank with horror. He kicked harder, causing the chair to jerk-scrape against the wooden floor. The ropes loosened. But not enough.

. . . *please God take it out on me instead please God on me instead please on me* . . .

Ronny cried out at last when Ruger cut his left eye from the socket. It was a guttural sound muffled by tape that pierced Cole's heart like an ice pick. And then the reek of urine saturated the room.

With a final, liquid motion, Ruger pushed the knife into Ronny's stomach, and then withdrew the blade and wiped it clean in the boy's hair.

Cole went cold with shock. Struggled to maintain focus. Through tears, he saw Ronny's chest rise and fall. Still alive! Still alive!

Ruger sheathed the knife. His white shirt was drenched with blood. He turned to Brandenburg and Watkins, who looked at him with their mouths hanging open. "Get out," Ruger told them. They did as ordered.

Ruger held a length of wire in front of Cole. "When the fire department comes to clean up the mess, they're going to pin it on you."

"How could . . . ?" Cole's voice was a croak.

"I *owed* you," Ruger replied, and then walked out the door.

Cole waited until Ruger was out of sight before giving his full attention to the ropes binding his hands. He had to hurry. Ruger meant to set off the mortar and burn them alive.

"Ronny! Can you hear me, son?"

Ronny's right eyelid fluttered.

"Hold on, okay? I'll be right there."

Cole took slow, deep breaths. Fight the shock. What you're feeling is nothing . . . nothing compared to what Ronny's been through. He curled his jittery fingers toward the knotted rope. Pinched it. Over and over. Felt it loosen, and then fall away.

He whipped his hands from the rope. Stood. Slumped to his knees. Shock had turned his legs to rubber. Clambering to his feet, he stumbled to Ronny's side.

His son's face was a scrimshaw of bleeding slashes. His T-shirt looked like a butcher's apron. With trembling fingers, Cole tore away the tape covering his mouth, which released a crimson wash of saliva.

So much blood . . .

"Dad?"

"We're getting out of here."

Cole struggled to loosen the rope that bound Ronny's hands

around the back of the chair. It was a simple thumb knot, but slick with blood. He couldn't get a good enough grip.

Too much time . . . I'm taking too much time . . .

He grabbed the seat of the chair to lift it, strained, nothing. Shock continued to sap his strength.

Whimpering in frustration, he tried to push the chair across the floor. First with his hands, and then by lying on his back and using his legs. But his cold limbs felt boneless. Without power. He stood, pushed again and heard the chair scrape hardwood as it moved only half an inch.

"They're gonna blow the house, Dad," Ronny murmured. "Leave me."

"Hush." It sickened him that his past had come back to hurt his son. Sickened him that his son felt he needed to make such a sacrifice.

He went back to the knot. The blood had dried enough for him to untie it. Hands unbound, Ronny slumped forward, and Cole shuffled around to catch him. The boy's skin felt clammy.

"Try to get up," Cole said, pulling Ronny's left arm across his shoulders. He struggled to keep his weakened legs from trembling as he levered Ronny off the chair. "You have to help me, son. I can't do it alone. Stand up. Stand up."

He wasn't sure that Ronny had heard when he felt the boy slowly, painfully, push himself to his feet.

"Good," Cole said, eyes filling with tears. Ronny was strong. Brave. They would make it out of here. They would live.

They took a few trembling steps forward, and then bigger steps as they gained momentum. When they were close to the door, he felt strength flood his legs. The shock was gone.

He shifted to bear Ronny's full weight. "We're going to make it, son."

Cole saw a flash. For a moment, he thought the morning sun was flooding the house with light. But then came an ear-splitting hiss of white noise, like a blaring out-of-tune radio, followed by a white-hot wave of flame that tore Ronny away.

Ruger watched the roaring tower of flame rise slowly, almost elegantly, from the incinerated stronghold until it blossomed into an eighty-foot wide, two-hundred-foot high orange and black fireball that sent blazing chunks of debris screaming into the night sky. As the flames continued to unfurl, he felt a wave of intense heat followed by the slamming shock of concussion.

There was no fucking way Cole could survive that blast. No fucking way. He was standing a quarter-mile distant, and the spillover felt like it could strip the flesh from his face.

Sucking a breath, he relished the reek of gasoline, and then smiled as the explosion ran like watercolor into his mind's-eye image of that night years ago in Iraq . . . the gunfire . . . the screaming . . . the explosions . . .

Victory tonight—just as victory had that night years ago—reinforced what he knew to be true: *The enemy was everywhere.*

Clad in desert fatigues, armed with Kalashnikovs, the enemy was ruthless. Relentless. Remaining hidden until they attacked. If they ever got the upper hand, he would die.

He also knew that David Cole had been one of them. Cole had left him rotting in a hospital cell, dressed in soiled whites, while death doctors exposed him to their "treatments." Cole had conspired to keep him in that cell forever.

But he had prevailed.

Yet he was no fool. He could never let his guard down. There were always more enemies to fight. *The enemy was everywhere.*

Turning, he noticed Brandenburg and Watkins staring at him. Keeping their distance. They feared him as sheep should fear a wolf. As it should be.

"Talk to the police, I'll do to you what I did to the boy," Ruger growled. "Now get the fuck out of here."

He watched the cowards run, and then turned back to the tower of flame. Finally, that motherfucker Cole was dead.

Chapter 4

Cole lay in a fetal position on the incline of a steep ravine. He had no idea how far he was from the burning house. He could still feel the blast that had launched him airborne, arms and legs tangling, heat scorching his body, slamming into the dirt.

He could hear his own ragged breathing. The distant chirp of crickets. That meant the concussion hadn't knocked out his eardrums. But the verdict was still out on his eyes. He blinked again. Everything stayed dark.

His body felt heavy, like he was pinned underneath sandbags. He ached, but the pain was muted, as if he'd been given a shot of morphine.

Maybe he'd gotten lucky. Come away with a few bumps and scrapes. But it was more likely that he was simply still in shock.

Maybe Ronny had survived the blast, too. He was a tough kid. He might be hurt, maybe even crippled, but at least he'd be alive.

Cole felt a surge of shame. His past had caught up with him, and Ronny had gotten caught in the crossfire. *I'm sorry, son . . . I'm so sorry . . .*

He'd never be able to forgive himself if—

He pushed aside the terrible thought. He'd find Ronny. He'd climb this hill and find his boy even if the attempt killed him.

Gritting his teeth, he strained to move his arms and legs. Couldn't. Like he was a marionette with its strings severed.

Concentrate, he ordered himself. He took deep, deliberate

gulps of air. Felt sharp pain under his right pectoral. A ruptured lung? He hitched another breath, then noticed the stench.

Grotesque. Cloying. He couldn't quite place it. But it smelled strikingly familiar—*oh, God.*

The smell was his cooked flesh.

His stomach clenched. If he succumbed to the burns, he'd leave Ronny all alone. He couldn't let that happen. Wouldn't let that happen. He had to keep going.

Son, forgive me . . . please forgive me . . .

Tears pouring down his face, he rolled onto his stomach. A bolt of pain beyond anything he'd ever experienced seared his chest.

"Gkkkkk . . . gkkkkkkkkkkkk . . ." he coughed, then vomited something wet and ropy.

An eternity later, the agony faded. Barely.

You have to keep going . . . for Ronny . . . for Ronny . . .

Gritting his teeth, he extended his left arm, dug his fingers into the soft earth. Dragged himself forward. Dirt scraped his skin like crushed glass. Twigs stabbed at him like sabers.

"Gkkkkkkkk . . ."

Jerking his torso like an epileptic, he used the momentum to throw out his right arm, and grabbed an exposed tree root. Hauled himself up the slope half a yard more.

Pain gouged his tricep. Razored his shoulder blades. Crashed the base of his skull.

Next stroke, his left arm. The effort started a mini-landslide above him that sent dirt cascading into his open mouth. Tasting grit, he spit out the debris.

Ronny needs you!

He whipped his head from side to side, praying that his vision would return. But there was only claustrophobic blackness.

He groped madly, hooked his fingers around a rock, wormed forward two inches more. When he retracted his arm, he felt tearing pain as flesh from his palm stuck to the rock's coarse surface like strands of chewing gum.

Suddenly, he could distinguish circular blobs. Scrub brush. His vision was coming back. He looked up the slope, saw a bright flicker near the top.

The burning stronghold. He was nearly there.

Keep going . . . keep going . . .

Like he was swimming upstream, he sucked another breath, threw out an arm, clawed dirt, pulled himself up. Flung out the other arm. Clawed. Pulled. Up. Inch by inch. Flung out an arm. Pulled. Searing pain. Pulled, clawed, pulled.

"Gkkk . . . gkkk . . . gkkkk . . ."

He swam up . . . through dirt and rock and pain. Up . . . up . . . and then with a burst of strength, scrambled over the hill's summit.

There, he struggled onto his knees, then finally, shakily, to his feet.

He looked at the stronghold. The fire he'd seen earlier had burned out. All that remained was a smoking ruin.

Ronny lay at its core. A melted, misshapen carcass.

Cole blinked, desperately hoping that his vision was playing tricks on him. He closed his eyes for several seconds—*please, God*—and opened them again. But his son was still there.

No . . .

He lumbered to a cratered wall, ducked through it, staggered to his son's side. Sank to his knees.

"Ronny?" he whispered.

Despair smothered him like a mudslide. Time froze as he found himself unable to move, unable to look away, unable to carry his son from that dark and ugly place as violent sobs wracked him.

Suddenly, he heard the distant wail of sirens. Turning, he saw cherry lights flashing on the horizon. He remembered what

Ruger had said about planting evidence. The authorities would think *he* was responsible for killing his son.

He had to get out of there.

Trembling, he stood. Looked down at his own body. His clothes had been burned away, and his chest was a ruin of blackened flesh.

As the wail of sirens grew closer, he shambled away—when he glimpsed a patch of blue in a pile of ash. Reaching down, he plucked the object free. Ronny's baseball cap. Almost black with soot, it had survived the holocaust.

Gripping the cap with both hands, he loped toward his truck, and prayed that he'd be able to escape in time.

"Dave, this is Ted. There's been an accident on the set of *Bringing Them Back*. We could use your help to sort it out. Call me as soon as you can."

After hanging up the cell phone, Ted Roberts parked his red Chrysler in the parking area, got out, then opened the back door and retrieved his turnout gear. As he shrugged into the greenish-yellow jacket and slipped the matching pants over his jeans, he caught a glimpse of his reflection in the window.

He had a whipcord body and short brown hair tucked underneath a red baseball cap. Sometimes he believed that his plain, sallow facial features kept him from having a social life. But when he was honest with himself, he knew it was because he kept obsessive hours on the job, and had commendations to prove it.

The department shrink called him a super-achiever—a condition she linked to Cole saving his life in the war. Whether or not that was true, it helped get the job done, which is all that mattered.

He briefly surveyed the scene. The Incident Commander had told him over the phone that the first-in crew had discovered a body, but he couldn't spot it from this distance. He suspected the victim was a resident from a nearby community who'd snuck onto set despite the posted warning signs. Sometimes people couldn't help but be attracted by the glamour of movie sets.

Finally, he stepped into the black turnout boots, strapped on a helmet, and then grabbed an unlined paint can to hold evidence samples. Heading onto set, he saw several paparazzi hovering outside the police tape. *Goddamn buzzards,* he thought. Fortunately, the perimeter had been set up fifty yards away from the scene, so the fire crews wouldn't be distracted by the commotion.

Among them was a woman confronting a sheriff's officer who stood guard.

"I'm the director of this movie," she said. "What happens on set is my responsibility."

"Maybe so, but I can't let you through," the officer replied.

Roberts knew that Cole was dating the film's director, and walked toward her. "May I help you?"

She whirled. "I won't let you throw me out of here!"

He raised his hands. "You're Jennifer, right? I'm Ted Roberts, a friend of David Cole. He's told me about you."

When she realized he wasn't the enemy, her face softened. "It's nice to meet you, Ted. David has told me about you, too. I'm sorry we had to meet under these circumstances."

"How did you know to come here? The production company hasn't been notified."

She hooked a thumb at paparazzi behind them. "At times they can be useful."

"I wish I could fill you in, Jennifer, but I haven't checked things out yet."

"Have you gotten in touch with David?"

"I left a message on his machine."

"Me too. He's usually available twenty-four, seven, when

working on a film."

"I know you film industry folks work long hours during production. He could be sleeping."

She glanced worriedly toward set. "You don't think . . ."

"Let me tell you something," he said firmly. "Dave is one of the very best, damn near equal to legends in the field like Joe Lombardi, Joe Viskocil, and Paul Staples. He wouldn't let something like this happen." Roberts considered telling her about the body—she might know who it was—then thought better of it. The information would only worry her. He would ask during a follow-up interview, if necessary.

"Of course, you're right," she whispered.

"Why don't you go home? I promise to fill you in after my inspection. And if I hear from Dave before then, I'll have him call you, okay?"

"I'd rather stay."

"I can appreciate that, but it will help if you're rested when we talk later. Remembering even the smallest detail could be relevant to the case."

She sighed. "If this is a brush off, Ted, you'll be hearing from me."

"I'll be in touch," he said, ducking under the police tape.

Jennifer seemed like a good person, he thought while continuing on. Strong. Independent. Pretty, too. And it was obvious that she cared for Cole very much. Roberts was happy for his friend. The guy deserved a good woman after losing Caroline. Maybe he'd bring her to the barbeque, that is, if he decided to come at all.

"Hey, long time no see, buddy!" came a voice from behind him.

Roberts turned and saw Otto Anderson approaching, all curly black hair and smiles in his blue ATF windbreaker. He couldn't help but smile back. Anderson was a forensic chemist and explosives expert with a penchant for arson investigation. They'd become fast friends while working a string of office park fires three years ago. Turned out the perp had been an arson investigator himself, and Anderson had helped uncover key pieces of evidence that broke the case.

"Good to see you too, Otto," he said. "Who's the primary detective?"

"Take one big guess."

Roberts rolled his eyes. "Shit, I thought Whittaker put in for a transfer to Internal Affairs."

"Denied on account of his charm."

"Too much of an asshole for the Rat Squad," Roberts grunted. "Unbelievable. Where's Mr. Personality now?"

"Canvassing."

"The farther away the better."

Anderson nodded. "Has anyone given you the rundown?"

"You really should let Whittaker brief me," Roberts said, smirking.

"Never tell me what I can't do," Anderson said, returning the smile. "The videographer did his thing, and the Incident Commander is waiting on you before calling the bomb squad."

"Won't be necessary. This is simple F/X stuff."

The two men walked briskly through clusters of responding emergency units. Since it was not quite dawn, work lights had been wired to aid with the mopping-up. Roberts could distinguish the hulking silhouettes of pumper trucks, and the more compact shapes of ATF vans and sheriff patrol cars. Some patrol cars still had their cherry lights spinning, and the intermittent glow made the desert appear unearthly.

"The 911 call came in at two-twenty," Anderson explained. "First respondents arrived fifteen minutes later."

"Who called it in?" Roberts asked.

"Anonymous."

"Where did the fire start?"

"Dunno. Place was a total loss by the time we got here."

"Mortar configuration?"

"V-shape cluster in the main room."

"Was it set off by a secondary fire?"

"We're hoping you'll tell us."

Roberts nodded. "And the body?"

"Near the mortar," Anderson grunted. "Hope you haven't had breakfast."

As the men stepped with practiced ease over snaking lengths of hose that crisscrossed the ground, it never ceased to amaze Roberts how fire could reduce something as complex as the human body into a pile of grease and bone. He'd seen hundreds of burned bodies during his seven years as investigator and three years on LAFD. And still he wasn't used to it. "What about the house?" he asked.

"In foreclosure until the bank sold it to Loki Productions. All the right permits were filed, everything was done by the book."

"Doesn't surprise me. David Cole, the lead pyro, is an old Navy buddy. Great guy, meticulous as hell. I called and left him a message about half-hour ago. With his help, we'll be able to determine cause in no time."

Roberts stopped when he noticed that Anderson was no longer walking with him. Turning, he saw a strained look on the man's face. "What is it, Otto?"

"What I'm about to say is by no means conclusive, okay?"

"What are you talking about?"

"The body in the house," Anderson said.

"Yeah?"

"One of the fire crew found a tool belt and walkie-talkie thrown clear from the blast. The belt has the initials D.C. stamped on it."

Roberts felt his stomach drop. No way Cole was in there. No

way. “Let’s not jump to conclusions.”

“Like I said,” Anderson said quickly. “But I thought you should know.”

“Okay, thanks.”

Nodding, Anderson continued on. Roberts pushed the fear from his mind, and concentrated instead on following Anderson through a large hole in the east wall of the house. The stench of gasoline assailed his nostrils. The room was a mass of wet ash and soaked, charred lumber broken into sharp angles. He noted that the engine crews had done their job well, dousing the fire with fog nozzles instead of solid streams to preserve evidence.

Roberts followed Anderson down a short hallway, ducked under a fallen beam, and then stepped through a cracked door-frame and emerged into the living room. He glanced at the mortar cluster, the V-pans streaked with soot. Now that they stood at the source of the explosion, Roberts could detect the clean, musky sharpness of black powder in addition to the gas.

“Where is it?” Roberts asked, throat tight with dread.

Anderson pointed to a pile of blackened lumber near the front door. “Take all the time you need.”

Roberts waited until Anderson was gone before releasing a shaky breath. *It can’t be Dave,* he told himself. *He’s too good to make a mistake like this.* He inhaled deeply to steady himself, and then walked to the pile of debris.

The body was there, lying behind the burned clutter, back fused to the floor. The ribcage had been split apart by the concussive force, exposing a stew of internal organs. The skull had also ruptured in the heat, like a boiler bag left too long in a microwave. The rest of the body was covered with full-thickness burns, the skin blackened, melted, misshapen. Where the flesh had charred even deeper was the hard line of bone.

As Anderson had said, there were no distinguishable traits. The victim could be anybody. And then he saw the melted remains of a wristwatch imbedded in the charred flesh of the left wrist. He blinked, then looked at his own wristwatch. The two watches were identical Navy SEAL issue.

After all they'd survived together, it had come to this. Dying on the set of a cheap action flick. *Dave. I can't believe it.*

He felt the paint can slip from his hands, and sat heavily on the wet hardwood. He stared at the corpse, wishing he could have saved Cole's life like Cole had saved his. *I'm sorry, man. I'm sorry I wasn't here to do something.* He continued to stare, chest tight, tears streaming down his cheeks, until sloshing footsteps approached.

"You okay?" Anderson asked.

"It's him," Roberts whispered. "It's Cole."

"Oh man. Jesus. I'm so sorry, Ted."

Roberts slowly climbed to his feet. "You mind giving me a few more minutes, Otto? I need to figure out what happened here."

"Sure, no problem," Anderson said. "Whatever you need. I'll keep everybody outside."

He watched Anderson go. *Pull yourself together. You can help Dave by finding out what happened.* He thought about Ronny, and how he would take the news. The kid loved his dad. Devastated wouldn't even begin to describe how he would react.

Roberts pushed the image from his mind. *Concentrate.*

The chance that Cole had blown himself up was as likely as him burning down his own house with a Hibachi. A secondary fire had to be at fault.

Pulling on a pair of blue surgical gloves, he walked to one side of mortar cluster and dropped to one knee. He tuned out the chatter of voices coming from outside as he brushed away debris around the base and then clicked on his penlight. As he expected, there was a two-foot corona of white ash where the wood had been incinerated by intense heat. Beyond that, in a much larger radius, the wood appeared scaly and shiny where it had been exposed to a lesser flash of heat.

He examined the alligatored wood carefully, tracing the blast zone, looking for a break in the scaly pattern. If a secondary fire had ignited the mortar, taking Cole by surprise, at least one portion of hardwood would show evidence of a slower burn, characterized by broader, duller scorch marks. But he didn't find anything like that.

Frowning, he repeated the procedure around the entire mortar cluster, feeling a growing sense of disappointment edged with disbelief—there was no evidence at all of a secondary fire.

He walked to a blown-out window that had been built above an outlet in the south wall. The electricity would have been shut off long ago, but that didn't rule out internal fuses that carried their own charges. One could have shorted out and started a fire inside the wall.

Holding a penlight in his teeth, he scraped his thumbnail against a charred piece of tempered glass that remained in the window frame. The carbon deposit peeled away easily, and had a loose, silky texture, which indicated quick scorching. Had a fuse started a secondary fire, he would have found baked, more resilient deposits.

Shit. If a secondary fire hadn't triggered the mortar, then what the hell had happened?

He began looking for signs of foul play. As tragic as it would be—and much as it would complicate the investigation—he hoped the evidence now pointed in this direction. He didn't want the reputation of his friend impugned by negligence after he'd served his country, and fought hard to create a good life after a career in the military.

Roberts scoured the sodden, trash-strewn floor for any sort of aberrant triggering device—a timer, blasting cap, mercury switch, even an out-of-place wire. But he came up empty.

"You've gotta give me something to go on, Dave," he said to the body in the corner.

He scraped the inside rim of each V-pan with a pocketknife, then deposited the samples into plastic bags, which he then placed in the paint can. And then, exhausted by emotional stress and frustration, he walked out the front door and down the steps.

The sun was beginning to rise, which cast the desert with a deep shade of amber. He'd been in such deep concentration that he hadn't realized that most of the engines had left.

Anderson approached. "Find anything?"

"We'll see," he said, indicating the paint can. "I'm headed to the detonator's shed now if you want to tag along."

When the men reached the shed, Roberts opened the squeaky metal door and shined his penlight inside. What he saw in the tiny circle of light made him stand dumbfounded. *I don't believe it.*

"What're the chances Cole could make a mistake like that?" Anderson said from behind him.

A hellbox lay on its side near an upended card table, its top panel yawning open like a wound. Cole could never have overlooked the exposed wires. It simply wasn't impossible. The mortar's power circuit began and ended there.

"Exposed leads?" Anderson said incredulously. "That means any bit of static could have triggered the mortar."

"Or it could have been detonated by radio waves from the walkie-talkie you found earlier," Roberts said. *It can't be true. It can't be.*

"What're the chances Cole could make a mistake like this, Ted?"

"Nil."

Anderson looked at him. "When you saw Cole last, did he give any indication that he wanted to commit suicide?"

"No," Roberts said quietly, knowing that he wouldn't rest until he found out why the man who'd saved his life in Iraq would take his own.

Chapter 5

"What the hell are we gonna do?" Brandenburg asked.

"Shut the fuck up!" Watkins said.

"It wasn't supposed to go down like that!"

"I said shut the fuck up, motherfucker!"

Brandenburg snapped his mouth shut and gripped the truck's steering wheel. Collecting the kid had been easy. They'd looked him up in the phone book, then gone to his apartment and knocked on the door. When he'd answered, they'd grabbed him. Actually, Watkins had grabbed him, clapping a hand over his mouth to keep him quiet, while Brandenburg had closed the apartment door and made sure the coast was clear of nosy neighbors.

Nobody'd seen the grab. Quick in, quick out. Fuckin' perfect.

Now this bullshit. He hadn't signed up for this, no fucking way. They were supposed to scare the kid. Make him watch as they worked over his old man. That'd keep 'em both quiet. Keep 'em from squealing on Uncle Gary. He mewled as Ronny's ravaged face flickered in his head.

"SHUT THE FUCK UP!" Watkins roared. "I've had enough of you crying like a bitch. What's done is done. All we need to do now is get paid."

"What went down wasn't supposed to go down. We gotta report back to Uncle Gary."

"We do that and we might connect your uncle to this mess. He wouldn't like that. Not one fucking bit."

"Uncle Gary will know what to do!"

"Listen to me, motherfucker," Watkins hissed. "I do *not* want your uncle siccing his mob goons on my ass because you're too much of a pussy to handle this. We act like it never happened. We get our money. End of fucking story."

"Think about what'll happen when Uncle Gary finds out on his own. He's gonna ask us why we didn't tell him. What're we gonna say?"

Watkins stared out the windshield like he was thinking things through, and then looked down at his boots. "Mother*fucker.*"

The sky wasn't black anymore, but deep blue. The sun would rise soon to shine light on what they'd done. He didn't know what made him feel like pissing his pants more: going to jail or Uncle Gary. It had been bad enough when his uncle found out about what happened on set. He'd been called into the office that afternoon, and without so much as a "How are ya?" Uncle Gary had beat him down with a golf club, voice calm the whole time, explaining he wasn't angry so much as *disappointed.*

He was twice his uncle's weight, but knew better than to hit back. Nobody hit Uncle Gary and lived to tell about it.

Veering onto an exit ramp, he took a canyon road and gunned the engine on the straightaways. Thirty minutes later, he screeched up the circular driveway to his uncle's mansion—an awesome place nestled in its own private beach canyon in the heart of Malibu.

After cutting the ignition, he scurried from the truck. There were no traffic sounds here, only the cry of gulls and lapping waves.

"C'mon!" he called to Watkins as he rounded the front of the truck. Watkins shook his head and yelled through the closed window, "Nuh-uh, motherfucker. He's your uncle, you fucking tell him!"

Brandenburg felt another spike of fear. The idea of confessing the fuck-up was one thing. But actually doing it . . .

He trudged to the front door like a condemned man. The house always reminded him of some kind of temple—bright white with tall columns on the porch. A temple where he'd be sacrificed now.

He jabbed the doorbell with a pudgy finger, and smiled weakly when his uncle answered wearing a purple silk robe over red silk pajamas. "Is it done?"

"I . . . we . . ." Brandenburg stammered, looking down at his shoes. He didn't know how or where to begin.

He heard his uncle sigh. "Let me rephrase the question, Ned: Are David Cole and his son dead?"

He looked up in surprise. "You *know?*"

"Answer me."

He dropped his head again. Of course his uncle knew. His uncle knew everything. "Yeah, they're dead."

"Ruger planted the evidence?"

He nodded.

"Very good."

Shuddering, Brandenburg's eyes filled with tears. He couldn't shake the bloody image of Cole's son tied to the chair . . . face cut up . . .

Suddenly, he felt his uncle's hand strike him across the face, the sharp *smack* echoing like a gunshot. Brandenburg looked up, wide-eyed and startled.

"For God's sake, Ned, get a hold of yourself. David Cole was a threat, and we took necessary action. If I'd told you the truth, you would have backed down."

Brandenburg mewled. "We were only supposed to scare them!"

"What would that have accomplished? Cole brought it on himself when he threatened to close me down. This way, we can use the insurance money to secure Anne Devereaux for *Mothers and Daughters,* though I suspect she'll forgo the money in light of this tragedy. God forbid she appears the ghoul."

Brandenburg closed his eyes, and saw Ronny bleeding. Heard him screaming. "Frank Ruger . . ."

"Quite a find, isn't he? I had Steven Huxley look into Cole's past. Cole and Ruger trained and fought together in the Navy SEALs, with no love lost by the end of their careers. As such, Ruger was the perfect choice for assassin. Better than any man in my organization, certainly."

"But Ruger is crazy!"

"Yes, literally. The man was committed in a military asylum for years until his release this month. A fortunate event to say the least." His uncle smiled grimly. "He was thrilled that I knew where to find Cole."

"Committed? How the hell did he get out?"

Brandenburg cowered as his uncle stepped closer. "He learned to play the system to his advantage, Ned. Exactly as I did. We're on the verge of a major breakthrough at Loki, and I won't let anyone stop us. David Cole learned that lesson the hard way. In light of this, it's time for you to take a more active role in the company. To become a man."

Brandenburg's head reeled with bloody images of Ronny. He didn't know if he could do this kind of work, but didn't want to look like a pussy, either. Not when his uncle had trusted him—really trusted him—for the first time, ever. Tears flowed down his cheeks. "I . . . I just wanna do what's right."

"Of course you do," Stanford said, placing a warm hand on his shoulder. "And you will."

At 7:30 a.m., Roberts pushed through the swinging doors of the Ventura County Morgue.

The burned corpse lay on a metal table, chest gaping open. As he'd expected, Paul Cortese was conducting the autopsy.

The man was middle-aged, with salt-and-pepper hair, and wore hospital greens under a black rubber apron that hung to his ankles. Cortese was always on duty, it seemed, no matter what time of the day or night. Roberts guessed that he was the most devoted medical examiner in all of southern California. A microphone was suspended from the ceiling next to him to record what he observed.

"Morning, Paul," Roberts said, standing opposite him across the table.

"Sorry about your friend," Cortese replied, looking up. "You sure you want to watch this?"

Roberts nodded.

"Detective Whittaker is on his way, you know."

"I know," he grunted. Whittaker was in charge of homicide while he was in charge of the arson so, technically, Roberts knew that he was overstepping his bounds. With most detectives, it wouldn't be a problem. But Whittaker was known for jealously protecting his turf, and making life hell for those who crossed him. Roberts couldn't let that stop him. He had to learn the truth about Cole firsthand.

"I just started my examination, Ted. But I can tell you one thing for certain: The victim is male."

He nodded, appreciating the verification. The body had been so severely burned that its primary sex characteristics had been obliterated. Gender had to be determined by the presence of a prostate or uterus.

Cortese plucked a scalpel from the dissection station and used it to incise the corpse's trachea. Inside, Roberts saw black paste.

"Heavy ash inhalation," Cortese said, stating aloud what they both knew into the microphone. "Which means that the fire didn't kill him outright." He pointed to the hands. "Spears of bone protruding through the skin at both wrists indicate defensive wounds."

Roberts frowned. Defensive wounds on a man who'd committed suicide? It didn't make sense. But then again, little about the case made sense. His thoughts turned to Ronny, and he made a mental note to call the boy after the autopsy. Better that he heard about his father's death from a friend than a stranger in the police department.

He felt a sudden flash of anger at Cole for leaving his son alone—and then doubt. No matter what the evidence, he couldn't believe that Cole would kill himself. The man had too much to live for: a wonderful son, a successful career, a new love. Besides, giving up on life wasn't in the man's character. Cole always had an extreme will to live. On some missions, he'd pushed the men past what they believed was physically possible to escape an enemy.

"Need something, Ted?" came a gruff voice from behind him.

Roberts turned to face Whittaker. The five-foot-five detective wore a brown suit jacket that was speckled with dandruff from what little gray hair he had left. "The victim is a friend of mine, Scott."

"Doesn't make the homicide yours."

"I understand that."

"Apparently not," Whittaker said as he approached the table. "I asked Anderson for a rundown of your arson investigation, so don't bother going into it. Now step aside."

Roberts bit his tongue, and let Whittaker take his position at the table.

As a SEAL, he'd learned to engage an enemy only when conditions were favorable, and now they were not. To get more involved, he'd have to fight against a man with seniority, and the ear of higher-ups in both the police and fire departments. Better to retreat and wait for a better opportunity.

"What do we got?" the detective asked Cortese.

"The victim is male," the medical examiner replied, and then leaned over to scrutinize the corpse's face. The flesh had been cooked away and only a charred layer of muscle remained. "There seems to be scoring on the cheeks."

Roberts looked closely, and noticed a series of fine, almost imperceptible crosshatches about an inch below each eye.

"Shrapnel wounds?" Whittaker asked.

Cortese slid the tip of the scalpel into one of the wounds, and then pulled it open so that it yawned like a tiny mouth. Inside, Roberts saw a glimpse of bone.

"Too precise for shrapnel," Cortese said. "A bladed weapon, most likely."

Whittaker looked over his shoulder. "Was your buddy in the habit of cutting himself?"

Roberts refused to lash out and give Whittaker reason to toss him from the room. "Cole was of sound mind, Detective," he said, but the message in his tone of voice was clear: *You'll have to do better than that, asshole.*

Whittaker smirked at the challenge.

Roberts turned his focus back to Cortese. Using forceps, the man peeled the black titanium SEAL watch from the corpse's wrist, and placed it into a plastic evidence bag.

Cortese handed the bag to Whittaker, and Roberts examined the watch over the detective's shoulder. The luminous dial lay underneath a glass face warped by heat. The band was smeared with soot, but otherwise undamaged. When Whittaker turned the watch over, Roberts noticed an engraving on the back of the band. He struggled to read the thin, tiny lettering through the plastic.

For my dearest son. May your time be filled with health and joy. Happy Birthday. Love, Dad.

"This is Ronny Cole," Roberts whispered.

"Who?" Whittaker asked.

"Cole's son. Dave must have given him the watch as a gift."

"I thought you said you had a positive I.D."

Roberts ignored the dig. Cole blowing himself up on set was tough enough to swallow. But Ronny? Had he been on set alone? If not, where was Cole?

Whittaker turned to face him. "Was the kid licensed to act independently?"

Roberts shook his head. "He was a trainee."

"Then the answer is pretty fucking clear. Cole is responsible."

He felt a tide of anger that he didn't bother to stem this time. "Watch it. Cole is my friend."

"I don't care if he's the fucking pope. The unshunted leads you found on set? Cole couldn't have missed them. You said so yourself. Unless the kid was on set alone, cut his own face, and triggered the explosives, then I'd say your *friend* is our primary suspect."

Roberts shook his head, mind a blur. None of this made sense. But there was no way Cole could have killed his son. He knew that much. "You're off base here, Scott. Way off base."

"If your buddy is innocent, where is he? Why isn't he doing everything he can to help us investigate his son's death?"

Roberts didn't have an answer. "I left a message on his answering machine," he said lamely. "He'll be here when he gets it."

"Yeah? I sent a unit to his house when I began canvassing the area. Routine procedure. You should learn it sometime. Cole wasn't there. In fact, his bed hadn't been slept in. I didn't give the detail much thought until now."

Roberts felt nauseous. Whittaker was right. Cole was MIA when he should have been home.

"Maybe your friend went nuts," Whittaker continued. "A lot of war vets do. He could have wasted his son, panicked after realizing what he did, then set off the charges to cover his tracks."

Roberts felt overrun as Whittaker made his case. The evidence against Cole was damning. Mutilated corpse, exposed wire leads, initialed tool belt. And, perhaps worst of all, his unexplained absence. But the part of him that had refused to believe that Cole could blow himself up—and he *had* been right about that—now refused to believe that his friend was guilty of murder.

"No way," Roberts insisted. "You don't know David Cole. He isn't capable of hurting his son. There's another explanation, believe me."

"A minute ago you believed that Cole was on this table," Whittaker said, waving his hands over the corpse, "so excuse me if I think you're full of shit."

"I'm telling you Cole is innocent."

"I won't allow your bias to interfere with this investigation, Ted. *Do you read me?*" the detective growled in mocking reference to his position as a radio operator for the SEALs.

While another detective might have given him a chance to exonerate his friend, Roberts knew that Whittaker would deny his request to participate in the investigation. Worse, once Whittaker's mind was made up about a suspect's guilt or innocence, little could sway him. He would interpret any future evidence accordingly.

To clear Cole's name, Roberts knew that he would have to act quickly, quietly—and alone.

"Yeah," Roberts replied. "I read you loud and clear."

Thump-thump.

Lawrence opened his eyes, jarred from a deep and drunken sleep on the recliner. He shifted, then groaned, as his expansive belly roiled and his temples throbbed.

After a day of target practice and BBQ with Cole and Ronny,

he'd spent the night with a case of Miller Genuine Draft and a few Elvis Presley and Jean-Claude Van Damme movies. After fourteen bottles, he'd passed out near the end of *Cyborg.*

He craned his head to look at the TV. The movie long over, the screen had defaulted to the DVD's opening menu.

Groaning again, he looked at his wristwatch. Six a.m. Way too fucking early to be awake when he didn't have to be on set. Rubbing his head, he wondered about the noise that had woken him up. A tree limb probably fell onto the roof, he thought. Or maybe a deer had—

Thump-thump.

He sat bolt upright. The sound hadn't come from outside the house, he realized. But from down the bedroom hallway. He grabbed his .44 Police Bulldog from the coffee table. Flipping off the safety with his thumb, he kept it aimed down the hallway as he lifted his bulk from the creaking recliner.

"I fucking hear you!" he bellowed. "Come out with your hands up!"

No answer.

Thanks to an elusive crossed wire, the alarm system messed with his TV picture quality, which is why it stayed off most of the time. He should have fixed the problem a long time ago. Now look what happened. Somebody'd snuck past his drunk ass.

Just like the night his baby, Crystal, was murdered.

He felt a surge of anger as he held the Bulldog with both hands, and crept slowly down the hallway. *Whoever you are, you ain't gonna get away this time.*

As he approached the closed bathroom door, could hear the hiss of shower water behind it. *What the hell?*

And then the smell hit. Rancid. Cloying.

Charred flesh.

As a cop, he'd helped the NYFD pull victims from burning buildings.

The smell sent his stomach into a tailspin. He leaned against the wall, swallowed thickly, forced himself to continue. By the time he reached the bathroom, the sickly-sweet stench hung in the air like steam in a sauna. He swallowed again, tasting bile, and then placed his ear against the closed door. No thumping now. Just the hiss of running water.

Taking a couple of preparatory breaths, he burst through the door and dropped to one knee, aiming the Bulldog.

"Freeze, mother—" he began, but then his voice choked in his throat when he saw the figure clinging onto the shower spigot. A man, his torso an open wound, needles of water peeling away ribbons of burned flesh.

"Dave?" he croaked.

He watched Cole grip a thick flap of charred flesh on his chest, and pull. The flap peeled away with a Velcro *skrrrrtch!* Cole emitted a strangled cough as he pounded the tiled wall with his fist.

Thump-thump.

A paramedic friend from New York had once told him about debridement. You had to wash away any charred skin on a burn victim or risk acute infection. The pain for the victim was beyond anything you could imagine and here Cole was debriding *himself.*

"Dave!" he yelled.

This time Cole turned his head.

Be cool, Lawrence cautioned himself. Panic and the victim panics with you. "I'm gonna call you an ambulance," he said, barely able to keep his voice steady.

Cole shook his head.

Lawrence took a step forward, and saw that Cole stood up to his ankles in greasy water, the drain clogged by chunks of blackened skin. It looked like the man had been grabbed by a massive, flaming hand—there was a third-degree burn across his chest, and four more burns across his back. His face was also burned from the corner of his right eye down across his cheek to the front of his chin.

"Dave, listen to me. You need a doctor."

Cole slammed his fist against the wall in protest.

"Don't make me come in there and grab you."

Cole pounded the wall a second time.

Lawrence moved to grab him, but stopped when he saw a desperate, haunting sadness in his friend's eyes.

"Dave . . ." Lawrence said, feeling his voice begin to shake. "Where's Ronny?"

Cole closed his eyes.

"Aw, man," he said, tears streaming down his cheeks. *Let Cole take care of himself, then he'll fill you in,* he told himself. *Until then, just be cool.*

With trembling hands, he fetched a sponge and washcloth from the cabinets beneath the sink and placed them on the edge of the tub. He turned to leave, but Cole grabbed the front of his shirt.

"You gotta give me a sec with this," Lawrence rasped.

Cole looked at him a moment, then nodded and let go.

Lawrence left the bathroom, closing the door behind him. He returned to the living room, popped *Viva Las Vegas* into the DVD player, and then fell into his recliner.

He wiped the tears from his face as he did his best to concentrate on the movie—such a cool cat, Elvis, crooning, making time with Ann-Margret. Cranking up the volume, finally, when Cole began to scream.

Chapter 6

Roberts pounded on the front door. "Dave! It's Ted!"

He wanted to check the house for himself. Cole could have moonlighted on another job, or spent the night with another girlfriend. Whatever the reason, Whittaker's officer could have simply left before Cole returned home.

"Dave!" Bile rose in his throat as he thought about giving Cole the news about Ronny. First the Team. Then his wife. Now this.

He'd do everything he could to help his friend cope. He owed the man that much, and more.

After knocking for a few more minutes, he tried the knob. Locked. He produced a pick set and defeated the lock easily, then drew a Smith and Wesson .40 semi-automatic from the holster on his belt. The perp who'd killed Ronny might be prowling around. If Cole were home, he would understand Roberts' precaution.

In his six years as an arson investigator, he hadn't used his weapon once. He hoped that record would stand.

Pushing the door open, he stepped into cool darkness. The entrance hall windows were covered by curtains that blocked the morning sun. He'd been in the house only once, years ago, when Cole invited him for a beer on Labor Day. Although cordial, the tension had been palpable. Too many memories. And his therapist was right—he felt compelled to prove himself to Cole because the man had saved his life. That day was no exception. Cole politely listened to him go on about his accomplishments. They rarely got together after that, big surprise. Not that he blamed the guy.

Roberts crept down the hall toward the living room, holding the pistol with both hands. If somebody was in the house, his pounding may have tipped them off. He could be walking into an ambush. Adrenaline surged in his chest, and he forced himself to calm down.

Take it easy . . . you'll be fine . . .

But what if Cole *was* guilty? And what if he was lying in wait?

There was no way he could take Cole in combat. The man had been a master at strategy and tactics, often keeping the Team alive against insurmountable odds. Until the odds finally caught up with them.

He forced away the ridiculous notion.

Idiot. Stay focused.

When he reached the doorway to the living room, he heard a rubbing squeak, and froze. So someone *had* arrived after the patrol officer. He took a calming breath, gripped the pistol. *Here we go . . .*

He strode quickly into the room, and then leveled his pistol at the woman asleep on the couch. That would explain why his pounding hadn't alerted her. He struggled to discern her features through the gloom, but couldn't.

"Arson Investigator," he said. "Raise your hands where I can see them."

She jerked awake, and unfolded into a sitting position.

"I said get your hands up."

"Ted!" she said.

Lowering the pistol, he switched on a table lamp, which flooded the room with light. "Jennifer? What the hell are you going here?"

"I went home like you said, but I couldn't sleep, so I came

here to wait," she said quietly. "He gave me a key at dinner two nights ago."

"The detective running the homicide investigation sent an officer. Did you talk to him?"

"That must have been before I arrived."

"The officer claims that Cole didn't spend the night here."

"It doesn't look like it, no." Taking a deep breath, she looked at him plaintively. "Please tell me that David is okay, Ted. Please tell me that he arrived on set after I left, and is away trying to figure out what triggered the explosion."

Roberts looked at her with an ache in his chest. She deserved to know what had happened, and he needed her to know that he was going to solve the case. Aside from Ronny, she was Cole's closest relationship, and her input would be invaluable.

"There was a victim inside the house," he told her. "But it wasn't Dave."

"I *knew* it. David would never make a mistake like that." She closed her eyes as tears ran down her cheeks.

"Jennifer," he said. She opened her eyes, expression buoyed by relief. He didn't want to dash her joy, but he had no choice. "Jennifer, the victim was Ronny."

Her expression crumbled. "Oh my God."

"We need to find Dave," he said. "Do you know where he is?"

"Let me think," she whispered and looked at her lap. Roberts could see that she was caught between conflicting emotions of relief and horror.

"I'll give you a moment."

Walking into the kitchen to give Jennifer privacy, Roberts saw an answering machine on the counter. He pressed PLAY. He heard the message he'd left earlier, followed by two messages from Jennifer. Beside the phone was a pad of paper with two additional messages written in blue ballpoint pen, both dated the previous day. One was a reminder to send Jennifer a dozen roses. The other was a reminder to meet Ronny for lunch.

These were the notes of a man who loved his son and the woman in his life. Not a man on the edge of a murderous breakdown.

"You mentioned having dinner with Dave recently?" he called to Jennifer.

"With David and Ronny, both, yes," she said with a tremor in her voice.

Roberts returned to the living room. Jennifer had an expression of resigned calm that belied her grief and exhaustion. "Did anything come up that might help?"

She paused. "David had an argument with Gary Stanford."

"Producer of *Bringing Them Back*?"

She nodded. "Gary hired his nephew, Ned Brandenburg, to work with David on the pyrotechnics. The man clearly didn't know what he was doing."

"Why did Dave keep him on?"

"Nepotism goes a long way in Hollywood. David had no choice until Ned and his partner, Levar Watkins, almost got everybody killed. That was when David confronted Gary about removing Ned from the set. David also wanted to rewire the stronghold for safety reasons, but Gary balked about giving him the time."

Her mention of time made him think about what time the 911 call came in, and how long the fire units took to arrive. Fifteen minutes from report to response. Why did that time frame bother him suddenly?

"Are you saying that Gary Stanford might be involved?"

"I don't know. David halted production while he and Gary talked things out, and the delay was costing Stanford a lot of money. The explosion just seems convenient, that's all."

She was flailing, desperately trying to make sense of the

tragedy. He knew how she felt. "Movie producer to murderer is a pretty big jump, Jennifer."

Her eyes flashed. "You're defending Gary Stanford?"

"No, I'm not," he said gently. "I'm just saying we'll know more after the ATF analyzes the samples I collected from the mortars."

"Can you at least ask Stanford a few questions?"

Had he been working with a detective other than Whittaker . . . "Actually, I can't. The homicide investigation falls under police jurisdiction."

"Then let them know what you think."

"It's not that simple."

She looked at him a moment, confused, and then her eyes widened. "The police think Cole triggered the explosion and killed Ronny. They've already made up their minds."

Too smart for her own good, he thought. "I'm afraid so, yes."

"We have to do something, Ted," she pleaded. "Before it's too late."

"Jennifer, listen to me. I don't believe that Dave is responsible any more than you do. But if I go after Stanford based on assumption when the physical evidence strongly points in another direction, the police will yank my badge and dismiss anything I've discovered as biased. And I can't say I'd blame them. It's no secret that Cole is my friend. Better to build a solid case before coming forward. At least we'll have a chance that way."

"If you believe in David so much, why did you come here?"

"I had my doubts, I admit. But now that I've seen the phone messages and talked to you, I'm convinced. I'll do everything in my power to get to the bottom of this. The man saved my life. It's time I returned the favor."

"If you ask Gary just a few questions, you might be able to—"

"I said no," he interrupted. "The moment Stanford asks for a lawyer, the cops will get involved, and it'll be over."

She looked at him, clearly frustrated, until finally she said, "You may not be able to investigate Stanford. But I can."

"You'll do no such thing."

"I care about David too, Ted. More than you know. I refuse to sit by and do nothing."

He could empathize with her all too well. The shock. The disbelief. The need for resolution. But the risk of involving her . . . "Jennifer, you're a civilian."

"I have a key to Gary's house. There might be evidence inside that ties him to all this."

"Without a search warrant, it'll be inadmissible," he said. "Give me the key."

"Not if I have a reason for being there, which I do. I'm his employee. I could be looking for production schedules, contracts, anything."

"I'll take care of it, Jennifer."

"What will you say if he catches you? If he calls the police?"

She was right. The opportunity to search Stanford's house was too valuable to pass up. And if he was caught, it would all be over. He couldn't take the risk—not when Cole's life hung in the balance. Still, he couldn't give Jennifer carte blanche to act as she wanted. She was emotional, reckless. "Okay. I'll let you search Stanford's house on the condition that you report everything you find to me. And I mean everything."

"If you do the same."

"If I deem it appropriate."

She nodded, probably realizing that he had no intention of compromising further. He was already risking too much, and more variables would only complicate the case.

Her shoulders sagged, the stress of confrontation sapping what little energy remained from her grief. "I'm going to stay here a few minutes to collect myself," she whispered.

Again, he felt distracted when she mentioned time. *What the hell is bothering me about that?* He thought about the time he'd arrived on set, about calling Cole, about the last wispy traces of fire in the stronghold. He thought about the watch on Ronny's wrist. The glass face had melted. The minute and hour hands had stopped to mark the time of the explosion. He did the mental math. *Wait . . . can that be right?*

"Don't stay too long, Jennifer. The cops'll be here soon to conduct a more thorough search." He handed her a business card with his cell phone number. She did the same. "I'll be in touch," he told her, and then hurried from the room.

"Give me morphine!" Cole rasped. "Now, goddammit!"

He sat naked on the kitchen floor, back against the refrigerator, legs splayed across the linoleum. The charred flesh on his throat had dried and constricted, making his voice sound like it was coming through a clogged tube. Clutching Ronny's baseball cap in his right hand, he looked at Lawrence, who knelt on the floor next to him. The big man pulled a two-foot length of open-celled foam bandage from a military medikit, and dipped it into a purple mixing bowl filled with iodine.

"Dave, this is crazy," Lawrence said, eyes bloodshot from crying. News of Ronny's death had hit him like a wrecking ball. "Morphine won't be nearly enough. You gotta let me take you to a hospital."

Cole knew the disinfectant would protect the burns from bacterial infection temporarily, and help prevent fluid and protein loss. No substitute for real medical care, but it might do the trick until he accomplished his mission. "The morphine will have to do," he said. "I can't let them get away with it. I won't!"

His anger flashed. Ruger, after so many years, it couldn't be, it just couldn't be. And then memories of that horrible night fifteen years ago flickered to life like some hidden-away movie dragged out of a vault. Flickered to life despite his best efforts to keep them away like he'd done for so many years, flickered between blur and algetic focus . . .

. . . as SEAL Team commander, he crouches at the head of the Zodiac raft, scanning the three-hundred-foot wooden hull that towers above them. Spots a silhouette, mid-ship.

Sentry. Armed with an AK-47, smoking a cigarette that glowed cherry-red in the dark.

"I say we kill 'em all," Ruger whispers, using the barrel of his AR-23 to point at other sentries farther down the moonlit dock.

"We'll do no such thing," Cole whispers back to his second-in-command. "We stick to the mission: Grab the captain and blow the boat."

"They deserve to fucking die."

Cole looks closely at Ruger. Face streaked with black camouflage paint, the man's eyes catch the red flicker of Kuwaiti oil fires burning on the horizon. Although Ruger continues to be an indispensable member of the Team that matched his own, the man seemed withdrawn lately. Contentious. Less in control. Cole thinks about switching duties—letting Ruger wire the underwater charges while he led the on-deck assault—but decides against it, knowing that a sudden change in procedure could throw off the Team's timing.

"You'll do as ordered, Lieutenant," Cole says. "Now move out."

Ruger sneers as he slides past. Cole watches him rappel the anchor line, black combat fatigues making him invisible in the darkness, and then silently climb up and over the stern. Returning his attention to the sentry, Cole listens for any sound that might give Ruger away, but hears only lapping water and the trilling of exotic bugs.

The sentry is still smoking when a shadow comes at him from behind. The blade of Ruger's K-bar knife flashes in the moonlight. And then it's over. No struggle. No cry for help . . .

"You don't have to let them get away with it," Lawrence said. "You can go to the cops."

Cole shook his head in an attempt to clear it. He didn't want the memories of the failed mission to compound his trauma. Didn't know if he could handle it. "Not with the evidence that Ruger planted. By now, the police think . . ." his voice trailed off. He couldn't bring himself to say it.

"Then let me talk to them," Lawrence offered.

"They won't listen."

Lawrence swirled the bandage to thoroughly soak it with iodine. "They will too listen. They'll listen if I have to fucking yell from the precinct steps. I used to be a cop, remember? I know how to talk to these guys."

"I can't take the risk."

"So going vigilante is the answer?"

"First, I failed my Team in the Gulf. And now I've failed my son. I'm not going to fail him again by letting the men who killed him get away. Not when I'm still able do something about it."

"You call this able?" Lawrence said incredulously.

Cole looked down at the charred flesh covering his chest. Since the shower, the wound had dried, forming a brittle scab that lay like red ice over a polluted lake. His wounds were bad, yes. But not impossible to overcome. "I can handle it."

Lawrence gave the bandage an angry swirl. "Your way is gonna get you killed. Any fool can see that."

Killed, what a fucking laugh. But he'd had no idea what was about to happen that night. How could he? If only he'd listened to his gut instincts and aborted the mission. If only . . .

. . . he gives the remaining four members of the Team a thumbs-up. They slide past him one by one and rappel the anchor line, following Ruger's lead.

"Maybe Ruger was right," Ted Roberts whispers, bringing up the rear. "Maybe we should take everybody out to be safe."

At twenty-two, Roberts is the youngest man on the Team by twelve years. The least experienced, eager-to-please, impressionable. Cole does not want Ruger to become a dangerous influence on him. "We're not butchers, Ted. We're soldiers. No unnecessary kills." He places a hand on Roberts' shoulder. "Remember your training. Block out fear, emotion, pain—everything—and focus on the mission. Do that, and you'll be fine."

Cole dispenses the advice with conviction, but for the first time, doesn't believe it. A deep feeling of dread has been churning in his gut since they'd left base. Not that it matters. He can't scrap the mission based on bad mojo.

"Got a Willy Pete in your launcher?" he asks. "If your radio gets wrecked, we'll need it to signal our evac."

Roberts glances at the grenade launcher attached to the barrel of his AR-23. "I made sure the other guys loaded up, too."

Cole nods, and watches Roberts climb the anchor line onto the boat. A good kid. If he keeps his head, he'll be fine.

Putting aside his AR-23, Cole slides the Draeger underwater breathing apparatus over his face, then grabs eight waterproof bladders—each with a half-brick of tetrytol inside wrapped with primacord—and eases himself legs-first over the raft's port side into the tepid marsh water.

When he dips below the surface, all sights and sounds snuff out. He feels suspended in a putrid, primordial soup that stretches to dark infinity in every direction.

He has six minutes to rig the charges before the team returns with their quarry . . .

"You think this is a joke?" Lawrence continued. "There won't be any burned-to-a-crisp handicap for you, man. Those motherfuckers'll waste you on sight. You're a walking, talking piece of evidence."

Cole slammed his fist against the linoleum and immediately regretted it as hooks of pain gouged his arm. He gagged until the agony subsided into a burning ache. "I know that this is no fucking joke," he panted through clenched teeth. "They killed *my* son, so we do this *my* way. Got it?"

"Jesus, Dave, I didn't mean . . ." Lawrence's voice faded as he continued to swirl the bandage.

Cole realized that Lawrence was suffering too, like he'd lost his own son. Or like he'd lost his daughter Crystal, all over again. "I know you didn't mean anything, big man. But I need you to shoot me up. Now. Before I lose my nerve."

Lawrence looked imploringly at him before retrieving a styrette from the medikit. He angled the tiny, single-dose syringe against Cole's right tricep, and then pushed needle through flesh.

Cole felt seeping warmth emanate from the pinprick, which dulled the knife-edge of pain throughout his body. To test the drug's effect, he took a deep breath. He felt several blossoms of pain underneath the rocky scab on his chest, but the pain was manageable. Barely.

"Let me give you another dose before I apply the first bandage," Lawrence said.

"No."

"Your body isn't in shock like it was in the shower, Dave. This time you'll feel everything . . ."

. . . even though the marsh water is piss-warm, he feels cold, suddenly, as lethal determination floods through his body—instincts, honed by years of training and battle. Fear and physical distraction fade away like stars eclipsed by storm clouds. His movements become measured. Efficient. Automatic. He welcomes the instincts. They emerge when needed, turning him into a weapon.

The mission is all that matters.

Wedging the bladders between his knees, he digs his fingers into the thick, warm algae coating the hull and spiders down until he is directly beneath the boat. With only his sense of touch, he attaches four of the eight bladders to the hull in a tight cluster, then spiders forty feet toward the bow and attaches the remaining four bladders. When detonated, the clusters will crack the mammoth wooden boat in half, sinking it.

Finished, he pulls himself back up the hull and resurfaces near the anchor line. After climbing back into the raft, he slips the Draeger apparatus from his face and flips open the cover of his black titanium dive watch. The luminous dial indicates that only five-and-a-half minutes have passed. Not bad for working blind.

He reaches for his AR-23 when he hears Akmed speak in Arabic above him, on-deck. The Royal Saudi SEAL is on loan, acting as an interpreter for the Team. He's speaking hurriedly, plaintively. And then another voice answers. Also in Arabic.

Cole crouches, adrenaline surging through his body. Akmed can only be speaking to an Iraqi soldier. As he slides across the raft toward the anchor line, he hears more voices.

"Don't you surrender for me!" Bradley yells.

He knew that applying the iodine-soaked bandages would be bad. But if he passed out from the pain, he could be revived quickly. Too much morphine was a different story. It would cloud his mind for hours when the cops were already on his trail. And who knew how long he had before his body succumbed to the wounds? One shot would have to do.

"Get on with it," Cole told him.

Lawrence pulled the bandage, dripping brown with iodine, from the bowl. "Shit man, are you fucking sure?"

"Do it."

"For Ronny," Lawrence told him, bringing the bandage close. "You're doing this for your son. Remember that."

"For Ronny," Cole whispered, and watched as Lawrence pressed the bandage against his left pectoral. For a moment, all he felt was cold iodine . . .

. . . the unknown Arabic voice barks, and Bradley screams—a pitched, slavering shriek that sends ice down Cole's spine.

"Motherfucker!" Roberts yells. "Akmed, make them stop!"

Akmed speaks more quickly, but Bradley screams again.

Cole's heart trip-hammers as he scales the anchor line. As second-in-command, Ruger should be handling the negotiations. Has he been taken out? On deck, he looks toward the bow, in the direction of the voices, but stacks of cargo block his line of sight.

The Iraqi soldier barks again. Akmed replies, and then translates: "If we give them the detonator, they'll let us go."

Thank God. The Iraqis will keep their boat, call it even. Nobody wants to die tonight.

Roberts says, "Frank, put the detonator on deck."

So Ruger is alive.

Cole creeps forward, weaving among oil drum pyramids and steel pallets stacked with grain until he reaches a pair of towering crates. He peers through the narrow space between them, and can see only Roberts.

"Frank, no!" Roberts yells . . .

Suddenly, pain exploded across his chest and body in stabbing, searing shockwaves. Crushing his eyes closed, he gagged then coughed a gush of crimson phlegm onto the kitchen floor. He clutched a knee to steady himself, and the contact sent more barbs of pain stabbing up his thigh into his balls.

"Dave!" Lawrence sounded a million miles away.

Cole opened his eyes. Saw only white splotches. He clawed at the baseball cap, digging his fingers into the smooth fabric, and then a bolt of terror struck. It was deep and razor-edged and went straight for his soul. What if he died right now? Before he was finished . . . before he even got started? He sucked air through his constricted throat. No! He would survive for his son.

"This is fucking insane," Lawrence said. "I'm taking you to the hospital."

"Don't!" Cole barked.

Lawrence turned away to prepare another bandage. Too soon, the brown, soaked dressing was ready to be applied. Cole clenched his teeth in preparation.

"Try concentrating on my voice, Dave," Lawrence told him, tears pouring down his cheeks. "Listen hard to every word I say—"

Lawrence's voice fell away underneath a rush of white noise as pain whipsawed through his chest and slammed his head back against the kitchen wall . . .

Cole sprints between the crates . . . just a few feet and he'll reach his Team before all hell breaks loose . . . please God, keep my Team safe . . . they're my friends . . . my family . . . my sons . . . please God . . .

He concentrated on the pain—on the slamming, searing agony—and used it to keep the final pieces of memory away. He couldn't handle them. Not now. God, not now. But he knew they'd return. It was inevitable. They'd catch up with him soon enough.

His head whipped back and forth so violently that Lawrence's face blurred.

"Dave! Jesus, Dave!" Lawrence whispered.

Cole strained to control his seizing muscles, but his body continued to convulse as one thought echoed in his mind: Ruger, the man he'd trained and fought with for so long, the man he'd once trusted with his life, was now his mortal enemy.

Chapter 7

Wearing a black tuxedo, Gary Stanford stood underneath a green-roofed pagoda that shaded the front of Grauman's Chinese Theater from the late morning sun. Hung high above the Fu Dog statues that flanked the theater's entrance was a multicolored banner that read: *Together Forever* starring Anne Devereaux.

Stanford thought it appropriate that a town based on illusion would hold its most prestigious premiers in a venue that was just as counterfeit. But now the gaudy façade loomed with the promise of riches and prestige that before this morning had been achingly out of reach.

Killing Cole had been regrettable, but he would not allow anyone to keep him from achieving his goal, least of all some below-the-line member of his crew. And now that he'd gotten rid of the man, he had only to close the deal with Devereaux to be on his way to A-list status.

He was among a select few that stood on *this* side of the velvet ropes, comfortably separate from the bustle of public, paparazzi and press. Anne Devereaux had deemed him worthy or, more precisely, Devereaux's agent, not that it made any difference. Stanford had called the agent yesterday with news that he'd raised the two-million-dollar retainer, and subsequently had been asked to offer Devereaux the part in *Mothers and Daughters* in person.

The red carpet stretched sixty feet from pagoda to street

curb, where Devereaux's limousine would deposit her like some precious cargo. When she walked into the theater's concrete plaza, adorned with the imprinted hands of Hollywood royalty, he would make the offer in front of the cameras. In that instant, major players in town would now take notice and recognize that he—Gary Stanford—was one of them. They would recognize, too, that Loki Productions was a force to be reckoned with.

"This is for you," Stanford whispered, thinking of his father.

He glanced into the theater's lobby. Huxley had excused himself to go to the restroom nearly twenty minutes ago. If he didn't return soon, he would miss Devereaux's arrival.

Stanford gritted his teeth. He could initiate contact without Huxley, of course, but the man's tardiness threatened to cast Loki Productions as less than professional. Even a minor blunder could jeopardize the deal. Up-and-coming actresses were notoriously skittish. They looked for any sign that a deal might go bad—the result of years of being rejected and exploited while fighting their way to the top.

Suddenly, the crowd surged forward. A moment later, the object of their excitement pulled to the curb: A white limousine. Flashbulbs popped, Beta Cam lamps beamed to life.

The goddess had arrived.

The back door swung open, and Anne Devereaux stepped from the limo. She wore a silver dress that shimmered as she stepped onto the red carpet, and waved to the crowd who called for her attention as plaintively as baby chicks for their mother. Her bejeweled neck glittered like tiny lights as she leaned forward to accept a kiss from her agent who stood nearby.

Stanford looked over his shoulder into the lobby. Still no sign of Huxley. *Damn you, Steven.*

Devereaux was even more stunning in person than she was on screen. Her bombshell-blonde hair, full lips and feline eyes beamed with confidence and sensuality—and something else.

Ah, yes, he realized. A touch of disdain for her adoring public. Understandable, since she'd been washed up for the past ten years until her indie film took top honors at the Cannes Film Festival. Suddenly, she was the hottest ticket in town, a reversal that had no doubt filled her with a sense of entitlement.

My kind of woman, he thought. It was clear now, more than ever, that the actress possessed "It." That elusive blend of looks, talent and attitude that would capture the imagination of the public she resented, and send *Mothers and Daughters* into the stratosphere.

Devereaux was making her way slowly up the carpet, heading for the VIP area. *Where the hell are you, Steven?* he thought, when a hand clutched his arm. He turned. It was Huxley. The man looked pale.

"Where the fuck have you been?" Stanford hissed.

Huxley handed him a copy of *Star Power,* an industry tabloid, which he had picked up from inside the theater lobby.

"Why are you giving me this trash?"

"Gary, open to page—"

Stanford waved Huxley off when he heard the crowd go quiet. Devereaux was about to answer a question from a balding reporter in a tweed jacket.

"There were so many great actresses up for this role," the man stammered. "Why do you think they chose you?"

Devereaux opened her mouth to speak and phallic boom mikes descended upon her from every direction. "Why, darling," she said, "because I deserved it!"

A wave of laughter and murmurs followed the answer, and then the questions began anew as Devereaux kept walking toward the theater's double doors.

"She's perfect," Stanford told Huxley. "With her on board, we can't lose."

"Gary," Huxley said. "Open the tabloid to page three."

Stanford tore his gaze from the approaching actress to focus on his colleague. "What?"

"Goddammit, Gary, page three. *Open the tabloid to page three.*"

Scowling, Stanford did, already furious with Huxley because he'd been late, when he saw the headline: ON-SET EXPLOSION CLAIMS VICTIM IN SANTA SUSANA MOUNTAINS.

Victim. The word stood out like a flashing neon sign. *Only one.* Stanford skimmed the article, eyes fixing on a passage that made his blood run cold.

> . . . this morning, special effects devices being used on the set of Loki Productions' latest action potboiler *Bringing Them Back* detonated prematurely.
>
> Early reports indicate that a victim was found inside the house and has been identified as Ronny Cole, son of David Cole, the head of pyrotechnics on the film. David Cole is missing while investigators are trying to determine the cause of the explosion, which still remains in question . . .

"I called our source at the *Times* to confirm," Huxley said. "It's true."

Stanford looked up and saw that Devereaux, led by her agent, was fast approaching. Beyond her, the crowd fell away into blackness as the abyss of failure yawned before him, threatening again to swallow him whole.

"We have to stop," Huxley struggled to be heard over the growing wave of commotion that heralded Devereaux's approach, "until we find out what's going on!"

"Are you insane?" Stanford shot back. "We won't get another chance like this again. We go forward as planned." He knew from bitter experience that business endeavors rarely succeeded without all the variables in place. But he had no choice. It was continue or lose everything.

"Gary, if Cole—"

"We go forward as planned," Stanford said, and then was blinded by Beta Cam lamps.

He smiled stiffly, like his lips were curling through concrete. He prayed that Devereaux wouldn't notice his awkward manner. Still blind, he felt tiny cool hands grasp his own and then heard Devereaux say with apparent sincerity, "Your call was a wonderful surprise, Gary, and just in time!"

"I always try to deliver a good cliffhanger, Anne," he heard himself say.

She laughed. "You have no idea how difficult it is to find good roles for women these days."

"It would be my pleasure to have you for dinner Sunday evening to discuss the details," he managed. "Your agent and attorney are also invited, of course."

Eyes adjusting to the lights, he noticed that Devereaux was still smiling for the cameras, but her gaze had hardened. He knew that she suspected something. He met her gaze, smiling himself. *You will not deny me this,* he thought. *I will cut your throat if you do, so help me.*

"Sunday is fine," she said, but the underlying message was unmistakable: *You screw up my career and I'll have your head on a platter.* And then she was gone, whisked away by her entourage of lawyers, assistants and bodyguards.

Devereaux had announced her intent to work with him in public, he thought. There was no turning back now.

"Sunday is the day after tomorrow, Gary," Huxley said as they followed the entourage into the posh theater. "That doesn't give us much time to find Cole."

"I had no choice. Her agent dictated the schedule when I called."

"You'll have to go underground until then. If Cole is alive, he won't go to the police. That much is clear from the way he barged into your office. He'll be out to settle the score."

Stanford nodded as they climbed a flight of purple-carpeted stairs, which led to a mezzanine that was partitioned into VIP boxes. He looked across the theater that was filling fast. The place held close to a thousand seats upholstered with burgundy velvet. Chandeliers made of multicolored glass hung from the ceiling, and the balconies were adorned with ornate moldings and plaster gargoyles. No matter how many times he entered this theater, he felt like he was back in the 1940s. Hollywood's heyday. When movie watching was an event.

He led Huxley to their assigned box on the right wing. He glanced at Devereaux who sat front and center, holding court with the guests around her. They would not be able to leave without her noticing.

"We take care of this Cole situation quickly and cleanly, do you hear me?" he told Huxley as they settled into the soft seats. "But first things first. After we get out of this premier, we'll have a talk with that motherfucker Frank Ruger."

Lawrence collapsed onto the recliner. He looked at Cole unconscious in the kitchen, finally free from the pain. He'd wait before waking the man up. God knows he needed the rest. It was amazing that he'd stayed conscious for so long. The guy was fucking superhuman.

Lawrence felt his eyes flicker. The adrenaline rush was finally wearing off. As he fell off to sleep, thoughts of Ronny drifted into his mind. The kid he'd cared for like his own nephew was gone. Burned by men driven by violence and greed.

If only he'd been able to protect him. If only he'd been able to protect Crystal, too. *If only* . . .

His cell phone rang, jerking him awake. He pressed it to his ear and said "Hello" before he realized it.

"Mr. Fuchs?" a woman asked. "This is Jennifer Shrager."

Lawrence breathed a quiet sigh of relief. Not the cops. "I know who you are, Jennifer," he said gently. "Please call me Lawrence, okay?"

"Lawrence, I—" she began when her voice hitched and she went quiet. "Have you read the trades this morning?"

The words triggered a new rush of sadness in him. Now he was the one who struggled to keep his voice steady. "Yeah, I know about Ronny."

"I'm so sorry. I know you were close to him."

"Thanks."

"I only have one question and then I'll leave you alone," she said, her voice beginning to waver again.

"It's okay, Jennifer."

"Do you know where I can find David?"

Even though he'd been expecting the question, answering it filled him with dread. Lying to her would be worse than lying to the police. Lying to her would be like lying to the people who he'd served and protected as a cop. Neighbors . . . friends . . . family . . .

Crystal.

"Have you tried his cell phone?" he answered lamely.

"He doesn't answer." She paused, and then words came rushing out, like water from a broken dam: "I stopped by his house, too, but he wasn't there and I don't know where he is or if he knows about Ronny or if he's lying hurt somewhere or anything at all not anything not anything . . ." She began to sob.

I used to be a cop, he thought. But was he protecting Jennifer by lying to her? Was he serving Ronny's memory by keeping his father out of the hospital?

He looked at his Crystal's photo on the mantel. She was smiling. Thin as a reed. Wearing her favorite blue-flowered sundress. It had taken a long time to come to terms that he—a decorated New York cop—had been fucking powerless to protect his own daughter.

He fought back tears of frustration. *Goddammit, Dave, if you'd only listened when I told you to walk away from Stanford.*

"I'm sorry, Lawrence," Jennifer croaked. "I thought if he contacted anyone, it would be you."

You have the chance to be a cop again. To do the badge proud.

But he couldn't betray his friend. Cole had accepted him despite his failure as a father, a husband, a cop. Cole had accepted him *as-is* and never tried to change him. Not once. Not even when he got drunk and laid into Cole because he was the closest available target. Cole understood real fucking pain. Now more than ever.

You were a good cop.

Yeah, good enough to know when the law should be bent. Even broken.

He couldn't allow Cole to feel what he'd felt after the death of his daughter. The man already felt like a failure. Lawrence would not let Cole feel powerless, too. And he would not allow a gentle soul like Ronny to be taken from the world without the men responsible paying the price.

If Cole wanted to do things his way, then he would help, no matter what that meant. Deep down—despite memories of the way his life used to be—he knew he had no choice. He owed it to Crystal, and to himself.

"If David contacts you, would you mind giving me a call?" Jennifer asked.

Lawrence closed his eyes. "I'll call you. I promise." He heard a soft, almost undetectable sigh of resignation escape her. The sound was nearly enough to make him tell her the truth. "Jennifer, wherever Dave is, I'm sure he's got a good reason for being there. He wouldn't stay away from you unless he had to."

"Thank you," she whispered, and hung up.

Lawrence listened to the dial tone for several moments, vowing to help his friend no matter what, wondering how long Cole could keep going before his body shut down.

"How long have I been out?" Cole rasped.

Lawrence was sitting beside him. "About an hour. Good news is that you're all bandaged up."

Mercifully, he'd passed out. Unconsciousness had saved him from excruciating physical pain, yes. But just as importantly, it had spared him from reliving every memory of that fateful night in Iraq. He couldn't bear to think about what had happened after he'd emerged from between the crates on that boat. Even after all these years, the memories were vivid. Too vivid. Hyper-real like some terrible, living nightmare. His stomach clenched. Now, thankfully, he had the strength to keep the memories at bay. But they were bound to recur. With Ruger back, and Ronny . . . he closed his eyes. There were too many triggers. It was only a matter of time.

He looked down at his body. Lawrence had double-wrapped his chest and stomach in thick bandages, and slipped burn nets over them to keep the dressings in place. Although he ached, the pain was nowhere near as excruciating as it had been. The morphine he'd taken earlier was working.

"I threw in silver nitrate bandages, too," Lawrence said. "To control the pain along with the morphine."

"Help me up?"

Lawrence grabbed his hand and pulled him to his feet. "Are the bandages too tight?"

Cole slowly flexed his arms, crouched, bent over and touched his toes. Not as limber as before, of course. But it would have to do. "They're fine, thanks."

"Dave, you need to call the police," Lawrence said. "Tell them about Ruger."

He shook his head. "We went over this, big man."

"By now LAPD knows that Ronny is dead. It was all over the trades this morning. If you don't come forward, they'll think you had something to do with his death."

Cole gritted his teeth. In fact, he had plenty to do with his son's murder. He'd allowed his past to catch up with him—and Ronny had paid the ultimate price. Now he would try to right that terrible wrong. "I said no."

Cole looked hard at Lawrence. His friend was holding something back, he knew. You work with and trust a man for so long, you knew when something was up.

"What's on your mind?" Cole asked. "And don't tell me it's the cops."

"Nah, it's nothing," Lawrence replied and turned to walk away.

Cole grabbed Lawrence's shoulder. The quick action sent tracers of pain up and down his arm. "You've helped me this far. Don't hold out on me now."

Lawrence stopped but didn't face him. He stood absolutely still for several moments, working out whatever was bothering him. Finally, he turned around. "Jennifer called this morning. She's looking for you. So's your friend Ted Roberts. I didn't want to say anything because I didn't want you to feel worse than you already do."

The news hit Cole like a sucker-punch. Of course Jennifer and Roberts were looking for him. But in the chaos of the morning, he hadn't given it any thought.

An almost overwhelming sense of shame washed over him as he thought about how Jennifer would be handling news of Ronny's death alone. About how his disappearance might seem to her. His shame multiplied when he thought about the confusion and sadness that Roberts must be feeling, too.

I can't dwell on them now, he thought. *Stanford and Ruger must pay for what they've done. The mission is all that matters. My son must take priority.*

But images of Jennifer stayed with him. The warmth of her smile. The gentleness of her touch. It took considerable effort to banish her from his mind.

"The phone call doesn't change a thing," he said.

Lawrence nodded—and Cole noticed the remains of struggle in his eyes. Jennifer's call must have triggered quite a dilemma, one that struck the core of what he'd stood for as a cop.

"Lawrence, you don't have to do this."

"I've made up my mind."

"You were a good officer. Dedicated. If you back out, I won't think less of you. You have my word on that."

"When Crystal died, I wished I'd had a way . . ." Lawrence's voice trailed off as he wiped tears from his cheeks. "Ronny was my family, too."

Cole looked across the living room to the fireplace mantel. On it was a silver-framed picture of Lawrence's six-year-old daughter. The frame was surrounded by little wind-up animals, flower magnets, and torn-out pages from coloring books. Cole felt a stab of sorrow every time he saw the girl's pretty face. She'd been murdered during a home invasion robbery, and the heartbreak from that trauma had sunk Lawrence's marriage and career. Obviously, no one could take Crystal's place in Lawrence's heart. Nevertheless, his friend loved Ronny as his own.

"You were the uncle Ronny never had," Cole said.

"I'm doing this for you both. And myself, too."

Cole nodded.

Lawrence sniffed loudly. "Yeah, well, I got some stuff that might help you do your thing. Be right back."

Cole breathed a quiet sigh of relief. The truth was, he would not have been able to continue without the ex-cop's help. He would need more than bandages and morphine. He would need new dressings. Logistical support. Equipment.

But he couldn't pressure his friend. Not when the man had lost a child, too.

Lawrence reappeared from the living room, pushing a green metal footlocker in front of him. He stopped, then threw open the lid and gestured Cole over. "I've been holding this stuff in case you needed it again."

Inside was SEAL gear . . . just like he'd used while still enlisted. Black fatigue jumpsuit, H-harness, sheathed K-bar knife, jungle boots, everything. Lawrence, always the collector. The man had added a Kevlar assault vest, aviator gloves, binoculars, a handheld smoke machine, a coil of det cord and blasting cap igniters, and various types of special effects wires and squibs to the stash. Lying on top was an MP5 machine gun and six clips of 9mm ammunition.

He sensed memories of the Iraqi mission begin to unfurl, and pushed them away. And then, in their place, he felt something cold rustle to life inside him . . . the instinct that had resurfaced at home in his bedroom, he realized. What he'd felt the moment before Ruger had knocked him out.

Trying to ignore the feeling, he began to climb into the jumpsuit. When Lawrence moved to help, he waved him away. He had to be self-sufficient.

"Where you headed first?" Lawrence asked, handing him a new cell phone. The police would monitor the old one.

"Stanford's place."

"Asshole doesn't deserve to live after what he did."

Cole swallowed thickly. The instincts slithered forward again, offering a more permanent solution. Threatened to turn him into . . . He pushed the cold feeling from his mind. "I won't tarnish Ronny's memory by sinking to his level."

"Take it from an ex-cop, Dave. If Stanford is dead-set against talking, there isn't much you can do."

"I've been giving that possibility some thought," he said, securing the assault vest and H-harness. He winced as he tightened each strap. "I don't need a confession. All I need is a recording of his voice to compare to the 911 tape."

"I see what you mean. Only three guys could've made that call. Four if Stanford did it himself after he got word. Hold on, I got just the thing."

Lawrence went back down the hallway and returned with a miniature tape recorder. Cole stashed it in a pocket.

He pulled on the aviator gloves next, and then slipped into the boots and laced them. Finally, he picked up and hefted the MP5. It was an SD3 model fitted with an integral silencer. The bolt slide was padded with rubber buffers to absorb noise.

The MP5 slid into his hands like a familiar beast—an extension of him and yet separate. It spoke to him, seduced him, made him want to forget the vestiges of civilized behavior. His fingers stroked the polished metal like a lover's skin . . . he knew it as well as any woman he'd slept with.

Cole choked on the disturbing emotions. He needed to be cautious to keep the cold, slithering instinct from dragging him beneath the muddy waters. If not, he could lose himself along with his son.

You've changed since the war. You can keep that side of yourself under control.

Lawrence handed him an ammunition clip. Cole slapped it into the MP5, then racked a round into the chamber. The familiar *chkk-chakk* echoed ominously in his ears. He slipped the remaining clips into the assault vest.

"You sure you're ready for this?" Lawrence asked. Cole nodded. "I pulled your plates. Every cop from here to fucking San Diego will be looking for you. Stick to surface streets, and take it easy. You don't wanna get stopped for speeding."

"Okay."

"Last thing," Lawrence said, and handed him a small plastic box with a clear lid. Inside were five morphine styrettes. "For whenever the pain comes back."

He tucked the box into the assault vest, knowing that he could take one at a time only and stay functional. Any more, and he'd be down for the count.

He moved to the front door and opened it. The afternoon sun was setting behind the hills. It would be dark in two hours, maybe three.

"Don't forget this," Lawrence said.

Cole turned, and saw that his friend held Ronny's baseball cap. The white Dodger emblem and blue fabric were still streaked with ash.

"Thanks," he said, taking the cap and fitting it onto his head. "I guess this is it, then."

"If it gets hard out there, Dave, think about Ronny," Lawrence said. "You're doing this for him. Don't forget that."

"I won't forget, big man," Cole said.

As he walked out the door and headed for the truck, he thought about how he'd failed. Again. He was always failing when it mattered. In the Gulf. Here at home.

Not this time, son, he vowed. *I'll do right by you this time, so help me.*

CHAPTER 8

Cole loped up the sweeping driveway of Stanford's home as barbs of muted pain jabbed the muscles in his leg. The morphine was keeping the pain at bay, but just barely.

But it was nothing compared to what Ronny had endured. He could take the pain. Nothing would keep him from accomplishing this mission. Nothing.

When he reached the top of the driveway, he cut across the sprawling front lawn, then veered around the southern corner of the house and crouched next to a side door.

No defensive fire. No enemy movement.

Slinging the MP5 over his shoulder, he picked the lock and entered a huge kitchen furnished with state-of-the-art stainless-steel appliances and a marble-topped island brimming with pots and pans. He crouched behind the island, listening again. Nothing. Not even a creaking door.

Was the house clear? Or was Stanford lying in wait?

Craning his neck over the island, he peered through the kitchen door into the living room. The area was spacious with white leather chairs and couches, similar to those he'd seen in Stanford's office. Spaced around the perimeter were marble sculptures on white, waist-high pedestals. A baby grand piano sat in the far corner.

He shook his head in disgust. The wealth. The pomp. The trappings of power common among men who had a flagrant disregard for human life, like the political fat cats that had sent his SEAL Team off to die.

Leading with the MP5, he moved silently through the living room, checking his areas of fire: front left, front right, back left, back right. Clear.

Moving exactly like he had across the deck of the Iraqi boat. Heading toward the voices. Bradley's screams. Like him, the Team had taken every precaution, but still . . .

He shook his head violently to clear it. He couldn't afford to break focus. Not now. Not when the man who'd masterminded Ronny's murder could be close.

Continuing through the living room, he passed a sliding glass door that led to a balcony with a wrought iron railing. Outside was an unblemished stretch of white sand, and a wooden pier that stretched fifty feet past the break line. To his left was a staircase leading down to what he assumed was an underground screening room, a common feature in Hollywood mansions since directors and producers often liked to view their dailies at home. The earth acted as natural sound insulation. He ignored the screening room in favor of another staircase that led to the second floor. Contrary to what people saw in the movies about buried stashes, the bedroom was typically where people kept what was most important to them.

Starting up the stairs, he grimaced as pain stabbed his legs. When he reached the top, his face was drenched with sweat, and he placed his hands on his knees to rest. *Your muscles are adjusting to the stress,* he thought, taking slow, measured breaths. *You'll be limber soon enough.*

He shambled stiffly into the master bedroom, feeling like some zombie in a horror movie. Everything in here was white as well—carpet, bedding, furniture. Floor-to-ceiling windows let in plenty of light. He began his search with the nightstand left of the bed. Inside were back issues of *Esquire,* a box of tissues, a hard case for glasses and a carton of cigarettes. He strode quickly around the bed to search the other nightstand when he heard the front door downstairs open.

Stanford. He stood rigid, and listened as the front door closed. As footsteps echoed on the hardwood floor. Stanford.

Trembling, he ducked into the walk-in closet, leaving the door open a crack so he could monitor the man when he entered the room.

He thought he was ready for this. Thought he could handle it.

Stanford. The man who'd ordered the death of his son. Was here.

He felt his upper lip curl. Fists clench.

The man who killed his son.

Motherfucker . . .

Was here.

He hitched a breath, listened as the footsteps continued to clatter below. And then the footsteps began to thump up the stairs. Burning rage lanced his chest. Motherfucker was here . . . motherfucker . . .

He yanked the K-bar knife from its sheath.

Motherfucker, I'll fucking kill you, he thought as the footsteps got louder. I'll fucking kill you . . . I'll fucking kill . . .

And then the memories hit.

Ronny on set rigging his own squib vest. Pounding nails into a nail board like a pro. Adjusting the brim of his Dodger cap. Waving to him. Smiling.

Screaming.

Cole shook his head, trying to force the scene away. But it came rushing in anyway . . .

Ronny tied to the chair. Straining against the ropes. Face smeared with blood. Screaming for the pain to stop. Dad, make it stop. Dad, please make it stop.

Cole gripped the doorframe, crushed his eyes closed. He

tried to focus on the good images of Ronny, but his thoughts were going haywire, hitting him rapid-fire.

Ronny bucking against the ropes. Knife blade flashing. Slicing. Blood spraying.

He felt wetness on his cheeks, realized he was crying. The K-bar slipped from his trembling fingers, thudded on the carpet.

Flash of anger at himself now. You're not up to the job. Impotent. Pathetic.

He sank to his knees.

Ronny screaming . . . help me, Dad . . . please . . .

He heard the footsteps grow louder as Stanford continued upstairs.

"You took my son," he rasped weakly in the dark confines of the closet.

Tears flowed freely down his cheeks as a string of mucus swayed from his lower lip like a noose. His heart felt crushed in a vise. "I'll kill you for taking my son . . . motherfucker . . . kill you . . ."

He heard the thumping footsteps grow silent as Stanford crossed onto the plush carpet of the bedroom. He saw a shadow cross the closet door. The man was here. A few feet away.

". . . kill you . . ." he whispered again, and sagged to all fours. Drained. Unable to stand.

Unable to accomplish his mission.

"I'm sorry for failing you again, son," he breathed. "Please forgive me."

And then he felt a sudden, icy determination.

No.

He'd felt the same determination when gearing up. When he'd picked up the MP5.

More than anything, he wanted to accomplish the mission. To bring Stanford to justice. But he didn't want this. Not this.

It meant returning to what he'd been as a SEAL. A calculated killer once again.

Gritting his teeth, he tried to push the feeling away, but it began to seep coldly through his chest. Without realizing it, his fingers had groped for the knife. The padded hilt felt good in his hand. Natural.

And then the terrible images and the burning pain of his wounds began to sink away, like a flaming ship into a cold black sea.

In its place came emotionless resolve.

He struggled again to keep the cold at bay, but it pushed back like a living thing. Gaining ground. And then a thought slipped into his mind like an ice pick. Dispense justice with the knife. It was the only kind of justice that mattered.

Pain nearly gone, he climbed to his feet. It was like he was in a theater, watching himself on screen. As he heard Stanford on the other side of the door, the muscles in his knife-arm jerked forward and up. Angled the blade, ready to plunge.

No! he commanded. He couldn't violate his son's memory with more death. But his body refused to obey.

He crouched as the shadow moved closer. Legs coiled like steel springs. And then he leaped forward . . .

"I'd like to speak to Gary Stanford, please."

The voice made him slam on the brakes inches before the door.

"This is Jennifer Shrager. I'm on hold for Gary Stanford."

Jennifer . . .

He peered through the crack in the door. She was there, back to him, cell phone pressed to her ear. She wore jeans and a simple green sweater. Looked as beautiful as he remembered on the night they'd had dinner. Seeing her flooded him with sudden warmth. He dropped the knife, sucking in a lungful of air, like he'd just broken the surface after being trapped underwater.

A flood of grief and burning pain came rushing after it, battering him to his knees again. But the warmth he felt for Jennifer continued to cut through the cold that filled his chest, causing it to retreat.

He ached for her, but knew that the same love that had pulled him back would compel her to try and stop him. And he couldn't allow her to compromise the mission, not when he had already come so close to failing.

But she was so close. Close enough to touch. He slipped his arm through the crack in the door and reached out, stretching, knowing that he was taking a terrible risk, but also knowing that to touch her, however briefly, would keep him going.

She was standing just out of reach. He stretched harder, splayed his fingers, and then the tips gently brushed her hair. The softness made him close his eyes for a long moment before he pulled his arm away.

"Steven, this is Jennifer. I want to talk to Gary," she said, and turned. He saw that her face was pale, eyes washed out. She'd been crying. After a few moments of listening to Huxley, she replied, "Do you honestly expect me to believe that Gary left town without telling you where he was going?"

So the fucking coward had gone underground, Cole thought. That meant the house had been cleaned of evidence.

He sat heavily on the floor. Emotionally exhausted. Although his mind began to fog, Jennifer's voice lingered in his ears like calming music. Keeping Jennifer in the dark was necessary if he wanted to accomplish the mission, but that didn't make being apart from her any easier to deal with. How he wished that they could be together, but of course that was impossible.

Or was it?

He pulled the mini tape recorder from his vest. If nothing else, he could listen to her voice. It didn't matter that she was simply making a phone call, the sound of her words would be enough to remember that he wasn't alone. He fumbled to press the record button, but the recorder slipped from his fingers and thumped softly onto the carpet.

He scooped it up as Jennifer shook her head and said, "Fine. Let me know as soon as he contacts you."

Finally managing to press the record button, he held the tape recorder to the crack in the door, but Jennifer had finished her call and slipped the cell phone back into her handbag. Too late.

"I love you, David."

Cole felt a bolt of adrenaline thinking she'd spotted him, then realized she'd spoken while looking up at the ceiling, as though in spontaneous prayer.

He kept still, mesmerized. He could hear her soft breathing as she looked up at the ceiling for several minutes, saying nothing else.

Finally, she collected herself and left the room. He listened to her footsteps thump down the stairs, and then the front door open and close.

She'd given him a wonderful gift without even realizing it.

Struggling to his feet, he scooped up the knife and MP5, and left the closet. He pressed the rewind button, held the recorder to his ear, pressed play.

"I love you, David."

Although the words sounded tinny over ambient static, they filled his heart with calming warmth.

"I love you, too, Jennifer," he said.

Saying the words felt good. And true. He ached to cradle her, to protect her, to whisk her away. But that would have to wait.

"I love you," he repeated, and then the left the room to continue the next phase of the mission.

"This way, Mr. Brandenburg."

Brandenburg looked up from his magazine. The woman who'd addressed him had blonde hair, big tits. Nice. If he'd known the executive producer was this hot, he'd have worn a better shirt. He stood and followed her from the plush lobby into a hallway. She walked quickly, and he hurried to keep up.

"This had better be an exclusive," she snapped over her shoulder. "So help me, if I find out you went to *Entertainment Daily* after talking to me . . . am I making myself clear?"

"Sure," he said, checking out her ass.

"Are we fucking clear?"

He looked up and found her looking back at him. He felt hot with embarrassment, caught in the act. "Yeah, we're clear."

Give a show an exclusive, and they'd spread it all over town like the clap. They didn't care if it was a lie. They only cared if they had it, and no one else did.

As they walked on, an image of Cole's son popped into his head. Bloody and screaming. He bit his lower lip, pushed it away. *This just ain't right.*

Sure, Cole was an asshole, but he sure as hell didn't deserve what happened to him. And for all he knew, the man was looking for payback. But if he ran, Uncle Gary would have his ass. Who was he scared of more? Uncle Gary or David Cole? Both made him wanna puke.

Either way, he knew one thing for sure: Being here wasn't right.

He followed the executive producer into a room done up with thick maroon carpet and leafy potted plants. Two chairs were set facing each other with a television camera positioned behind each one. A half-dozen 1K lights shined from a ceiling grid.

"Sit," she said. He did. "In our business, weekends are slow. We'll be able to run this story for two days straight. But it has to be an exclusive, Mr. Brandenburg. *An exclusive,* do you hear me?"

"Yeah," Brandenburg said, trying to get comfortable. The

chair was too small, the bright lights blinded him, and this executive producer was a fucking bitch.

He sat up straight as a man wearing a red baseball cap and brown cargo pants clipped a tiny microphone to his T-shirt collar.

"No more monosyllables, Ned," the executive producer said, clipping on her own microphone. "Try to answer in complete sentences. Think you can do that? And don't stare into the camera."

"Yeah, okay." His stomach curled into an icy ball and Ronny appeared again. Screaming. Dying. He shouldn't be doing this. *He shouldn't be fucking doing this!*

"Mr. Brandenburg, are you ready to go?"

The woman's voice sounded a million miles away. No he wasn't fucking ready. He wanted to bolt from the studio. Bolt from the fucking city. But if he did, he knew Uncle Gary would send Ruger after him.

"Mr. Brandenburg!"

"Yeah, yeah, I'm ready!"

The executive producer nodded at the cameramen, who in turn gave her a thumbs-up. The red light on top of the cameras blinked on.

"Welcome back to *Star Power,* your powerful news source to the stars!" she said, voice all sugar and blowjobs now. The bitch sure knew how to turn it on and off. "Mr. Ned Brandenburg is with us today to give us a glimpse into the mind of pyrotechnic killer, David Cole. Tell us, Ned, you worked closely with Cole. Did you have any idea that he was capable of such a heinous crime?"

Brandenburg opened his mouth, but couldn't make his voice work. He felt sweat roll down his left temple. *I shouldn't be here. This is fucking nuts.* But he didn't really have a choice. Deep in his gut, he'd known it all along.

"Yeah, I had some idea," he managed. "David Cole is one screwed up dude, let me tell you . . ."

Roberts punched the Chrysler's accelerator and sailed through a traffic light that had just turned red. A chorus of honks followed him through the intersection.

He grabbed his cell phone from the passenger seat, dialed it with his thumb. Whittaker answered on the fourth ring. "What do you want, Ted?"

"I think I have a break in the David Cole case." Silence. The detective wasn't giving him any leeway whatsoever. Still, he had to try. "The fire was called in at three fifty-three, two minutes after the glass face on Ronny Cole's watch melted. We know this because the watch face was frozen at three fifty-one. Our units took fifteen minutes to respond, which means the glass melted in less than twenty minutes. No way a petro fire could do that." More silence. "Scott, we should put a rush on the chemical analysis. I'll bet there was an aberrant compound in those mortars."

"The fire could have burned long before the tip came in," Whittaker said.

"Not likely. The mortar would have engulfed the house immediately. If the tip had come much earlier, the fire would have burned itself out before our first-responders arrived."

Whittaker sighed. "Thanks for the tip, but we've got things under control."

"I'm sure you do, but this might—"

"We sent men to Cole's house," the Detective interrupted. "Intelligence tapped his cell phone and hard line. We also have authorization to reverse tap any calls that come in. We're chasing down his acquaintances and colleagues. Get the picture? We're tightening the noose on this prick."

Roberts took a slow, calming breath. "The aberrant compound might point to another culprit. We're talking about a substance than burns at fifteen-hundred degrees, maybe hotter."

"What did I tell you about pursuing this case?"

Roberts' stomach sank. So this was less about collecting evidence than it was about spite. He'd stepped on the detective's toes, and now Cole would pay the price. "Scott, I have every right to request those results."

"You've made your bias in this case painfully clear, and I won't let it interfere with my investigation. From this moment, I'm barring you from the Federal Building. If you take any further action, I'll toss you from the case altogether."

Roberts heard a click as Whittaker hung up.

He clutched the steering wheel. Technically, his job as an arson investigator was done. The cause of fire had been determined. As such, Whittaker had every right to restrict his participation in the homicide for whatever reason. If he went against orders, he could earn a serious reprimand, possibly much worse. Continuing meant putting his spotless career in jeopardy.

It was a no-brainer, really.

He dialed the phone.

Chapter 9

Stanford sat on the cabin's sun porch, watching his nephew on a 70-inch flat screen television hanging on the wall. As he'd expected, *Star Power* had begun airing the taped interview immediately to take advantage of the exclusive.

On screen, Brandenburg shifted uneasily in his chair. "David Cole is one screwed up dude. Let me tell you, on the day before the explosion, he went off and threatened me with a knife."

The camera cut to a plastic-looking blonde reporter. Her brow was furrowed with what Stanford knew was practiced concern. It was an expression that he, too, had perfected. "Oh my God," she said.

Cut back to Brandenburg, nodding solemnly. "Yeah. In my opinion, resorting to violence is bullsh—" He snapped his mouth closed, mid-curse. The reporter glared, clearly annoyed by the transgression. Obviously, she thought his nephew would know better than to use such language on network television. Obviously, she didn't know his nephew.

"Did you feel like your life was in danger?" the reporter continued, regaining her composure.

Brandenburg nodded again, like a horse performing for a lump of sugar. "Don't get me wrong. I can take care of myself in a fight, you know? I wasn't afraid of the guy. But it was pretty clear he meant business."

"What did you do?"

"I told myself, 'Ned, this just isn't worth it' and walked away.

I didn't wanna sink to his level."

Stanford smiled. Although scripted, his nephew was coming off as a Samaritan who'd bravely stepped forward in the aftermath of tragedy. A crude but effective performance. *Very good.*

"You wanted me, Gary?" Huxley stood in the front doorway, sipping a glass of orange juice.

"Did Anne Devereaux's people call?"

Huxley nodded. "I just spoke to her agent and lawyer. The Sunday meeting is still on, and they forgave the retainer, as you predicted."

He'd known that Devereaux wouldn't want to appear like a ghoul by demanding a payday while he coped with the accident. He'd gone from being cash poor to liquid, literally overnight. "What about Ruger?"

"On his way to the stronghold. He'll report back when he completes his reconnaissance." Huxley paused. "I don't trust him, Gary. He's too volatile. And I don't need to remind you that he failed."

"He performed well enough."

Huxley blinked. "Are you serious?"

"Ruger did what we asked him to do. Luck happened to be on Cole's side that night is all," Stanford said. He knew the difference between incompetence and bad fortune, and this was clearly a case of the latter. The explosion should have killed Cole, but hadn't for some inexplicable reason. There was no use dwelling on the twist of fate. But they had to remedy the situation. Now. "Ruger is the best candidate to track Cole. He knows how the man thinks and fights."

"But can we control him?"

"Anyone can be controlled if handled properly."

"Gary—"

"Enough," he said. "What about my nephew?"

"Ned arrived at his secure location a short time ago, where he'll stay, awaiting your instructions."

"And Levar Watkins?"

"As you and Ruger discussed."

"Fine," he said, and returned his focus to the television.

Back on screen, the blonde asked, "Did you call the police, Mr. Brandenburg?"

Cut to Brandenburg running fingers through his ratty red hair. "We didn't want to bother other people with a problem we thought we should handle on our own. Ask me, and Cole would have fought with anyone, you know? Even the cops. He was fu . . ." Brandenburg stopped, catching himself. "He was *fricking* crazy."

Stanford relaxed into his chair. Public and police opinion would be firmly on his side now. And since the planted evidence was airtight, he didn't care whether the police or Ruger got to Cole first, as long as the man was removed from the equation.

Roberts stood on the southeast corner of Hope and Second Street in downtown LA, clutching a paint can that held chemical samples from *Bringing Them Back* in one hand, and a box of Krispy Kreme donuts in the other. He knew that every ATF agent in the downtown office would follow Whittaker's orders, and dutifully restrict his ability to collect evidence.

That is, every ATF agent but one.

He saw the blue-and-white ATF truck approaching from the direction of the Walt Disney Concert Hall. A repurposed ambulance, the truck carried every piece of chemical analysis equipment that an arson field unit could ever need. When the truck pulled to the curb, Roberts held up the box of donuts to the open driver's side window.

"Thanks for coming, Otto."

"Glazed, right?" Anderson said, reaching down to take the

box. "I'm not gonna find any of those nasty chocolate donuts in here."

"A dozen glazed," he confirmed.

"I swear, Ted, one of these days you're going to get me fired. Now get your ass in back before somebody sees you."

Roberts jogged to the back of the truck and climbed through the double doors. "Okay, I'm in."

Feeling the truck lurch as Anderson pulled into traffic, Roberts strapped himself into a seat that was bolted to the floor. In front of him was a desk that held an array of equipment, including a portable gas chromatograph/mass spectrometer that could quantify the chemical make-up of accelerants. Popping open the paint can, he removed a large plastic test tube and emptied half its black powdery contents into the reservoir at the base of the spectrometer. He then returned tube to can, and punched a few buttons on a laptop keyboard.

He expected to find gasoline, black powder and 100-grain high explosive in the mix, but he suspected that there was something else, too. A compound that burned hot enough to melt the glass face of a SEAL watch in only a few minutes.

A voice crackled over the truck's dash-mounted radio. "Truck number four, this is dispatch, what's your twenty?"

Roberts looked up. "Please tell me you signed out the truck, Otto."

Anderson turned, gave him a sheepish look. "Technically speaking, I'm not cleared to drive these trucks. So I used the name of a buddy who is."

"Then please tell me your buddy is out sick today."

"Sort of. He was out to lunch."

"Jesus, Otto."

"Best I could do on short notice," Anderson said. "How long till the results come up?"

Roberts looked at the horizontal status bar crawling across

the laptop screen. The sample was heating and separating into its basic components. Under normal circumstances, the processing of the portable unit was considered very fast. But now . . . "Twenty minutes."

"If we don't respond immediately, they'll hone in on our GPS signal and send out units."

"How long till they get here?"

"We're only a few blocks from the office. Ten minutes, tops."

The radio crackled again. "Truck four, this is dispatch, requesting your location. Please respond."

Roberts gritted his teeth. Yes, he needed this evidence to pursue the case, but he couldn't ask his friend to compromise his career and reputation, not when he had a family to support. Cole wouldn't want it this way, either. The man would not allow the sacrifice on his behalf. "Head back, Otto."

"I can give them a run for their money until you get what you need."

He shook is head. "If you run, they'll fire you, Otto. If they drive out here and catch you with me, you'll be cited for insubordination or worse. The only thing you can do is go back, let me off, and hope they buy some bullshit excuse."

Anderson shook his head. "Helping clear your friend's name is more important—"

"I said no," Roberts interrupted. "Not at your expense."

Sighing, Anderson picked up the radio mic and spoke into it. "Dispatch, this is truck four. I'm inbound. See you in a few." Then he swung the truck around and said, "Okay, Ted, you've got six blocks."

Roberts stared at the laptop screen. He didn't need a complete readout. All he needed was evidence of the mystery accelerant. The success of his investigation hinged on which chemical component the software chose to diagnose first.

"When you're in a hurry, you get red lights," Anderson

growled. "But now it's green as far as I can see."

Roberts continued to stare at the screen when a blue bar graph began to form slowly, identifying the molecules that comprised the first compound. In ninety seconds that felt like an eternity, the graph was finished to complete the chemical fingerprint.

Black powder. *Shit.*

Roberts peered through the windshield, and saw the ATF headquarters building ahead. They'd be there in no time. "Slow down, Otto."

"I'm going twenty miles per hour, as it is, Ted. But you got it."

Other cars honked and sped around them as Roberts kept his eyes glued on the screen. A yellow graph was forming. From the few molecules visible, he knew it was the fingerprint for gasoline. An endless sixty seconds later, the yellow graph was complete.

C'mon, he urged, and then the truck lurched to a stop. They were outside the parking garage.

"We're here," Anderson said. "And we've got company." He pointed through the windshield at two approaching agents. He waved at them good-naturedly as he said, "Whatever you need to do, Ted, do it now."

Roberts looked at the screen. A red graph was forming. He blinked in disbelief when he saw the first molecule.

"Ted . . ." Anderson warned.

To be certain of his suspicion, he'd have to wait for the entire readout. But there was no time. "Otto, toss me your water bottle!"

"You have twenty seconds before those agents reach us and you're asking for a beverage?"

"Otto!"

Anderson grabbed the bottle from the cup-holder, and pitched it over his shoulder. Roberts caught the bottle, twisted off the top, and then retrieved the test tube from the paint can and poured the remaining sample into it. When the black grains hit the water, they sparkled and hissed violently, and then the bottle exploded, dousing his shirt.

That clinched it. He knew the chemical. He'd seen it used to horrible effect that night during the mission . . .

. . . the Iraqi commander totters against the rail of the boat, his pitched screams mingling with a sharp, chemical hiss as the meat of his stomach melts away. Finally, mercifully, he falls overboard. When his body hits the marsh, it flares with supernova intensity, and continues to spark and hiss and flash even after it sinks below the murky surface . . .

"Willy Pete," Roberts said.

Anderson turned. "Jesus. That would explain the melted watch face. But what the hell is white phosphorous doing in a special effects mortar?"

Roberts felt his stomach curl into an icy ball. *No way. It can't be . . .*

"Ted, you've gotta get out of here," Anderson warned again.

"Thanks, Otto, I owe you," Roberts said, and bolted out the back doors, unable to shake the feeling that he'd just put his own life in serious jeopardy.

Ruger drove his Jeep past a small cluster of union workers who shoveled the charred debris from the demolished Iraqi stronghold into a dump truck. In a couple hours, it would be as though the stronghold had never existed.

He'd wanted the same fate to befall Cole—charred remains reduced to garbage.

But Cole was alive.

An hour ago, Stanford had called to let him know. The enemy who had fucking betrayed him and then handed him over to Navy death doctors had survived. Now he had the opportunity to make sure Cole stayed down.

Stanford could have tossed him after the failure, but instead that man had given him a second chance . . . something he hadn't gotten from Cole or the Navy. He felt a swell of loyalty for Stanford that he'd once felt for flag and country. Loyalty and deadly determination.

Yes, the enemy was everywhere. But Cole *would* stay down this time.

Ruger drove around the demolished set. As he scanned the workers, pressure at the back of his skull made him feel as if he were going to pass out. He gripped the steering wheel, shook his head, and blinked . . . *saw a squad of Iraqi soldiers instead of union workers who clutched AK-47s instead of shovels . . .*

Keeping his eye on the soldiers in his rearview mirror, he parked at the edge of a deep ravine. He tensed as he climbed from the cab, ready to evade if attacked—but the enemy soldiers ignored him. Good. He had work to do.

Peering into the ravine, he noticed that the dirt in direct trajectory from the house had crumbled. So Cole had been thrown clear by the explosion. He'd suspected as much. There was no way Cole could have remained in the house and survived.

He stepped onto the slope and slid on his feet to the bottom. There he examined the dirt beneath the crumbling area above. It had also been disturbed. To the untrained eye, the cause could have been any number of things—an animal or weather, maybe. But he knew better. A human being in pain had made the gouges. *Cole.*

Something caught his eye up the slope. He clambered a short way up the incline until he came to a large rock. One side was gummed with a dark substance. He knelt, took a closer look.

Charred flesh. Cole was alive, but seriously fucking hurt. Going to the hospital would have involved cops, which meant Cole was treating the wounds himself.

Without proper medical care, the burns could kill Cole in a few days. That meant the man would be acting fast, with less precision.

Not that he needed the advantage. He was more than Cole's fucking equal. But the man's sloppiness would make his job that much easier.

Ruger sat Indian-style in the dirt. The late afternoon sun felt warm on his skin, and the smell of sweet grass was strong. He closed his eyes and blocked out the construction sounds of the Iraqi soldiers above him.

Cole would act tonight, he knew. The man had no other choice.

Ruger rolled up his left shirtsleeve. The flesh on his muscled forearm was crosshatched with thick, white scars. He drew the K-bar from its sheath, and drew the blade across the area with short, controlled strokes, opening a new ladder of wounds.

It's your turn to suffer now, Commander, he thought as blood ran down either side of his arm. *Enjoy the fucking ride before you die.*

Chapter 10

Cole sat in the truck, and with trembling fingers pulled a styrette from the box and plunged the needle into his upper thigh. He exhaled slowly as a warm rush of morphine reduced the screaming pain to a dull moan.

But it did nothing to numb the terrible realization of what had happened in Stanford's closet. He'd felt out of control. Out of *himself.* His SEAL instincts had returned, transforming him into the ruthless soldier he once was. A trained killer. Worse, he'd almost hurt Jennifer. God . . .

He would have to be more careful. Plan every aspect of this mission to make sure that nothing took him by surprise . . . maybe then, he could keep the horrible feelings away.

When his hands were no longer shaking, he dialed the cell phone.

Lawrence answered on the first ring. "You okay?"

"Yeah, but Stanford's gone underground. We need to find Brandenburg or Watkins."

"Just so you know, Brandenburg was on *Star Power* dissing you. I got half a mind to call the station."

So Stanford was using Brandenburg to influence public opinion. Now there would be a thousand concerned citizens on the lookout for him. "Thanks, but I don't want you making your loyalties known, big man."

"I figured as much. I taped the chump's voice off the TV for you."

"Good, but I still need to pay him a visit. He might know where his uncle is hiding."

"I'll try to track him down. Call you in a few."

Cole sagged back into the driver's seat. Riding the warm rush of morphine, he turned his thoughts to Jennifer. He was surprised at how quickly he'd fallen in love with her. The mere sight of her had energized him, like a second wind during a marathon. He closed his eyes and remembered when she'd leaned over to kiss him. He smiled, feeling the whisper of her lips against his. Her simple, loving gesture had made him feel like he'd never gone to war, or taken a human life, or failed the men in his Team.

And her simple presence had banished the instincts that had struck without warning within him. He felt relieved that the instincts were gone, yes, but wondered if he could accomplish the mission without them since they'd numbed the pain from his wounds at Stanford's house.

It's not worth the risk, he countered. He'd spent years after the war suppressing those terrible instincts, and today, in one fell swoop, they had returned. He shuddered, realizing that he'd almost lost himself in that cold, lethal determination. He couldn't disrespect his son's memory by becoming the calculated killer he once was. By relying on skills that embodied everything he'd tried to leave behind.

I won't do it, son, you've got my promise on that.

He pulled a Thomas Guide from the glove compartment so he could find whatever address Lawrence gave him. As he did so, his thoughts returned to Jennifer. What had she been doing at Stanford's house? Looking for location permits? Contracts? Unlikely, since *Bringing Them Back* had been shut down.

Evidence, he realized. Against Stanford. She was trying to clear his name. That meant she believed in him despite the evidence that Ruger had left behind. He felt even greater love for her, followed by fear. By pursuing the case, she was putting herself in Ruger's line of fire.

Ruger . . .

The simple thought caused memories of the failed mission to hum to life, but he was too physically and emotionally spent now to keep them away . . .

. . . Cole sprints between the crates and emerges to see Ruger firing full-auto at over two hundred Iraqi soldiers crowded on deck. A troop transport, Cole realizes, not a munitions boat at all. Intel got it wrong.

Ruger fires with suicidal intensity . . . it's an act with no strategic purpose . . . the Team had been moments away from escaping with their lives . . . but from the look on Ruger's face, it's obvious to Cole that the man snapped . . . his expression is vacant, lost, but his eyes are full of bloodlust and hate . . .

Ruger keeps firing and everyone—friend and foe—is too stunned to do anything but watch . . . beneath the automatic thunder of Ruger's AR-23, Cole can hear the mad scraping of combat boots as the front-rank Iraqi soldiers slip-scurry away in a vain, blood-soaked attempt to escape . . .

. . . and then the night explodes with crisscrossing green and red tracer rounds as the Team and battalion of Iraqi soldiers finally get their bearings and enter the fray . . .

. . . Ruger doesn't take cover as the firefight goes full throttle . . . he calmly stands his ground as bullets sizzle past, missing him somehow . . . his AR-23 flash, flash, flashing . . . the fear of death absent in his eyes as though his spirit was already dead . . . and Cole screams, unable to help himself . . . screams orders to retreat, screams in horror, all of it drowned out by booming chatter as the Team engages two hundred enemy soldiers . . . rounds chew up the deck, punch through crates, shred sails . . . and then the inevitable happens all too soon . . .

His cell phone rang, jerking him back to reality. He shook his head to clear the dark hangover of nightmare, willed himself to keep his voice steady so Lawrence wouldn't freak. "Talk to me, big man."

"I called Brandenburg's apartment and the places he hangs out, including that titty bar on Van Buren," Lawrence said. "No go. He's MIA, like his uncle."

"What about Watkins?"

"Chump answered on the first ring."

Cole frowned. It didn't make sense that Brandenburg had gone into hiding while Watkins was home. "It's a setup," he said.

"Fuckin'-A it's a setup," Lawrence replied. "Leaving Watkins open is the best way for Ruger to get an idea of your capabilities."

Although Watkins was a risky target, he couldn't afford to wait. His body was deteriorating—his skin felt tight, a sure sign of fluid loss. "It has to be tonight."

"Setup aside, Watkins is a big dude. There's no way you can take him hand-to-hand," Lawrence warned.

"I plan to use the MP5 to soften him up."

"That'll tell Ruger what he wants to know."

"I don't have a choice."

"What if Ruger springs an ambush?" Lawrence pressed. "No offense, but he'll take you down easy."

"Ruger won't be there."

"Willing to bet your life?"

"If he's gone to the trouble of setting up a forward element, he'll wait before launching a counterattack. He'll want all the advantages. He's methodical like that."

"You sure you're up to this? You sound off. More so than before. Don't be a fucking hero, Dave. Take the morphine if you have to."

"I'm fine." He felt guilty about lying to his friend, but didn't want to argue about going to the hospital. Besides, the physical disadvantage was the least of his concerns. The instincts, and how they'd kicked in without warning, filled him with dark terror. Would he be able to control them this time? "Give me Watkins' address."

Cole hung up and checked the Thomas Guide. The house was across town. He'd have to take Watkins down quickly, not only for himself, but for Jennifer, too. If she were conducting her own investigation, it wouldn't be long before she called attention to herself. If perceived as a threat, Stanford and Ruger would take her out as ruthlessly as Ronny.

He cranked the ignition, and the simple movement triggered razor blades of pain in his wrist and elbow. Wincing, he put the truck into gear and drove away, promising himself that he wouldn't stop unless his wounds—or Ruger—killed him.

Jennifer stepped into the air-conditioned luxury of the Hollywood Roosevelt Hotel. She knew that Gary Stanford used the Oscar Room upstairs as a makeshift office and audition space, and guessed that he hadn't been as meticulous about clearing it of potential clues as he had his home.

The hotel hadn't changed in fifteen years. She tried to keep the memories at bay as she walked past a seated bronze statue of Charlie Chaplin and entered the Blossom Room. Thick palms stood like sentries around brightly colored couches and glass-top tables. Above her, an ornate gold-leaf chandelier hung from a hand-painted ceiling. To her left was the legendary Cinegrill piano bar that hosted such celebrities as Clark Gable and Carole Lombard in the 20s and 30s.

Fifteen years ago, she'd wanted nothing more than to be like Carole Lombard: Revered and rich. How needy she'd been. As she headed upstairs, she couldn't help but remember the casting sessions that she'd attended here. The rejections, the empty promises, the constant come-ons from low-rate directors and producers who'd offered her walk-on parts in exchange for . . .

She closed her eyes, feeling hot with shame.

She wasn't that person anymore.

Pushing away the thoughts, she continued down the hall until she reached a door labeled Oscar Room in script gold lettering. After making sure the area was clear of hotel employees, she pulled a credit card from her purse, used it to jimmy the lock, and then peeked inside.

The L-shaped room was spartan compared to the hotel's lobby and ballrooms. She couldn't see around the corner, but against the opposite wall were a metal desk, computer, phone and file cabinet. Gary used this satellite office when he couldn't afford the time to travel across town to Loki headquarters. If he were hiding anything about David or *Bringing Them Back,* it would be here, away from prying eyes. Although she believed in David's innocence, tangible evidence of Gary's involvement would buttress her resolve.

Closing the door softly behind her, she walked across the room. Suddenly, she heard a rustle of papers from around the corner. She froze, heart leaping into her throat.

Someone was here.

Get out!

Even though she was an employee of Loki Productions, she had no reason for being in Gary's private office. If caught, she'd be fired. What's more, she'd be blackballed from the industry. Hollywood studios welcomed drug dealers, rapists, murderers, and all manner of criminals onto their payrolls. But they could not tolerate people of conscience. One whistleblower could dismantle an entire studio. Honor among thieves was paramount, second only to the bottom line. Make a mistake here, and everything she'd achieved since those desperate days of casting couches and drug abuse would be gone in an instant.

She took a step back toward the door, but stopped when she thought of David.

He was so different from other men in this industry who felt like they had something to prove. From the beginning, he'd revealed his feelings freely, not because he was weak, but because he understood that the rewards outweighed the risks. When she'd kissed him at the dinner party, it was like she'd fallen into him, but without losing herself. She felt buoyed, not dominated, by his masculine influence—a new experience for her. He'd made it clear that he respected who she was and who she wanted to be. Most importantly, he did not complete her. Rather, he *complemented* her. She felt like they were equals.

If helping him meant leaving the film business, so be it. She'd be happy doing anything as long as it was with him.

Taking a deep, calming breath, she walked to the file cabinet, and tugged gently on the top drawer. Locked. Scanning the desk, she grabbed a paperclip and slid the end into the lock, trying to pick it. No go. She threw a nervous look over her shoulder. The sound of rustling papers had stopped. She checked the floor for an approaching shadow, saw none, returned to the lock. Tried again to pick it. Nothing. And then she heard footsteps approaching. Heavy footsteps. A man.

There was no way she could make it out the door in time. With no other choice, she darted around the file cabinet and pressed her back to it. She'd be safe as long as he didn't look too carefully in this direction.

She heard the thumping footsteps stop in front of the file cabinet. If he took one step to the side . . . She closed her eyes. Held her breath. Heard a key click into the file cabinet lock, and then felt a hollow bang against her back as the drawer was opened. After a rustle of papers, the footsteps receded.

She peered around the cabinet. The man was gone—and the drawer was still open! Quickly walking her fingers over the files, she found scripts, headshots, and financial statements for an array of Loki film projects. Folders for *Bringing Them Back* were conspicuously absent. She looked back over her shoulder for any sign that the man was returning, when she noticed a thick manila folder on the desk that hadn't been there before. It was labeled *Bringing Them Back—5 of 5.* The man must have removed it from the drawer. She couldn't believe her luck.

Undoing the folder clasp, she pulled out contracts, payroll receipts, and production budgets. Even with a quick glance, it was obvious that Gary was pulling off a juggling act of allocating and reallocating funds. The producer also had millions of dollars in outstanding bank loans, taken out against future earnings.

Loki is having serious money problems.

And then she remembered that Stanford had been given right of first refusal to hire Anne Devereaux for *Mothers and Daughters.* That would cost two million dollars, at least.

How would Gary come up with the retainer? A thought chilled her: Could Gary have orchestrated the on-set explosion to collect insurance? The payoff would cover Loki's losses, plus provide for Devereaux's retainer. It certainly made more sense than David making such a careless mistake. But could Gary have been so ruthless?

Although she had no proof, her instincts screamed that her supposition was on target. That these files were being removed only strengthened her supposition.

She heard the heavy footsteps approaching again. She quickly slid the papers back into the folder, and returned to her hiding place behind the filing cabinet.

The clasp. Oh God. She'd slipped the papers back into the envelope, but had forgotten to refasten the clasp.

She heard the footsteps stop in front of the file cabinet again. There were several moments of silence.

Oh God.

The drawer banged closed. She held her breath. Please . . .

"Step away from the file cabinet," said a male voice. Steven Huxley. Her heart sank. Had it been anyone else, she might have been able to keep word of the break-in from Gary. But Huxley was Gary's number two.

She stepped from her hiding place. Huxley was there, wearing his trademark dark blue suit and black tie. In his right hand he held a large, silver-plated pistol. His eyes widened in surprise.

"Hello, Steven. Would you mind not pointing that gun at me?" Caught, it was all she could think to say.

"What are you doing here?" he asked, keeping the gun steady.

"Steven, the gun."

"I asked you a question."

She struggled to keep her voice from shaking. "I thought Gary might want to reshoot the final scene of *Bringing Them Back*. I wanted to be ready if that was the case."

"Don't lie to me, you junkie whore."

His viciousness hit her like a slap. For a moment, she felt a pang of real terror. She realized that Huxley—for all his supposed class and refinement—was capable of extreme violence, and would have no hesitation directing that violence at her if he felt justified.

But his tone told her something else, too: He was hiding something. Had he greeted her graciously, she might have doubted her assumption about Gary's involvement. Now she had no doubt whatsoever.

"Steven, I'm telling you the truth."

"Bullshit. Why not call Gary first?"

"I tried, but spoke to you instead, remember?" she said. If he only knew that she'd called from Gary's house. "You told me that he was out of town."

A flicker of doubt crossed his face, but the gun didn't waver.

"No. You're trying to clear the name of that murderer you call a boyfriend."

Anger surged. He was baiting her, she knew. Trying to provoke a truthful response. She wanted to scream into his face, but held her tongue. And then before she could stop herself, she slapped him hard across the cheek. "Go to hell."

Huxley smiled, and the condescension shattered her restraint. She slapped him again, then again, his face tough and leathery against her palm. This man wasn't fit to be in the same room as David . . . wasn't fit to mention his name.

Finally, Huxley caught her wrist with his free hand. "I don't know what you're up to, Jennifer, but I do know that you're lying. Consider your employment with Loki Productions terminated."

She was about to respond when she noticed a business card pressed back against the open desk drawer with a tattered face and dated design that read, "Lydia's Diner." The address was in Brooklyn, New York. Gary Stanford's hometown. Was this a card he'd forgotten to throw away? Or was there a more significant connection?

"I'm sorry," she told Huxley with feigned contrition, and then slumped against the desk, pretending to feel faint.

As he grabbed her shoulder, she quickly palmed the business card.

"Get the fuck out," he said.

"I'm sorry," she repeatedly softly, pocketing the business card, and then hurried from the room.

As she retraced her steps down the hall, a feeling of resolve flooded her. When she'd left the Hollywood Roosevelt Hotel for the last time fifteen years ago, she'd vowed that she'd never return. Yet here she was again, but for the right reason this time.

I'm coming, David, she thought. *Hang on, baby.*

★ ★ ★ ★ ★

The last time Roberts had been at the Bucklew Center for Naval Special Warfare in San Diego was after the failed mission in Iraq, only weeks before he left the service for good.

Driving through the gates today had felt like coming home—but to abusive, controlling parents.

"You must have some pretty important questions to drive all this way," Commander Dana Burke said, peering through a pair of binoculars. They sat together in a two-story observation post watching a phalanx of haggard-looking recruits wearing white T-shirts and orange life jackets slog through the surf toward an array of wooden obstacles. Each group of six carried a black, rubber raft over its head. Roberts' arms and legs ached in sympathy.

"I do," Roberts replied, and couldn't help think about how little Commander Burke had changed. Burke had been a junior instructor in the Basic Underwater Demolition School during Roberts' training. Now a man in his mid-sixties, Burke was still lean and exuded the same strength that had awed him as a recruit.

"I read the case file you faxed over," Burke told him. "But before we begin, I want to make one thing clear."

"Of course."

"You're pathetic."

Roberts blinked. There'd been no hint of hostility when he'd called Burke to set up the interview. Apparently now that they weren't on a monitored phone, the man felt free to express his feelings. "Excuse me?"

"Your Team failed in Iraq."

"Navy intel sent us to the wrong target," he said, trying not to sound defensive. "We were equipped to board a munitions boat carrying fifteen enemy troops, not a transport carrying two hundred."

Burke put down his binoculars and appraised him with dark eyes. “In Vietnam, my SEAL Team ran into a battalion of NVA after we’d accomplished our op. We lost one man.”

He’d been in the military long enough to know that Burke’s hostility was a test. The man wouldn’t have granted the interview if he hadn’t wanted to divulge information. But like all officers, he was trying to determine whether the man in front of him was worthy.

Refusing the bait, Roberts said, “I’m here to discuss Frank Ruger.”

“What makes you think he’s involved in this case?”

“There were traces of white phosphorus in the special effects mortars.”

“And?”

“Ruger killed an Iraqi soldier with a WP round.”

“Hardly conclusive, Investigator. Ruger was merely using every weapon at his disposal to escape.”

“We both know Ruger wasn’t himself that night.”

Burke turned away and surveyed the beach. The drenched men were now scaling a cargo net propped on sixty-foot wooden poles. “What I know is based entirely on testimony. Ruger’s. Cole’s. Yours. Regardless, the matter is moot. Ruger is no longer in our care.”

“So you told me over the phone. Where is he?”

“We can’t track soldiers once they leave the base.”

“Can’t or won’t?”

“You’re lecturing me about responsibility, Investigator? We spent a lot of time, energy, and money raising you as a SEAL. What do you do with those skills now? Track down insurance cheats and pyromaniacs?”

“I didn’t want to make killing my career.”

“Some men consider being a SEAL patriotic. Or don’t you believe in patriotism anymore?”

Roberts forced a pleasant smile. Burke's comments were like harassing fire, designed to break his morale. Another test. "I looked up Ruger's psychological evaluation. According to his doctors, he was cured of sociopathic behavior."

Burke's mouth constricted.

"You disagree?"

"SEALs are masters of camouflage and deception," Burke said.

"If he's still sick, why protect him?"

Burke looked down at the clipboard he was holding. On it was a list of physical tasks and their required completions: One-mile bay swim without fins, seventy minutes; four-mile timed run, thirty-two minutes; obstacle course, fifteen minutes; drown-proofing test, pass/fail. Among many, many others. "I'm not protecting him," the man said finally.

"You're doing exactly that. I'm telling you that Ruger may have committed murder, yet you insist on throwing me evasive answers. You are protecting him, Commander, whether or not you'd like to admit it."

"No."

"Then what are you doing?"

Burke looked up. "I'm protecting *you.*"

Roberts leaned back in his chair. The man was tireless in his diversionary tactics. "Don't do me any favors."

"The man you're pursuing and the man you call your friend. They're . . ." Burke's voice trailed off. "You have no idea."

"I have every idea. That's why I'm here."

"About Ruger, maybe. But not Cole."

Roberts felt a spike of anger. Who was Burke to question his friendship with Cole? "I've known David Cole for years both inside and outside the Navy. I also know that he saved my life on that boat."

"He saved your life and now you want to save his life in

return, which is admirable. But this case isn't only about Frank Ruger, Investigator. Not by a long shot."

It was obvious that Burke was finally prepared to speak openly, but would the disclosure shake his opinion of Cole, as the Commander believed it would? "Tell me what I need to know."

Burke regarded him evenly. "If you repeat what I am about to say, I will deny ever having said it."

"Fine."

"As you know, I was part of the disciplinary tribunal that investigated the failed mission. We interrogated Cole and Ruger separately, as we did you. Cole testified that Ruger's reckless action put the Team in harm's way, and Ruger vehemently denied the charge."

"I was there, Commander," Roberts interjected. "Ruger opened fire recklessly during my negotiation with the Iraqi officer."

Burke nodded. "Ruger corroborated your testimony on that point. That particular action was never in question. However, the tribunal did not regard the consequences to be of critical import."

Roberts blinked in disbelief. Had he heard the man correctly? The Team had been expendable? "So what *did* the tribunal consider to be of critical import?" he asked incredulously.

"Control," Burke said.

Roberts shook his head, still in shock from the admission. "I don't understand."

"Ruger insisted that he had no choice to act as he did because Cole was not present to lead, when, in fact, that choice was not his to make. He dismissed military protocol."

Burke's point suddenly dawned on him. "He went rogue."

"Worse," Burke told him. "When Ruger opened fire that night, he betrayed your Team and the Navy, yes. But more importantly, he betrayed *himself.* Consciously or subconsciously, he enlisted in the Navy to keep himself in check, as most recruits do. To control his own savage nature. If not in the military, he would have become a soldier in the mafia. Or in the police force. Or in the fire department."

"My nature is just fine, Commander," Roberts said, even though Burke's assessment struck a chord. He remembered that joining the Navy had fulfilled some vague, undefined need. Had it been the violent nature that Burke described?

"Ruger allowed that fundamental control to slip away," Burke continued. "After we heard Ruger's testimony, we knew what had to be done. We gave our recommendation to SPECWAR-COM who overturned our decision, for unspecified reasons, in favor of Level One psychiatric treatment."

"What was your recommendation?" Roberts asked with a growing sense of dread. He thought he knew where Burke was going with this, but how did it relate to Cole?

"Again, if you repeat what I am about to say . . ."

"I understand."

"In our opinion, Lieutenant Ruger should not have been put away as SPECWARCOM decreed. He should have been put down. Permanently."

Roberts felt stunned for the second time in as many minutes. No wonder Burke refused to divulge this information over the phone. Such talk could be considered treason. Yet the tribunal had not been disciplined for making the recommendation, which meant that SPECWARCOM had found it to be justified.

"Doesn't Level One treatment require total isolation?" Roberts asked.

"It does."

"What about Ruger's wife? His two sons?"

"After fourteen months, the family stopped trying to see him. Shortly after that, they dropped out of touch altogether.

Understandably, the loss drove Ruger even deeper into his psychosis."

Jesus, Roberts thought. Sentenced by the tribunal. Stripped of rank. Abandoned by his family. Ruger's motives against Cole were stacking like cordwood. "How does this relate to Cole?"

"During testimony, Ruger displayed severe symptoms of post-traumatic stress. Outbursts. Hallucinations. At one point, he had to be restrained." Burke looked at Roberts. "Cole showed similar symptoms. Not as severe, but they were present."

Roberts shook his head. "No way. I've never seen Cole crack. Not during the mission, not after we left the Navy, not ever."

"What you think you know is irrelevant, Investigator. The fact remains: Cole lost his command in a manner devastating to the military psyche. He may not have acted out during the mission, but it's only a matter of time before he does. All it will take for Cole to become like Ruger is the proper trigger."

Roberts still couldn't believe what Burke was telling him. It simply didn't jibe with what he knew about Cole as a friend. A father. *But could it be true?* He felt a sick, bottomless dread, knowing that post-traumatic stress could be triggered by something as simple as smell, sound, even an offhand comment. And here Cole had lost his son.

"If what you say is true, why wasn't Cole held for observation?"

"The man was exonerated. He received a few weeks' counseling at the behest of a superior officer, but that's it. I doubt even Cole realized how fragile he was when he left."

Roberts looked out at the beach. It was empty now. Only a confused swath of footprints indicated that the recruits had been there.

He still believed that Ruger was responsible for killing Ronny, but if what Burke said was true, he had to find Cole before the man went over the edge and gave Whittaker more justification to press his case. That is, if Cole hadn't already gone over the edge.

"Make no mistake. Both Cole and Ruger are extremely dangerous. If you find them, I urge you to do what the tribunal and SPECWARCOM failed to do those many years ago," Burke said, and then added quietly, "Please don't fail this time around, Investigator."

Chapter 11

Cole pulled into an abandoned gas station on the corner opposite the house and parked. He looked back at the intersection. Not one car had driven by since his arrival. The place was like a DMZ: deserted, desolate.

He grabbed the silenced MP5 and smoke machine from the passenger seat, and climbed from the cab. The reek of gasoline lingered, reminding him of how Ronny and he had rigged the mortar cluster inside the stronghold. He felt a tear trickle down his right cheek and soak the bandage there, stinging the burn underneath. He reached up, gently brushing the brim of Ronny's baseball cap with his fingers, and then turned the cap around so that the brim wouldn't get in the way as he worked.

Here we go, son.

A dry, hot wind snapped across his face as he walked to the partial concealment of a rusted gas pump. He pulled binoculars from his assault vest, and through them saw that the setting sun illuminated the house's tinted windows, revealing the hazy silhouettes of furniture inside. And then a figure moved past a window. Watkins was home.

He'd been able to glimpse the man through the tinted glass because of the angle of the setting sun. But come nightfall, he'd have to think of another way to zero him.

Next he examined the windows of nearby homes. All were dark. He doubted that people in a neighborhood like this would call the cops, anyway. No doubt inundated with violence, they would lock their doors and draw their blinds, thankful that they weren't involved.

But he couldn't take the chance that someone would spot him. He'd have to wait until nightfall. He retreated into a shadowed corner of the garage to wait for the sun to set. It felt like knives were slashing him everywhere. The pain was bad, but not crippling. At least not yet. And he knew it was better to endure the pain than take another hit of morphine, which would slow him down and give Watkins an even greater physical advantage.

He closed his eyes, concentrated on the cool heft of the MP5 in his hands to take his mind off the pain. The weapon, so like the AR-23 he used that night in Iraq. His eyes snapped open, but too late. Before he could stop the train of thought, the ultimate horror of that night unfolded before him . . .

. . . he can only watch helplessly as Ruger fires full-auto into the ranks of Iraqi soldiers, without provocation, blowing apart any chance the Team has of getting out alive . . . Akmed pleads in rapid-fire Arabic, trying to contain a situation that's already out of control, when his head snaps back in a spray of meat and bone . . . Moscone tries to reload his grenade launcher when automatic fire cuts him in two . . . Shannon, shotgun empty, digs frantically through his assault vest for extra rounds when a round shears away his face . . . Bradley, already dead, face and arms a mess of bloody knife slashes, jerks like a marionette as bullets slam into him . . . while Ruger continues to fire his AR-23 full-auto . . . and just like that half of Cole's men are dead . . . his teammates . . . his sons . . .

His son.

Ronny.

He felt tears streaming down his cheeks. He'd failed Ronny as he'd failed his Team. And now it was time to right those terrible wrongs.

He needed one clear shot—a bullet in the shoulder or leg

would take Watkins down, and then he could start asking questions about Stanford and Ruger.

He winced at the stabbing pain, which continued to grow more intense, knowing that he'd have to be extremely careful during the attack. And quick.

"Get over here, you fuckin' cracker. We got work to do," Watkins growled into his cell phone.

Brandenburg made a mewling sound on the other end. "I'm telling you, man, Cole is bound to be seriously pissed off."

"Let him come by, then. I'll cap his fucking ass."

"I'm not saying we should leave permanently. Just for the next few days until this all blows over."

"Where you calling from?"

"I can't tell you that. Ruger said not to."

"You Ruger's bitch now?"

"Levar, we gotta lay low. If we get connected to Cole, we'll put Uncle Gary at risk. And if that happens . . ." His voice trailed off.

Watkins scowled. Bad enough he had to deal with a stupid white boy, but a stupid *chickenshit* white boy? "You don't get over here *now,* and all proceeds from tonight's transaction are mine, got that motherfucker?" he said, and then slapped the cell phone closed.

Shaking his head in disgust, he thumped down a short hallway into the bedroom where he opened the closet and pulled a thick black briefcase out from behind a moving box filled with greasy engine parts. Then he reached around a measuring scale on the top shelf and grabbed the nickel-plated Mossberg 500 shotgun that he'd scored at a gun show in Pomona, already loaded to capacity with six blue-slug rounds that could punch through a bulletproof vest. He hefted the weapon in both hands, racked the slide.

Come get me, motherfucker.

He grabbed the briefcase and thumped back into the living room. After turning off the overhead light, he sat on the couch and switched on an end-table lamp. Beyond the circle of light, everything disappeared into shadow.

Cole deserved what had happened to him, he decided, as he propped the shotgun barrel-up against the couch, then opened the briefcase and pulled out a Ziploc bag of coke. Talking to Brandenburg and him on set like he did, the man was asking for it.

What went down with the kid though . . . Frank Ruger was one crazy fuck. A man ought to enjoy his work, sure, but Ruger liked hurting that kid way too much. But what was done was done.

He opened the bag and poured a small heap onto an IKEA coffee table. Without Brandenburg here to harp about keeping inventory, there was no reason not to try the supply. He pulled a razorblade from the briefcase and used it to divvy the pile into four lines, and then pulled a glass straw from his pocket and snorted two lines into each nostril.

A warm rush jolted his body, causing him to drop the straw onto the threadbare rug that covered the hardwood floor. The blow was bonafide, definitely high grade.

Grabbing the shotgun, he walked to the window and looked out across the neighborhood. He felt a tingling in his nose and the tips of his fingers. Everything outside took on a fucked up, almost iridescent sheen—the sun-scorched grass, trash overflowing from his garbage can, the limp, dying fronds of the palm tree in the next yard over. Light from a street lamp pulsed like a living thing.

And then a thick white fog rolled in from the left. It crawled across the ground, first obscuring the garbage cans and shrubs in a billowing cloud, and then it grew thicker to consume the taller bushes, lamppost and most of the palm tree. Soon, all he could see were the palm fronds, sticking out of the glowing fog like the hair of some cartoon character.

What the fuck? You only get fog this thick at the beach.

He shrugged it off when he noticed his ghost image reflected in the window. Bald head, bulging muscles. At thirty-two, he could still do major harm. Looked like a badass in his frayed military fatigues.

Let Cole try to take him down. Pansy white motherfucker. Let him try.

Fingers trembling with adrenaline, he reached out to his reflection, and it to him. Time to commune with his clone, get twice the mojo. He slid his fingertips across the cool surface of the glass when white sparks flashed suddenly along the left edge of the windowpane.

He dropped to his knees, body flooding with jittery adrenaline.

Drive-by?

Couldn't be. No gunfire.

He crept to the pane, looked close. Half a dozen tiny wires had been taped along the wood. *What the fuck?*

He stood for a closer look when the window exploded.

Something sledgehammered his left shoulder, flinging him ass-back onto the couch in a rain of splintered glass. His elbow caught the lamp and it toppled from the end table, bulbs smashing against the hardwood floor. The room pitched into darkness.

Watkins answered with instincts honed on the street. He racked the shotgun and fired blindly through the shattered window into the swirling fog, the explosive report bashing his eardrums, the discharge flashing like a lightning strike.

In the flash, he saw the buckshot splinter the window frame, and beyond that, he saw something else. A dark figure dart through the fog.

Cole! And then the tactic became clear: Spark hits along the window frame so Cole would know where to shoot through the tinted glass. And fog from a handheld smoke machine to cover his approach.

"Die, motherfucker!" Watkins racked another shell and leveled the gun when stabbing pain ripped his left shoulder, causing him to drop the barrel just as he pulled the trigger. The shot missed the window, pulverizing the wood and cinder-block shelves underneath.

And then everything went still. The streetlight's pale yellow glow created long shadows in the living room. The wind howled as it flapped the curtains and ruffled the porno mags littering his floor. The smoke from the shotgun blasts was dissipating quickly, but the peppery smell of cordite still seared his nostrils.

From the floor, he peered through the shattered window. Cole was gone. So Brandenburg hadn't been full of shit.

Watkins ran to the wall to the right of the shattered window where he flipped a switch. With a high-pitched whine, metal shutters slid along a groove in the pane and locked into place. He'd installed them as a precaution against drive-bys. Now they'd protect him from an asshole out for revenge. He lumbered across the living room and flipped a similar switch to seal the opposite window.

Gasping, he flipped on the overhead light and looked down at his chest. The front of his shirt was soaked with blood and bristling with glass shards. His left shoulder was slick with blood, too.

I've been fucking shot! Gotta take something before the pain hits.

He lurched to the coffee table, upended the Ziploc bag, and snorted more coke, sticking his nose into the powder this time. His vision went stark white for a moment, then cleared as adrenaline surged through him.

That oughta do it.

After pushing the couch down the hallway to barricade the bedroom door, he returned to the living room and sat against the wall opposite the front door. He'd custom-built that, too: sheets of 14-gauge steel mounted on heavy-duty hinges and set into a reinforced frame. Add to that high and low six-inch double-bolts, and there was no way the guy was getting inside. No fucking way.

Taking slow, even breaths, he listened intently for any sign of break-in. Nothing. Maybe the guy left? Scared shitless by his armed response? Chickenshit cracker.

And then he heard the tread of heavy boots on the porch, followed by scraping against the metal door.

He felt a spike of rage. Cole was attacking him where he lived. Making him a prisoner in his own house. Fuck him and his dead son. Nobody attacked him in his house. Nobody! Scrambling to his feet, he leapt at the door.

"Eat this!" He thrust the shotgun barrel against the door and fired. The shotgun kicked back as the blue slug punched through the metal plating with a *whang!* He bent forward to peer through the baseball-sized hole. He could see the porch, the front lawn, a patch of street. But no corpse.

Shit.

The edges of the door disappeared suddenly in a sizzle of white sparks.

Det cord! Motherfucker had wired the door with det cord! He staggered back as the door fell in with a clattering boom. He fired the shotgun three times through the smoking doorway, each blast shaking the walls of the living room. When the smoke cleared, he saw that the porch was still empty. No corpse, no blood.

He kept the shotgun trained on the breach, prepared for Cole's inevitable assault—but none came. He held his breath and listened past his hammering heart.

Scratching. On the porch, to the right of the door.

So it's gonna be games, motherfucker? Fine by me.

He crept to the doorway, gripping the shotgun with both hands, then whipped around to the right. Cole was there, curled on the porch, writhing in pain.

Cole gritted his teeth, saw red behind closed eyelids. *Get up!*

He struggled to roll onto his knees and pain speared his stomach. Sliding a hand into his assault vest, he fumbled for the plastic box that held the morphine styrettes when he heard the stomp of heavy boots on the porch.

His eyes fluttered open. He saw the MP5 a few feet away, where he'd dropped it, through the dissipating smoke. He reached out to grab the weapon when it disappeared.

"Mine now, motherfucker," Watkins said.

A massive hand clamped onto the collar of the assault vest and yanked him to his feet. Watkins' face appeared in his dulled field of vision.

"Looks like my shotgun blast made you move too quick," Watkins growled, looking him over. "You fell on the trigger, too, dumbshit. A man in your condition really shouldn't pick a fucking fight."

Watkins whipped Cole through the doorway with such force that he went airborne before slamming into the far living-room wall. Pain ripped through Cole's body as he landed on all fours and retched up phlegm. *Morphine . . .*

One dose would cut the pain. He could get up. Fight. One dose. To keep from failing Ronny again.

He tried for the styrettes in his assault vest when the heavy stomp of boots came again. He looked up, vision fogged by agony, mucous connecting his lips to the hardwood floor.

Watkins bore down on him—a muscled, murderous giant.

"This is for cappin' me in the shoulder!"

The man kicked him in the stomach. Pain exploded through him as he lifted off the floor, then collapsed onto his side. *Get up . . . get up . . .*

Watkins snatched Ronny's baseball cap from his head, put it on, then rifled through the pockets of the assault vest. He yanked out the ammunition clips, flashlight, and K-bar knife, which he dropped clattering to the hardwood floor, stopping when he found the plastic box of morphine.

"What the fuck is this?" Watkins asked.

Cole grabbed for the box, and Watkins slapped his hand away. Cole needed the styrettes to numb the pain. To have a fighting chance.

Watkins took the styrettes from the box, clutching them in his fist with the needles pointed up like tiny daggers. "You take these for pain, right?" he snarled in realization. "Well, you ain't gonna need 'em anymore. For the record, I think what Ruger did to your kid was fucked up. Way over the top. But nobody attacks me in my house, you got that, motherfucker? Nobody."

Watkins clutched Cole's throat with his free hand and squeezed, fingers strong as metal rods. Cole clawed at the man's forearm, but felt like a child against his brute strength. He sucked air . . . *ktchuuuhh!* . . . *ktchuuuhh!* . . . *ktchuuhh!* . . . until he strained for another breath, mouth gaping like a fish, and got nothing.

Cole saw a ghoulish grin of satisfaction creep across Watkins' face as he writhed, bucked his legs and heaved his chest, ignoring the wracking, burning pain, trying desperately to get some air, to break free.

But Watkins held him fast, choking . . . choking . . .

Blackness pushed into his vision. He'd pass out soon. *I've failed you again, son. I'm sorry . . .*

Suddenly, he knew what he had to do. The realization struck

deep and filled him with dark terror.

No . . .

He sensed the distant cold like an approaching storm over a dark sea. The sensation was erratic, fluctuating, but definitely *there.* He struggled toward it, terrified, but aching to feel its kiss because it was the only way he would survive.

Ronny . . .

Cole closed his eyes and let his body go limp. Let his internal defenses down. His legs bowed and his arms fell, slapping against the hardwood floor.

Suddenly, the cold rushed forth in a black flood. He trembled as the icy torrent flowed through his limbs, snuffed the burning pain, infused him with strength.

He felt mired to his waist in the frigid morass, then gaped in silent horror as it began to rise, filling him with lethal, emotionless resolve.

The mission is all that matters. The words echoed in his head, relics from the past. Becoming louder. *The mission is all that matters.*

The morass rose to his stomach, threatening to consume him. Focusing his will, he pushed *hard.* It kept coming, the cold stretching across his torso like fingers of frost. He pushed again. Stopped it. *The mission is all that matters.*

His eyes flew open. Watkins peered down at him, still grinning, but the smile faded quickly.

Fueled by icy resolve, Cole balled his fists and boxed Watkins' ears. The man howled, released his death grip. Cole sucked in a cool lungful of air, then smashed a fist into Watkins' face, which propelled him up and off his stomach.

Watkins tottered, slashing the air with the styrettes he clutched in his fist. The man had obviously taken some of the cocaine on the coffee table to numb the pain of his bullet wound, and the drug was now going into overdrive.

Cole leaped to his feet as Watkins continued to sway, relishing the cold power in his legs. He stalked forward. All he needed was one word for a voice match. One word before the man lost consciousness.

With a groan, Watkins toppled like a felled buffalo. But what began as a grunt of pain on impact soon escalated into a shrill screech. The man rolled over and Cole saw that the he had fallen onto the styrettes, which protruded from his throat. Overdose.

Rushing to Watkins' side, he yanked out the needles. Too late. Watkins convulsed as white froth bubbled from his mouth, and then he stopped breathing.

Cole pressed his ear to the man's chest. Heard nothing. Slammed his fist over the heart once, twice. Listened again. Using two fingers to clear the froth, he gave Watkins mouth-to-mouth. Watched the man's chest rise and fall. Rise and fall. Then stop. Watkins was dead.

Fuck!

As muted barbs of pain gouged him, Cole rifled through the man's pockets, found a cell phone, and saw that the most recent call had been from Ned Brandenburg. Lawrence would be able to trace the call, no problem.

He slid the phone into his assault vest, and tried to clear his head. But the coldness inside him *surged.*

Panic shot through him. He struggled to contain it, but it seeped from his stomach to his ribcage. The morass kept rising, encasing him in a frigid vise.

He concentrated, pushed, icy sweat pouring down his forehead, but the cold continued, seeping through his chest.

Jennifer.

He tried to conjure her face, but her features appeared blurred, like he was looking at her through dense fog. As though his memories had been numbed.

And then he remembered the tape recorder. With trembling fingers, he tore it from his assault vest, and pressed PLAY. A few seconds of empty tape hissed by as the cold slithered through him like a living thing . . . and then her voice crackled over the speaker.

"I love you, David."

Her words blazed across his mind like flares in a night sky. But the icy morass continued to rise. His teeth began to chatter. He pressed REWIND, then PLAY again.

"I love you, David."

More flares, each word burning brightly. He pressed the buttons again. And again. *"I love you, David . . . I love you, David . . . I love you . . ."*

Suddenly, the coldness receded. He pressed the buttons again, closing his eyes, letting the warmth of Jennifer's words wash through him.

He'd almost lost himself. He'd almost become the remorseless soldier he'd vowed to leave behind forever.

And then the pain hit. Without the cold, it returned with a vengeance. He gagged, collapsed to his knees.

Hand trembling, he snatched Ronny's baseball cap from Watkins' head, and then crawled toward the destroyed metal door. His vision began to tunnel.

Pass out and you'll be a sitting duck for Ruger. He fumbled for his cell phone to call Lawrence. The big man would come get him.

Don't pass out, he thought as blackness took him.

Chapter 12

Cole blinked against sunlight that streamed through the front door. He checked his watch. 5:30 a.m. He'd been unconscious for over eight hours. Watkins lay next to him like a downed redwood tree, froth on his lips dried to white crust.

Shaking his head to clear it, he sat up and gasped as pain gouged his abdomen. He ran his hands over his body to search for new wounds, and felt a warm, gummy wetness on his chest and thighs where blisters had ruptured and soaked through the jumpsuit. Other than that, nothing.

He'd gotten lucky. Watkins could have easily broken his arms, crushed his ribcage.

Struggling to his feet, he felt a profound sense of shame when he saw his scattered equipment. He'd been overpowered, disarmed. Was he really up to the mission?

It didn't matter. He owed it to Ronny to keep going no matter what. But he couldn't rely on the instincts again. From now on, he'd have to use morphine to dull the pain. He'd come too close to losing control. To losing *everything.*

Shuffling around the room, he scooped up the equipment and slung the MP5 over his right shoulder. He retrieved the cell phones last. Both were useless. He hadn't noticed earlier, but the keypads had been crushed during battle. Although he couldn't call Lawrence, Watkins' cell phone had Brandenburg's number stored in its call log. A valuable piece of intel.

He slid the phones into his vest, then froze when he heard

the soft crunch of footsteps on the front yard grass. The rapid approach of a soldier.

Ruger. Coming in for recon.

He felt a surge of seething anger. Pushed it away. As much as he wanted to tear Ruger's heart out, he couldn't. Not after the abuse his body had just taken. He needed to recoup. Fresh bandages and morphine. A plan.

All he could do now was retreat.

Feeling helpless, he lurched down a hallway. At the end was a couch barricading the bedroom door. He gripped the armrest with both hands and pulled, wincing as pain stabbed his elbows and shoulders. After sliding the couch a couple of feet, he opened the door and slipped through.

Behind him came the thump of footsteps on hardwood. Ruger was in the living room.

He moved to the window, slid it open, pried off the screen. The footsteps thumped down the hallway, getting louder.

After leaning the screen against the wall, he stepped onto the window frame, but overextended his leg, tearing blisters along his inner thigh. He gasped, lost his balance, and tumbled out the window, landing hard on the brown grass. Fiery hooks gouged his stomach and chest.

He heard the couch slide across the hardwood. The bedroom door bang open.

Not having the strength to run, he looked for a place to hide. Saw a grille set into the foundation of the house. He wedged his fingers under the metal lip, popped it free, and wormed into the crawlspace. Once inside, he shuffled around, wincing, and replaced the grille behind him.

He heard thumping directly above. A shuffle. A scrape. And then a pair of combat boots landed in front of the grille. Cole's anger flared when he saw the polished black leather, the thick black laces. The boots were close enough to touch.

Ruger didn't move. Was he surveying the scene or toying with him? Cole angled the MP5 toward the grille. If Ruger attacked, he had no room to evade in the cramped space. But he might get a shot off.

Cole could hear the man's breathing. It was deep and labored like a wild animal. Like it had been the night the mission went wrong.

What happened, Frank? What drove you over the edge?

He closed his eyes as nightmare flashes of what had been, and foreshadows of what might be, stormed into his mind . . .

. . . still screaming, Cole sprints to Ruger's side . . . shouts into the man's face, spittle flying from his lips . . . How could you? How could you? . . .

. . . Ruger doesn't turn but keeps firing, face slack, breath rasping . . .

. . . no response . . .

. . . a virtual zombie . . .

. . . Cole screams, tears pouring down his cheeks . . . How could you? . . . and then spots more Iraqi soldiers approaching from farther down the dock . . . whirls to confront them . . . opens fire again for what seems like a blood-soaked eternity . . . smells fresh gore . . . ruptured intestines . . . burned flesh . . . the sharp, chemical signature of Willy Pete . . . hears the shrill screams of the wounded and dying . . .

. . . he switches clips, keeps firing, weapons and instincts on full-auto . . . half his Team is already gone . . . God . . . just like that, gone forever . . .

As is Ruger . . . gone deep within himself . . . within some dark abyss . . .

Bullets pock a nearby mast, forcing him to take cover behind an oil drum. He jerks a grenade from his vest, tears out the pin, and lobs it onto the pier. The grenade explodes with a blinding flash, and seems to bring Ruger back to sanity for a few precious moments. The man blinks, stops firing.

"Frank!" Cole yells. "Get overboard! Now!"

Ruger yanks up an Iraqi corpse to shield himself from enemy fire. The corpse twitches with each bullet strike as Ruger backs to the edge of the junk, then jumps overboard.

Cole unloads a clip into more soldiers on dock to cover Ruger's escape, and then scans the boat for Roberts . . .

The sound of crunching grass pulled him back . . . Ruger . . . walking away toward the front of the house.

No. He would never become like Ruger.

Never.

Cole quietly popped out the grille, crawled from the crawl-space, and loped toward the chain link backyard fence to collect the handheld smoke machine. The less evidence the better.

He was careful to stay out of sight, knowing he could only attack Ruger on his terms. It was far too risky otherwise, and he couldn't risk failure when Stanford was still at large.

After collecting the equipment, Cole headed toward the gas station and the truck. He would never become like the man who'd taken away his sons, he vowed.

Ruger was an out-of-control animal. An animal that had to be put down.

Ruger felt a throbbing pressure at the back of his skull, closed his eyes. When he opened them again, he peered at a row of shrubs in a nearby yard, at a backyard fence further down the street, at a cluster of rusted trashcans on the corner. All could be hides for Iraqi soldiers.

The enemy was everywhere. Cunning. Lethal.

But none more lethal than David Cole.

Anger boiled as he massaged the scars on his left forearm. The man who'd betrayed him was still at large. But not for much longer.

He walked back into the living room where Watkins was growing ripe on the floor. Cole had taken the fucking bait.

Two days ago, he'd raided Cole's house. He'd found plenty of guns and high explosives like C4 and det cord—which he no doubt used to demolish things on set. Cole wouldn't have had the equipment to stage a raid, which meant that someone was helping him.

Judging from the dimension and spacing of the bullet strikes in the living room wall, this "someone" had supplied him with an MP5. He pressed a finger into the holes. They were shallow, which meant the weapon had been modified with a silencer. And that meant this "someone" knew his shit.

Ruger crouched to examine Watkins' body, and saw powdery residue on his nostrils, probably cocaine from the bag on the coffee table. His left shoulder was a ruin of flesh and bone where Cole had winged him with the MP5.

And then he noticed that the man's knuckles were smeared with a gummy black substance. *Charred flesh.* It backed up what he'd learned on the movie set: The explosion had fried Cole.

Ruger walked to where five styrettes lay on the floor. He'd ignored the needles on his first pass, thinking they belonged to Watkins. Now he wasn't so sure. He picked up one and smelled the tip.

Morphine.

A grin crawled across his face. *Does it fucking hurt, Commander? It did for fifteen years as my life was stripped away.*

Watkins had been able to get close enough to Cole for hand-to-hand combat, which meant that Cole wasn't fighting at full capacity. The man was weak. Vulnerable. But Ruger knew better than to underestimate him. Even wounded, Cole was still dangerous.

He rolled the styrette between forefinger and thumb. He hadn't found styrettes at Cole's place, which meant the person arming him was also taking care of him. Helping him manage the pain. Keeping him alive.

Sacrificing Watkins had been worth it. Now he had valuable intel about Cole's weapons, tactics, and capabilities. But more importantly, now he knew that attacking Cole directly wasn't his only option for victory.

The lodge was nestled in its own canyon in the Angeles National Forest, near Mt. Baldy. A perfect haven for skiing, Stanford thought, but cramped when it came to running a business.

He was sitting on a couch in the darkened living room, watching digital dailies from *Bringing Them Back* projected onto a large white screen. The scene playing had been filmed MOS—or "without sound"—and featured hero Rocky Slaughter in a bar fight. Heightened sounds of fists smacking flesh, gunshots, and crashing furniture would be added in post-production when the film was finished. Because it would be finished, he had no doubt. Banks, private investors, even other film studios would prostrate themselves to invest, anxious to sate the morbid curiosity of the public. He mused possible headlines: Coming this Fall! *Bringing Them Back,* featuring movie-set murderer David Cole!

Whether Cole was ultimately killed or captured didn't matter. Interest would be a feeding frenzy, earning him a fortune in addition to the retainer that Devereaux had so conscientiously declined. Loki would be back in business.

There was a knock at the door.

"Come," he said.

Ruger entered, shadowy bulk filling the doorway, and stood opposite the couch to the left of the screen. Even in the flickering darkness, Stanford could see that Ruger's eyes were dialed into him as keenly as a laser sight.

"Cole took the bait," Ruger said.

Stanford nodded. Leaving Watkins vulnerable had been a brilliant tactic. He was disappointed that he hadn't thought of it himself. Cole's resilience notwithstanding, Ruger's military expertise had proven useful. As had his savagery. "What did you learn?"

"He's well-supplied."

"I thought you cleaned out his backyard cache."

"I did. Someone's helping him."

Stanford frowned. That meant another witness who might link him to the explosion. He would take no chances here. Not when the future of Loki Productions was at stake. Anyone aiding and abetting Cole must die. "Who?"

"You tell me."

Stanford thought for a moment, and then remembered the argument he'd had with Cole at the office. "Cole wanted to hire a man to replace my nephew on *Bringing Them Back.* A weapons handler."

"Where is he?"

"I don't have the contact information, but I know who does."

Stanford stood and walked across the room toward his desk when Ruger appeared in front of him suddenly, blocking his way.

Yes, of course, Stanford thought. He'd expected this from the moment Ruger had arrived. The man could have reported this information over the phone, but had delivered it in person instead. That could only mean one thing.

"How much?" he asked.

"Two targets, double the price."

Stanford knew that he could not simply agree to the terms, and then have Ruger killed when he left the room. Ruger was the key to success. He knew how Cole operated—the gambit with Watkins had proved it. But Stanford also realized that if he gave in, he would be in thrall to Ruger from now on.

"You were hired to complete this job regardless of variables," he said.

Ruger reached out and clutched his arm. "I'm not asking, motherfucker."

Stanford gave Ruger a measured look and saw eyes that were cold, bottomless, devoid of mercy and remorse. The man could kill him easily, well before Huxley responded to a call for help. Even so, he felt no fear—for he'd learned what *true* fear was as a young boy.

True fear was witnessing your father's murder. It was watching your mother come apart with grief. It was doing whatever necessary to support your mother and survive.

He knew that Ruger was formidable. A man whose mind and body had been forged by the government's most lethal military branch. But Stanford had been trained on the street by forces just as powerful: unrelenting anguish and pain.

Keeping his gaze steady, he said, "Do not make me ask you to stand down a second time, Mr. Ruger. You will adhere to our original contract. You will follow my orders to the letter and without question. You will also remember that my organization looks after family, and if you betray me, my associates will find you no matter where you try to hide."

Ruger's eyes remained dialed into him, searching for weakness. Stanford continued to look back with eyes just as cold and bottomless, knowing that Ruger would not—could not—break his resolve.

Finally, Ruger let go of his arm.

That's a good dog, Stanford thought as he stepped around Ruger to retrieve a business card from the top desk drawer.

"She'll know how to find the weapons handler," he said, handing the card to Ruger. "But you're not to hurt her unless necessary. Is that clear?"

Ruger regarded him with diminished intensity as he slipped

the card into the breast pocket of his jacket.

"Now get out of my sight," Stanford told him.

After Ruger left the room, Stanford turned off the projector and flipped on the overhead light. Then he called in Huxley and briefed him.

"I'm telling you, when all this is over, we should take Ruger out," Huxley grunted, shaking his head.

"Like any attack dog, all he needs is a firm hand," Stanford replied as he sat back down on the couch.

"What about Watkins?"

"Let him rot."

"Gary, considering the neighborhood, the body could stay unreported for days. We should call in an anonymous tip."

Stanford nodded, pleased. "You're right, of course. There's no reason why the police shouldn't learn sooner rather than later how dangerous a fugitive David Cole truly is."

Chapter 13

"You the asshole who helped Ted Roberts?"

Otto Anderson looked up from his desk. He knew Detective Whittaker by reputation only, but the unkempt man standing here with the sparkling tact and charm could only be him. Anderson knew that there was no use lying to protect Roberts. Whittaker was doing what detectives often did—asking a question he already knew the answer to.

"I helped Ted, yes," Anderson said.

"I don't give a shit if you're ATF. My authority supersedes everyone's, got it?"

"With due respect, sir, I was helping a fellow law enforcement officer pursue an investigation that I thought had merit."

"It's not up to you to decide shit. It's up to you to do as I fucking say."

Anderson repressed the urge to give Whittaker the finger. "Sir, Ted Roberts is not only a fellow officer, he's a trusted friend. If he says David Cole is innocent, I believe him."

Whittaker scowled. "You listen to me, Agent. The evidence indicates that David Cole murdered his son in cold blood, a member of Cole's own crew is all over TV calling him a fucking psycho, and we just received a tip that Cole has killed again." He placed his hands on the desk, and leaned forward. "So I guess my question is: When is Roberts gonna get with the fucking program?"

The new murder was news to Anderson, but the interview

was not. *Star Power* was airing the interview with Ned Brandenburg with O.J. Simpson–like fervor. Brandenburg wasn't very articulate but his message was clear: Cole was unpredictable and dangerous. At times, Anderson was tempted to believe the hearsay. But Roberts stood by Cole, and the man's instinct for truth was beyond reproach.

"The truth will come out soon enough," Anderson said.

Whittaker straightened. "Roberts has allowed personal feelings to influence his actions, as have you. For the duration of this case, you will sit at this desk. You will not assist any agent in any way, particularly Ted Roberts. Do I make myself clear?" Without waiting for an answer, the detective stormed away.

Never tell me what I can't do, Anderson thought, hoping for the sake of his family, reputation and career that Roberts was right. He picked up the phone.

Roberts sat cross-legged on Matador Beach and stared out at the morning ocean as he let details of the case sink in. The ocean always filled him with calm. As a young recruit, his SEAL instructors had taught him to treat the water as sanctuary—a calm refuge from dangers on land. As the sun slowly revealed itself behind him like some blazing, all-seeing eye, he wondered if the inky depths could provide answers as well as protection.

After arriving home from San Diego last night, he'd fallen asleep on the couch and slept the night through. He knew that he should have kept working on the case, but he'd been too drained from his meeting with Burke.

His cell phone rang. He answered, grateful for the distraction. "Hey, Otto."

"You sitting down?"

He felt an anticipatory rush of dread. Anderson was usually low-key. "As a matter of fact, I am."

"Levar Watkins. You know him?"

The name sounded familiar, but he couldn't place it. "I'm not sure."

"The man worked with David Cole on *Bringing Them Back* the day before the explosion."

Now he remembered. Watkins was working with Ned Brandenburg, the movie producer's nephew, and it was no secret that Cole had little respect for them. "What about him?"

"Turned up dead this morning. Whittaker is on his way to the man's house right now."

Roberts' stomach dropped. He thought again about what Commander Burke had said about Cole's frame of mind during the court proceedings. Could that volatility have carried forward thirteen years? Could it have impelled Cole to murder his son? No way. Cole had loved Ronny with all his heart. But who knew what Cole was capable of now that his son was dead.

"Thanks for the tip."

"I'm sorry, man. I know this doesn't look good for your friend."

"What's the address?" he asked, and then wrote it down. "Want to come along, Otto? Whittaker could be right. I might be too close to judge things objectively."

"I appreciate your faith in me, Ted, but Whittaker busted me to a desk after our joyride. Don't worry, I didn't tell him you were involved. That said, I'm stuck until my boss decides what to do with me."

Roberts felt terrible. The last thing he'd wanted to do was cause trouble for Anderson. The man had a family, a reputation to protect. "Shit, Otto, I don't know what to say."

"Not your fault, Ted. It was my decision to help you. I'm telling you about Watkins now as a 'fuck you' to Whittaker, sure, but mostly because I know how important this case is to you. I also want to tell you to be careful. Whittaker busted me without thinking twice, and I think the guy actually likes me."

Roberts knew that Anderson was right. Pursuing this lead might mean the end of his career when he had no family, no social life to speak of, and few friends outside the department. He'd turned into an overachiever-workaholic since the war, admittedly obsessed with earning the second chance that Cole had given him.

If Whittaker felt even remotely threatened by his presence, there was no telling what he would do. Roberts felt a twinge of hesitation that was quickly overwhelmed by his sense of duty to Cole. In fact, he felt guilty for hesitating at all. Cole had saved his life. He would be proud to return the favor.

"Thanks again for the tip, bud. I'll keep you posted."

No sooner had he hung up when he remembered Commander Burke's warning: *All it will take for Cole to become like Ruger is the proper trigger.* The words lingered menacingly in his head like a hand grenade with its pin pulled. All the more reason to find Cole quickly—before he hurt others, himself, or validated Whittaker's line of investigation.

The phone rang again. "Yes, Jennifer?"

"Do you have time today to compare notes?" she asked.

"Did you find something?"

Her voice was tense with excitement. "I plan to do research this afternoon to verify, but I think I might have evidence linking Stanford to organized crime."

"That's good news," he grunted.

"Your voice is different, Ted," she said. "Is everything alright?"

"Fine."

"I don't have to be an investigator to know something's up. Please tell me what it is."

He considered telling her about the interview with Burke and the Watkins case, but decided against it. It would only break her focus. "It's nothing. Really. How about six o'clock at Santa

Monica Pier?"

"You learned something about David, didn't you?" she said softly.

She was quick, he had to give her that. "I'll see you at six," he said and hung up, resigned that he was about to sink his career, and possibly learn more secrets about Cole that he didn't want to know.

An hour later, Roberts was kneeling over the pungent body of Levar Watkins as forensics people worked around him. Apparently, Whittaker was still en route. Roberts didn't have long to get the information he needed before the detective tossed him from the scene.

He examined the white powder around Watkins' nostrils, the dried mucus on his lips and the constellation of puncture wounds in his throat. It was clear that the man had died from a morphine/cocaine overdose. But that didn't explain the bullet wound in his shoulder.

Was Cole responsible? Or had Ruger attacked Watkins in an attempt to further implicate Cole?

Next, he examined the shattered glass that lay on the floor beneath the metal shutters. In the opposite wall were bullet holes. Nine millimeter, and shallow. Slowed by a silencer. It wasn't difficult to guess what had happened: Watkins had been shot through the window. He'd closed the shutters. The intruder had breached the reinforced door with det cord, and had taken him down. Textbook urban assault: Harass the flank, follow-up with a frontal assault.

The tactic would be second nature to Cole and Ruger both.

"You've gotta be kidding me," came a voice from behind him. Roberts turned to find Whittaker scowling in the doorway. "You've got balls coming here, Ted. I'll give you that."

"Hold on, Scott. There might be a third party involved," he

said, hoping to supplant Whittaker's hostility with curiosity.

"You breached protocol to tell me that?"

"Hear me out. A guy who served with Cole and me in the Gulf was just released from a psychiatric hospital in San Diego. This guy, Frank Ruger, has a serious axe to grind. I think he's worth investigating."

"Third party, huh?" Whittaker said, eyes darkening with anger.

"Remember the errant mortar compound I mentioned? Turns out it was white phosphorus. We used white phosphorous to fight in the Gulf."

"Third party, that's your story?" Whittaker shook his head incredulously. "My men already dusted for prints. Most match the victim. The others match the prints David Cole has on file with the State when he registered for his pyro license. There are no other prints. No third party."

The news hit him like cold water. Cole had been here. But why? He'd known Cole as a soldier and as a civilian—and the man never did anything without sound reason. "Maybe Cole was trying to find who killed his son," he suggested. "Why else would he attack a target that would further implicate him?"

"Because he's fucking nuts."

"That still wouldn't explain the phosphorus."

"So phosphorus isn't used to blow shit up, okay, fine, but even I know it's used in fireworks. He could have put some in by mistake."

"Cole wouldn't make that mistake."

"He did this time, and that's not the only one. He keeps killing people on my turf. For that, he's going down, no matter what you say."

Roberts gritted his teeth. He was losing control of the situation. Whittaker was even more hostile toward Cole, and Roberts realized his presence was making things worse. He shouldn't have come.

"I know it looks bad, Scott, but again, I have to go on my gut," he said. "I served with Cole. I know him better than anyone, and I'm telling you there's an explanation for all this."

"The explanation is that Cole is guilty. If you had any fucking objectivity, you'd see that."

"Frank Ruger is involved somehow, I'm telling you. I recommend—"

"You're not in the position to recommend anything," Whittaker spat. "I've been on the phone with your boss, Ted. He's forwarded me the arson files. You're done with this case. I wouldn't be surprised if you were done with the fire department as well."

Even though he'd expected the possibility, he still couldn't believe that he'd been forced off the case. He'd overstepped his bounds, yes, and the evidence he'd disclosed had been circumstantial. But his investigation had merit. Didn't it? He wasn't so sure, anymore. There was so much conflicting evidence.

"My job is to make sure David Cole pays for what he's done. Now get the hell off my crime scene or I'll have you forcibly removed," Whittaker said, and then walked across the living room and disappeared down the hall.

Facts from the case swirled in Roberts' head. He had to get away. Think. Reassess. Maybe Whittaker was right. Maybe he saw a connection with Ruger because he wanted there to be one. There was hoping a man was innocent—and then there was believing what you wanted to believe.

Turning to leave, he looked down and noticed four lateral scabs on Watkins' left forearm. He'd been so focused on staying clear of Whittaker that he'd missed it before.

Ruger had made similar cuts on his forearm with a K-bar

knife during the months preceding the failed mission in Iraq. Ruger had never told anyone, but Roberts had noticed.

Whittaker would see the cuts as circumstantial, he knew. But to him, the evidence was clear: Ruger had been here after Cole. The man's presence didn't fully explain Cole's involvement, but now he had proof that he was on the right track.

He had no choice but to continue his investigation, even when doing so meant disobeying orders and proceeding without backup.

But what would be his next step? The police would have searched Cole's house and confiscated any weapons. That meant somebody had armed Cole for this little raid, and he had a pretty good idea of who that might be.

"Goddammit, Dave, let me in!" Lawrence said.

Standing in the tub, Cole looked at the bathroom door, which bowed every time Lawrence slammed it with his fist. BAM-BAM-BAM!

"I'm fine," he croaked, struggling to focus his thoughts through the morphine euphoria. After returning to the cabin, he'd injected himself with a styrette from the medikit, and then barricaded himself in the bathroom before Lawrence had realized he was there. If his friend saw how much his wounds had deteriorated, he'd take him to the hospital no questions asked—overpowering him if need be—even though the mission was far from over.

"Yeah, you're the picture of health! Now let me the fuck in!" BAM-BAM-BAM-BAM!

Even though the door had been reinforced—Lawrence was anal about security—Cole knew it wouldn't be long before the big man busted his way inside. So he had to be quick.

With trembling hands, he unhooked the assault vest and laid it on the bath mat. Underneath the vest, the black jumpsuit was even darker with the Rorschach pattern of bloodstains. He unbuttoned the front and shrugged his shoulders free so that it fell around his ankles. As he'd suspected, the bandages wrapping his chest and stomach were shriveled and crusted with blood.

Using the K-bar knife, he carefully sliced away the bandages. The burns covering his chest seeped yellow pus. Worse, they'd dehydrated and constricted, making him feel like he was wrapped in gaffer's tape. He took a strained breath. If he didn't correct the problem soon, the burns could constrict tightly enough to suffocate him. He also noticed that the charred flesh on his stomach had split during the fight with Watkins. A jagged, vertical tear ran the length of his abdominal wall, and had rejoined badly within a lumpy island of scab.

"DAVE!" Lawrence yelled, voice an unrestrained boom now. "YOU LISTENING TO ME? I SAID OPEN THIS FUCKING DOOR!"

Ignoring the racket as best he could, Cole took a deep, preparatory breath as he clutched the K-bar knife with both hands, and then pushed the razor-tip into the burn covering his left pectoral, near the armpit. He inhaled sharply through clenched teeth, but kept pushing, slowly, slowly. When the tip was buried about an eighth inch, he dragged the knife steadily across his chest, creating a lateral incision. The ravaged flesh split easily, like rotten cheesecloth, oozing yellow pus and purplish blood. Thanks to the morphine there was surprisingly little pain—just a sharp, crackling sting, like he was dragging a live wire across his skin. He continued to cut until the incision reached his right armpit. Inhaling again, he felt the pressure ease a bit.

"I SWEAR TO GOD I'M GONNA BUST DOWN THIS DOOR! I'M NOT KIDDING!" Lawrence bellowed.

Cole made the next incision a half-inch below the first, slicing his chest above the nipples, creating another weeping, bloody furrow. He made another cut below the nipples, and then three more, each a half-inch lower than the next, until he'd created a ladder of horizontal cuts that stretched from the top of his chest to the scab on his stomach. He then pressed the tip of the knife into the soft skin underneath his Adam's apple, and sliced down, bisecting the lateral cuts until he reached the scab at his midsection. He made more vertical incisions on either side of the center cut, each a half-inch apart, creating a scrimshaw that covered his chest.

"OKAY, THAT'S IT!" Lawrence yelled. "YOU GOT ONE MINUTE TO OPEN THIS FUCKING DOOR BEFORE I OPEN IT FOR YOU!"

He inhaled deeply. The incisions yawned like gills as his lungs filled with air, the pressure gone. He pressed a clean towel against his chest to soak the excess blood, and then rewrapped his chest with fresh bandages as quickly as he could, starting from the top and working down.

". . . THIRTY SECONDS . . . !"

Satisfied with the dressing, he tore the bandage from the roll, and tied off the end.

"TEN SECONDS . . . !"

After throwing the bloody towel into the hamper, he stepped carefully from the tub, and opened the door. Lawrence was there, right shoulder forward, ready to turn his mammoth body into a battering ram.

"I said I'm fine," Cole told him.

Lawrence pushed into the bathroom, and pointed accusingly at the crusty jumpsuit and bandages littering the tub. "Yeah? Then what the hell is that?"

"I had to change my bandages," he said matter-of-factly, and then slowly made his way toward the living room. Lawrence thumped past him and stood in the hall, blocking his way.

"You ain't going anywhere until you tell me what happened out there."

"I already told you through the door."

"Watkins died from an overdose of morphine and coke. You passed out. Ruger was on your ass and you ditched him. I got all that." Lawrence glared at him. "But that ain't the full story. We agreed we'd never lie to each other, Dave. Tell me everything is fucking fine. Tell me your body and mind are healthy enough to keep going, and still get to the hospital in one piece after this is over. Go ahead, tell me."

He could see that Lawrence's stubbornness came from a caring place. The man didn't want grief to push him past his limits.

He could not tell his friend that the pain was beyond terrible, that his body was rapidly deteriorating, and that the instincts had almost consumed him. But he didn't want to lie, either, especially when the man was betraying his own instincts as a police officer to protect him. Yet the simple fact remained: Ronny took priority. He would sacrifice anything to accomplish this mission, including his life. And he needed Lawrence's help to do it.

He looked into Lawrence's eyes and said, "I'm okay, big man. You got my word on that. And my word counts."

Lawrence eyes softened with relief. "You had me plenty fucking worried."

Cole felt a pang of guilt that Lawrence had fallen for the deception so quickly and unequivocally. "I didn't mean to scare you," he said. He'd already failed too many people who'd made the mistake of relying on him. And now that Ruger was on his trail, he couldn't stop until he was done.

"Scared? Nah . . ." Lawrence said, turned quickly and continued into the living room before any emotion could play across his face. Cole felt lucky to know Lawrence. He was a good man. A good man, indeed. "Hey, I took the liberty of checking out Watkins' cell phone while you were in the bathroom. Brandenburg's call was relayed through a tower in Antelope Valley."

Cole thought for a moment. "Loki Productions owns soundstages out there."

"Exactly what I was thinking. Perfect place to hole-up."

Each soundstage would be the size of a jumbo jet hangar: two hundred feet high, made of concrete, sealed with a thirty-foot sliding metal door. He might as well be attacking a bunker. "Have anything that'll tip the balance?"

"You gotta ask? Wait here." Lawrence disappeared through the backyard door.

As he waited for the man to return, his thoughts turned to Watkins. Until now, he'd ached for vengeance, but faced with the morbid reality of violence, he didn't know how to feel. It had taken him so long after the war to come to peace with having killed at all.

Even though Watkins had died from his own hand, the battle had proved how consuming the instincts really were. *Bravery. Loyalty. Valor.* The justifications for killing that he'd used during war rang hollow now.

Ronny and Jennifer were all that mattered to him, but could he launch another assault and hold it together?

Lawrence returned, kicking through the door with a *bang.* His arms were loaded with a fresh jumpsuit and assault vest, a bulging green rucksack, and a sniper rifle.

Cole was familiar with the rifle: M40A1, heavy barreled, bolt action, magazine-fed with a five 7.62mm round capacity. Lawrence placed the rucksack and assault vest on the floor, then handed him the jumpsuit and laid the sniper rifle on the kitchen counter.

"Brandenburg is bound to have protection, and this," he said, indicating the rifle, "means you can pop the bad guys from a distance. No more of that through-the-front-door Rambo shit, got it?"

"I've learned my lesson," Cole said, stepping into the jumpsuit. The rifle was perfect for a ranged strike, true. More importantly, it meant that he wouldn't have to rely on his instincts to fight. He shuddered, feeling them beneath his consciousness, waiting like a shark in deep water.

Lawrence opened the rucksack and pulled out several large smoke pots, each the size of a coffee can with four-inch black fuses, followed by a black canvas harness fitted with several interlocking straps and buckles, and a spool of 1/8 inch wire rope—a stuntman's flight rig. "In case you attack from the roof," he explained. "And don't worry, the harness has a load limit of two thousand pounds to account for the weight of your gear."

Cole nodded. But as thankful as he was for Lawrence's help, guilt nagged at him. He'd lied to his friend. Worse, he was putting his friend at risk. "Lawrence."

The man looked up from repacking the wire rope.

"Stay here and there's a chance . . ." He stopped, as though not voicing the danger would minimize it.

He saw fear in Lawrence's eyes that faded quickly under an expression of determination. "I ain't afraid of that motherfucker."

"We can set up camp somewhere else."

Lawrence shook his head. "Nobody knows these hills like me, Dave. I can defend myself best right here. Besides, I'm not letting some psycho chase me outta my home. Let Ruger come looking for me. Let him try to pick on somebody his own size, someone who ain't tied up and helpless."

Cole felt hot with shame. Lawrence's continued involvement was based on a lie. But it couldn't be helped. Angry with himself, he walked to the kitchen counter, snatched up the sniper rifle and began to break it down, laying the pieces neatly in front of him. Everything was oiled, clean, in perfect working order. No surprise.

Lawrence said, "The new assault vest has everything the old one did, but it's also rigged up special, the way we discussed, okay?"

Nodding, Cole slapped the broken-down rifle back together, then jammed in the magazine, yanked back the slide to chamber a round, and pocketed the remaining shells.

"I put another box of styrettes in there," Lawrence continued. "You might want to slip an extra in your boot, so you don't run out like you did last night. Now you should get some rest."

"A couple hours at most," he said. "Every minute I spend here is another minute Ruger could be shoring his defenses."

Lawrence nodded. "I'll let you know if I hear anything over the police band."

Cole walked down the bedroom hallway, stopping in the bathroom to retrieve the mini tape recorder from his old assault vest. Practically, he didn't need it during this phase of the mission since Lawrence had taped Brandenburg off the TV. But with the push of a button, he could listen to Jennifer's voice whenever he needed strength and courage.

As he continued down the hallway, he thought about how she, Lawrence and Ted were putting themselves at risk for him. He was filled with a profound sense of gratitude . . . and sadness. His friends were enduring too much.

But he also knew that in a few hours, it would all be over, one way or the other.

CHAPTER 14

Roberts pounded on the front door of the cabin. The man who answered was far bigger than he expected. "Lawrence Fuchs? I'm Arson Investigator Ted Roberts. I'd like to talk to you about David Cole."

"I don't know where he is."

"Can I call you Lawrence?" Roberts asked. The man shrugged. "I'm not accusing you of anything, Lawrence."

"Ronny Cole was like a nephew to me, so you'll understand if I'm not in the mood to play twenty questions right now."

Even though Fuchs was contrite, Roberts noticed that he was looking at him intently. He noticed, too, that the man was using the door as a shield—as though afraid that his body language might give him away.

"I served with Cole in the Navy. Did he ever mention me?"

"Yeah, of course."

"I wish we could have met under better circumstances."

Lawrence shrugged again.

"Why don't you let me come in? There are a lot of people looking for Dave right now, and I'm as concerned about him as you are."

Roberts knew the man was an ex-cop, and would recognize implied threat. Sure enough, he caught a flash of resentment in Lawrence's eyes as the man stepped back and opened the door.

He entered and quickly surveyed the room: second-hand recliner and couch, cluttered bookcase, dirty plates. On a scuffed glass coffee table were a tool belt, beeper, 411 directory, and .44 pistol. No sign of Cole. At least not yet.

"You used to be NYPD, so I'll assume you have a permit for this," he said good-naturedly as he slid the pistol into his belt. "But I'll hold it for the time being, okay?"

"You ran a check on me?" Lawrence asked.

"Just the history you submitted with your union application. You ever work with the Red Caps back in New York?"

Lawrence shook his head.

"Best arson guys in the country."

Roberts moved to the fireplace mantel and examined a silver-framed picture of a little girl. Cute, had her daddy's eyes. "You mentioned your close relationship with Ronny. How would you characterize your relationship with Cole?"

"He's my best friend."

Roberts nodded, surprised at the pang of jealousy he felt. Cole had been like a father to him in the SEALs before the failed mission had torn them apart. "Has weapons handling been your only job since leaving the force?"

"What's that got to do with Dave?"

He turned. "How about some professional courtesy, Lawrence? I'm just trying to do my job."

"I don't like anyone invading my privacy."

"I can appreciate that, but you never know which details will help with a case."

Lawrence sighed. "Yeah, weapons have been my only gig."

"Thanks to Cole?"

Lawrence nodded.

"Seems like he went out on a limb, considering you had no experience in the movie business."

"I know my way around guns from being on the force."

Roberts moved toward the kitchen. "Can I look in here?"

Lawrence shrugged. Roberts went into the kitchen and peered

through a window into the backyard. In the lengthening shadows he could distinguish a copse of trees, a shaggy lawn, lots of junk. But no movement. Still no sign that Cole was here or had been. "You ever work with Dave on a movie produced by Gary Stanford?" he asked.

"You talking about *Bringing Them Back*?"

"Am I?" He returned to the living room, and glanced down what he assumed was a bedroom hallway. It was too dark to see the end.

"Are you?"

Roberts smirked. The man knew the interrogation technique—let the suspect answer his own questions—and refused to be trapped into offering information. So be it. "Yeah, Lawrence, I'm talking about *Bringing Them Back.*"

"That would've been my first."

"Who booked you?"

"Dave."

"Did you know you'd be replacing two other men?"

"Yeah."

"Dave must place a lot of trust in you."

Lawrence shrugged.

"What weapons would you have used on a job like that?" Roberts asked.

"Whatever's needed."

"My old man used to have a Colt .45 revolver, one from the Old West. Pretty rare. Could you get one of those if they needed it?"

"Depends."

"On what?"

"If the weapon is still in production. If there's a local supplier. There are a bunch of variables." Lawrence crossed his arms. "We almost done here?"

"Yeah, just about."

Lawrence was demonstrating again that he knew how the interrogation game was played. He'd made it clear that he was competent enough to earn Cole's trust, but was also noncommittal about his ability to procure any specific weapon. That meant Roberts couldn't pin him down about supplying the modified MP5 that Cole had used against Watkins.

"Lawrence . . ." he began, intending to tell the man flat-out that Cole was in trouble—that Frank Ruger was on his trail—to provoke an honest, emotional response, but stopped when he smelled something. An odor, sharp and strong.

It reminded him of the burned-out hatchback he'd found on a dirt road south of San Juan Capistrano nine months ago. The immolated victim inside had been rotting inside the vehicle for two days before being called in by a passerby. He remembered the ammonia-like stench . . . not chemical ammonia, but the stench given off by bacteria infesting burned flesh.

The ammonia smell was here. Faint, but present.

Roberts' eyes went wide as he made the connection: the on-set explosion that killed Ronny had burned Cole, and Lawrence had helped clean the wounds.

"Stay right where you are, Lawrence," Roberts said sharply, placing a hand on his holstered pistol.

"What the fuck?" Lawrence growled, but did as he was told.

"Dave, this is Ted. I know you're here," Roberts yelled. "Come out with your hands in the air!"

There was no answer. Roberts indicated the dark hallway with his gun. "Is there a light switch?"

Lawrence shook his head. Roberts pulled a pair of handcuffs from his belt and approached.

"Oh, no you don't," Lawrence said.

Roberts leveled his gun at the man. If Cole was here and decided to put up a fight, he didn't want a potential enemy behind him. "I'm not fucking around. Give me your wrist."

Lawrence glared, but held up his right hand. Roberts locked one end of the cuff around Lawrence's wrist and the other to the bookcase. He knew the bookcase couldn't keep Lawrence from moving, but at least it would make noise and act as a warning.

"Stay put," he said. "I mean it."

Roberts moved into the hallway. Three doors appeared in the gloom—the first was a few paces away to his right, the second further to his left, and the third at the end.

Again, he was in a position where he could be fighting Cole. If Cole didn't want to be brought in, he'd be trying to take down the man who'd taught him everything about guerrilla combat. *You can do this . . . you* have *to do this . . . it's for Cole's own good . . .*

Taking a deep breath, he burst into the first room. The shades were drawn, but he could still make out a queen-sized bed and a mound of dirty clothes overflowing from the shallow recesses of a small closet. *Nothing. Keep moving.*

He left the room and continued down the hall. The ammonia smell was stronger now.

The door at the end of the hall was closed. He pressed his ear against the cold wood. Nothing. Taking another breath, he flung open the door. The room was pitch dark. Realizing that he was a sitting duck framed in the doorway, he quickly slid his hand along the inside wall until he found a light switch. A single bulb set into the far wall illuminated a small garage cluttered by cardboard boxes, tools, and other detritus. *Nothing behind curtain number two.*

He glanced over his shoulder. "Lawrence! You still with me?"

"You got no right to search my place without a warrant!" the man yelled back.

"I can detain you until I get one," Roberts told him, hoping he wouldn't call the bluff. It may have been true before he'd been tossed from the case, but not now. "I'd be happy to call in a bunch of friends, too."

Roberts moved to the last door, which was also cracked open. He could see bathroom tiling in the gloom. He took a final, preparatory breath, and bolted through the door. Empty. But the ammonia smell was strong.

Frowning, he strode back into the living room to find Lawrence still shackled to the bookcase. "When was Cole here, Lawrence?"

"I don't know what you're talking about."

"Don't start with me."

"I said he ain't been here."

"I can smell him."

"*Smell* him?" Lawrence said incredulously. "You fucking kidding? That's it, man, we're done. Get outta my house."

Roberts seethed. First Whittaker had tossed him from the case, and now Lawrence was shutting him out.

He got in Lawrence's face. "I understand how Dave must feel. Ronny gets murdered and there's nothing he can do about it. Nothing except payback. So he went to his best friend for help. *You.* A friend who owes him a favor. A friend who has the tools and expertise to get the job done."

"You high, man."

"Levar Watkins. Name ring a bell? The man was attacked last night with a modified MP5. Cole's prints were on the scene. Do you deny giving Cole the weapon?"

"I'm telling you—"

"Lawrence, do the right thing here."

"The right thing for who?"

"Help me stop Cole before he gets in more trouble. Before Frank Ruger finds him."

At the mention of Ruger, Lawrence blinked like he'd just bitten into a piece of rotten fruit, but recovered quickly. "Man, I'm telling you, I haven't seen—"

"Goddammit, you're a cop!" Roberts barked. "Start acting like one!"

"*Ex*-cop, motherfucker!" Lawrence yelled back, brown eyes burning with fury.

Roberts glared back but knew the fight was lost. If Lawrence had disregarded the badge, then he'd made up his mind to protect Cole regardless of consequences. "I can help him, Lawrence," he said quietly. "You know I can."

Lawrence looked away. Roberts pulled the .44 from his belt and set it back on the coffee table, then unlocked the handcuffs.

"One more chance. Let me help before things get worse."

"Things are shit already," Lawrence said, rubbing his wrist, "and I ain't got nothin' to hide."

"This isn't over," Roberts said, and then walked out the door.

Cole knew he was taking a terrible risk. Jennifer might be home, spot him, and call the police. Or a neighbor might do the same. But he couldn't help himself. She'd kept him sane when everything else had failed.

Pulling a white rose from the plastic-wrapped bouquet he'd bought on the corner, he climbed from the truck, and jogged across the street to her front walk. The last time he'd seen these jade bushes was with Ronny. How he wished it were three days ago . . . when he was having dinner with his son and the woman he loved.

As he approached the front door, he saw his reflection in the living room window. Even if this god-awful mess turned out right somehow, this was Hollywood, a town known for beautiful people. How could Jennifer ever love a monster like him?

He knelt, holding the rose gently between forefinger and thumb. The flower matched the bouquet he'd sent as a thank-you for dinner, and would let her know he'd been there. More importantly, it might convince her to call off her search—the knowledge that he was alive might be enough for her. He doubted it, but had to try. If she continued, Ruger and Stanford might consider her a threat, and he couldn't bear the thought of her in danger, especially on his behalf.

After pressing the white rose to his lips, he laid it on the stoop. Standing, he felt an almost overpowering urge to knock on the door.

How he ached to see her . . . to hear her voice, not just on tape, but in person.

He imagined her opening the door, her long brown hair swept back, her green eyes widening with shock, and then softening with love and relief despite his appearance. He would hold her, and she, him. He would feel her body pressed against his, her radiant warmth.

He could knock on the door. He could. And if she wasn't home, he could slip inside and wait for her.

As he stood on the doorstep, he played the possibility over and over in his mind. He could end the nightmare. Right here. Right now.

Would Ronny understand?

It would be so easy.

Jennifer crossed the parking lot, passing underneath the Arizona Street pedestrian bridge, and climbed a wooden staircase up to the pier. Pacific Park, the pier's summer carnival, was in full swing. Among the attractions were the Santa Monica West Coaster, the Pacific Wheel Ferris wheel, and the Sig Alert bumper cars. The carnival had drawn throngs of visitors: couples, families, tour groups wielding cameras. Jennifer could hear the mechanical clinks and clanks of the carnival rides, children's cries of delight.

She envied the fun that these people were having, and wished that she were here under different circumstances. Smiling wistfully, she looked up at the Ferris wheel. Its fire-engine-red carriages rocked gently as they rose into the dark sky. David had taken her for a ride in one of those carriages last spring—before they'd had the courage to express their attraction for one another. They'd been on location on the Third Street promenade, only blocks away.

She remembered looking out along the coast, all traces of air pollution replaced by a twinkling carpet of lights. The pier itself was a finger of bright, flashing colors below them extending into the black ocean . . .

"Are you okay?" Jennifer asked.

"Fine," he said through clenched teeth. He sat opposite her, back straight, gripping the edge of the seat with both hands. "Nice view."

Jennifer cocked an eyebrow. "David Cole, are you afraid of heights?"

He shook his head vigorously, but was sweating as the carriage swept past the wheel operator. The operator registered his fear too and smirked. "How long does this ride last?"

"Only a few minutes," Jennifer said. "You should have said something."

"I'm fine."

"An ex-SEAL who's afraid of heights." She chuckled.

"Very funny," he said, smiling back.

That night she'd discovered an aspect about him that ran contrary to the man most people knew: the military veteran, the explosives expert, the tough guy. And she realized that he'd opened up because he didn't want to ruin the Ferris wheel ride. He'd made her feel very special that night.

"Jennifer," said a voice from behind her. She turned and saw Roberts approaching. She attempted a smile. He didn't smile back.

"Let's talk while we walk," he said, heading west toward the end of the pier.

She noticed again that his voice was lifeless, almost resigned. The first time she'd noticed it had been when she'd called to set up the meeting. Something wasn't right. "Are you having second thoughts about the case?" she asked.

He ignored the question and looked out at the water. "Over the phone you mentioned new evidence?"

"About Gary Stanford, yes," she said, letting the matter go for now. Although she felt growing dread, she sensed that Roberts would only retreat if pushed. The only thing she could do was wait. "Stanford keeps an office at the Hollywood Roosevelt Hotel," she explained, leaving out her confrontation with Huxley. She didn't want to give him any excuse to pull her from the case. "I let myself in yesterday and found this." She pulled the business card from her purse and handed it to him.

"Lydia's Diner," he said, reading it. "Did you call the phone number?"

She nodded. "It's an auto body shop now, but the manager told me that the diner was family-owned before it closed down."

"Which family, and when?"

"It'll be easier if I show you."

She fished into her purse and pulled out a photocopied article, which she handed to him. "Courtesy of *The New York Times* online historical archive."

He read the headline aloud, "Mom and Pop Caught in Crossfire: Police Suspect Drugs." And then he was quiet for a few moments as he skimmed the article. "Says here that a Mr. and Mrs. Cappinnini ran the place from 1955 to 1963 until Mr. Cappinnini was shot dead on the premises during a drug deal."

"A deal he was involved in," Jennifer added. "The diner was a front."

"Okay," Roberts said, still looking over the article, "but I don't see the connection."

"Look at the photo, Ted."

She re-examined the grainy black and white photo as he looked at it for the first time: A mother held the hand of her young son, who looked to be about twelve years old, as they stood in front of Lydia's Diner. Police tape stretched around outside tables to keep a crowd of onlookers at bay. The mother wore a lost, sleepy-eyed expression as the police bustled around her. The boy looked up at her, obviously for consolation, but she was clearly incapable of giving it as she struggled to deal with the trauma.

Finally Roberts said, "The kid."

Jennifer nodded. Even as a child, Stanford had the down-turned mouth, the piercing eyes. "I thought the resemblance was too close for coincidence, so I did some checking. Seems young Gary changed his name after moving to Los Angeles."

"So Stanford was born and raised in New York City," Roberts said. "He certainly doesn't publicize the fact. Why'd he move?"

"His mother passed of natural causes shortly after his father was murdered."

"He has family out here."

"I assume so, but I don't have a line on them yet. That might be the connection we're looking for, though."

"Nice work here, Jennifer," Roberts said. "Can I keep these?"

"Absolutely."

She allowed a tiny smile to cross her face as he slipped the photocopies into his jacket pocket. She was pulling her weight in this collaboration and it felt good. More importantly, she was helping David. It wouldn't be long before she uncovered Stanford's connection to organized crime. Of that she was certain.

Even so, Roberts was uncharacteristically subdued. She'd hoped the information would have cracked his morose veneer. What was he keeping from her?

Just then, they passed a gaudy booth that featured faded, life-sized cutouts of celebrities and a sign that exclaimed GET YOUR PICTURE TAKEN INSTANTLY WITH YOUR FAVORITE STAR ONLY $5!!! She and David had stopped here too, she remembered. He'd taken his picture with a cutout of Sharon Stone, she with Steve McQueen. She looked at the couples in line at the booth. All led simple, uncomplicated lives, no doubt. How badly she wanted to be among them with David.

"How about you?" she asked. "Did you find anything?"

"I went to the Bucklew Center for Naval Special Warfare in San Diego."

"Where you and David were trained?"

Roberts nodded. "I learned that a man who served with us named Frank Ruger is gunning for Dave."

She gasped. "Are you sure?"

"This morning Levar Watkins was found dead in his home."

"Oh my God."

"I was called to the scene this morning by a colleague and found clear evidence of Ruger's involvement." He paused as he looked away from her again. "I found evidence of Dave's involvement, too."

Her earlier feeling of dread grew tenfold. Yes, David had had words with Watkins and Brandenburg on set. But she refused to believe that he was capable of hurting anyone. Was this the information that Roberts had been hesitant to divulge? Or was there more? "You don't think that David was responsible, do you?"

Roberts kept his gaze fixed on the sea. "I don't know what to think, Jennifer."

"His presence doesn't prove anything. He could have been defending himself."

"I know," Roberts said halfheartedly.

Why is he doing this? she wondered. She knew that Roberts owed David his life, yet here he was giving up so easily. Something must have shaken him, and maybe he didn't want to share it because he was afraid it would shake her, too.

"David is acting the only way he can. We have to keep believing that," she said, mind racing. "Do you think Frank Ruger is going after David on Gary's behalf?"

"Ruger has enough motive to go after Cole on his own."

"Which would make him all the easier to recruit. You don't know Gary Stanford like I do, Ted. Manipulating people is standard business practice for him."

"We're talking murder, not manipulation."

"Not too far a stretch if he's involved with organized crime."

Roberts sighed. "This is all speculation, Jennifer, based on our hunch that Cole is innocent, based on a motive that we don't yet have for Stanford. Detective Whittaker doesn't buy any of it and, given recent events, I'm starting to doubt myself, even with Ruger's involvement."

She felt a bolt of fear. He couldn't be giving up on her. He couldn't be. "We can't stop now. I'll keep digging up information on Stanford and you can coordinate with Whittaker to find Frank Ruger."

He looked at her, the defeat in his eyes achingly apparent. "Whittaker took over the entire case. I'm no longer in charge of the arson investigation."

They had reached the end of the pier. Next to them was a group of fishermen with faces as weathered as the metal rail that propped up their homemade poles. A small, handwritten sign warned against overhead casting.

"That's okay," she said, refusing to be deterred. "We'll continue on our own."

"No," he said.

"Excuse me?" she said, feeling sick because she knew what

had to come next. So *this* was what he'd been holding from her.

"I'll keep going, but I can't allow you to put yourself at risk," he told her. "Not with Frank Ruger involved. He's a trained killer."

She clenched her fists as adrenaline surged through her body. So he'd been careful to collect her information before dropping the news. How dare he pull this underhanded crap. How dare he take away her right to be involved. She sensed that he was keeping other information from her, too, and it only fueled her anger. "You can't honestly think I'll stop."

"I expect you to do precisely that."

"You don't have the authority," she said, her voice beginning to tremble with frustration. "You're off the case, remember?"

"Don't make me cite you for obstructing justice."

"Please, Ted."

"It's for your own protection."

"But . . ." she began when her voice faltered. Now it was her turn to look away. A red sun was touching the water, causing it to shimmer. She wished desperately that this ordeal was over and David was there to enjoy the sight with her. Blinking back tears, she looked at Roberts again. "I love him," she said.

"Dave has lost too many people he cares about. I won't let you be added to the list."

Abruptly, she turned and walked away before Roberts could see her break down. How dare he ask her to sit by and wait while everyone involved in the case was losing faith in a man who she knew in her heart to be innocent.

Chapter 15

Two hours later, Jennifer arrived home. She parked and walked to the front door, still fuming about her meeting with Roberts.

There had been a time in her life when such an episode would have defeated her, but now it made her more determined. *Ted, you can go to hell.*

As she pulled the house key from her purse and slid it into the lock, she noticed a flash of white on the step. A rose. She must have missed it on her way out.

Who . . . ?

She felt a rush of adrenaline. David had sent roses as a thank-you for dinner. Strength draining from her legs, she slumped to the steps. *You're alive!* She'd told herself that from the beginning . . . but she'd also known, deep down, that she was denying any other possibility. Now she had proof.

Where Roberts had condescended to her, David was trying to dissuade her from looking for him in the most loving way he could under the circumstances. She loved him even more for taking the risk to warn her, but he had to know that she would never give up the search.

She clutched the flower to her breast. *Thank you for this wonderful sign!*

She looked across the front yard and street, searching. Was he watching her now? And then she caught her breath. Or was he inside?

Trembling with anticipation, Jennifer stood, unlocked the

door and stepped into the cool darkness of the foyer. She placed the rose underneath a table lamp, and then turned the lamp on. Soft yellow light flooded the foyer.

There was a man sitting on her couch, shrouded in gloom.

David . . .

Her doubts and fears disappeared, chased away by his mere presence. Now that he was here, they could overcome any challenge. Together. She tried to say his name but her throat closed with emotion. All she could manage was a plaintive mewling.

He stood in reply but said nothing, obviously overcome with emotion himself.

She rushed toward him, eyes filling with tears, wanting to hold him forever, wanting to tell him that everything was going to be all right . . . when she realized that his body was all wrong.

She froze, no longer seeing whom she wanted to see, but who was actually there.

Clad in a black suit and white dress shirt, the man was huge, with broad shoulders and steely eyes that regarded her in the way a lion regards a bloodied gazelle.

Frank Ruger, she realized with a bolt of fear. On the pier with Roberts, she'd expressed a stubborn need to continue the investigation despite the danger. Now the embodiment of that danger was here, *in her house.* She felt foolish in her bravado, and prayed that she could escape the brutal consequences of her naiveté.

Looking over her shoulder, she judged the distance back to the front door. A couple dozen feet, give or take. She could try for it. Ruger didn't have a gun that she could see—but somehow, that frightened her more than if he'd had one.

She whirled and bolted. Suddenly, he was beside her, and yanked her head back by the hair. She yelped, amazed that he could move so fast.

The man was a monster, over six feet tall with thickly corded arms that strained against the fabric of his suit jacket. She sensed a barely restrained anger in him, as though it was an effort to keep from tearing her limb from him.

"Where is David Cole?" he asked.

"You stay away from him," she whispered, not knowing where her courage came from. She only knew that every part of her wanted to protect David from a man like this.

Ruger raised his right hand, and slid a cold index finger behind her right ear slowly, gently, like a lover. Clenching her teeth, she fought the instinct to recoil, afraid that if she moved or screamed that he might kill her outright.

"I don't think you heard me," he said, and moved his finger.

Pain exploded through her head in a white, fiery nova as every muscle in her body went limp. She cried out and dropped to her knees. He lifted his finger, and the onslaught of agony stopped. "I know Cole is hiding with a friend. I know you know who that friend is."

She sucked a breath, head throbbing. All she could see were disconnected blobs of color. *No more,* she thought. First Roberts had tossed her from the case like some desperate actress from a casting couch. And now Ruger wanted her to betray the man she loved.

She was done feeling powerless. Done being bullied.

"I don't think you heard *me,*" she hissed, preparing for the inevitable. "I told you to stay away—"

Her voice blew apart under a lightning strike of pain. Ruger kept his finger in place as she sank to all fours in helpless, saw-toothed agony. She ground her forehead against the cold tiles, praying that the jagged pain would stop . . . please stop . . . when finally, after what seemed like an eternity, it did.

Tears streaming down her cheeks, she hiccupped for breath. Ruger gripped her hair, yanked back her head.

"Don't make me ask you again," he said.

"Go to hell!" she said, glancing at her appointment book, which lay on the dining room table. Ruger caught the gesture and let her go.

"No!" she wailed. Whether the glance was an accident or an instinctive act of self-preservation, she didn't know. Not that it mattered. The result was the same.

Still on her knees, she watched helplessly as Ruger leafed through the book, and then stopped on a page near the end before closing it.

The page where she'd written Lawrence Fuchs' contact information, she realized. Lawrence had the expertise to help David heal and fight. It made perfect sense. And now Frank Ruger knew where to find them both.

She moaned in regret, felt anguish that made Ruger's torture seem like child's play. *David, I'm so sorry . . .*

Ruger walked back to her. "You're lucky I was told not to kill you."

Then he gripped her shoulder with his left hand to keep her upright, and slapped her hard with the other. She cried out, head snapping to the side. It felt like she'd been hit with a brick. He followed up with a vicious backhand, but this time she didn't feel a thing.

"How much longer do we haveta stay here?" Brandenburg said, the chaise lounge creaking under his weight.

The guard standing in front of the grand piano looked at him like he was an idiot for asking the question. Like Uncle Gary looked at him sometimes. "Until we get orders."

"When's that gonna be?"

The piano guard adjusted the AK-47 slung over his shoulder and turned away, ignoring him.

Brandenburg grumbled, looked again at the props around him: Antique chairs covered with flowery blue fabric. Windows covered with green velvet curtains. White porcelain vases. A Persian rug that cost more than he made in a month.

A Victorian parlor, one guard had said. He shook his head disgustedly. After doing his uncle's dirty work, he was hiding on the set of a chick movie.

Why not hide on the starship bridge instead? Built in the middle of the cavernous soundstage, the bridge was mounted on a huge, circular platform with a black handrail around the edge and cool-looking computer panels. It also had a swiveling captain's chair and futuristic elevator that opened automatically with a *shhk-shhk* sound, so fucking cool. The cemetery on the far side was just as cool with rolling hills, open graves, plastic skeletons and headstones. There were even life-size crypts made of plywood and huge, gnarled trees made of plaster.

But neither was close to the door for a quick getaway. So he was stuck in the parlor.

Even though the parlor was spacious, it felt like the walls were closing in. He shut his eyes . . . *saw Ruger push the knife into Ronny Cole's stomach . . . saw the kid cough streamers of blood . . .*

He couldn't shake the horrible images no matter how hard he tried. They'd been playing in his mind like a constant film loop for the past thirty-six hours.

He tried to imagine himself at the Star Strip on Hollywood Boulevard, a crowd of empty beer bottles on the runway in front of him, watching his favorite redhead do her thing. A spinning buzz and a nice pair of tits could do wonders. It'd be just what the doctor ordered.

But the fucking guards wouldn't let him leave. Ruger's orders. After all, David Cole could be hunting him. The idea filled him with a vague sense of fear, like crossing the street. Sure you could get hit, but how likely was it? If the man hadn't struck by now, he'd probably skipped town to get away from the police.

Besides, any fear he had of Cole paled in comparison to

thoughts about his kid. Helpless. Tied up in that chair. Mother-*fucker.*

Shifting on the chaise lounge, he wondered how long he'd be cooped up. Probably until after Uncle Gary's meeting with Anne Devereaux on Sunday. That meant another twenty-four hours *minimum.*

He clutched a flowered throw pillow, fingers punching through the thin fabric.

He knew that Uncle Gary wanted him to take a more active role in the family, but he never thought it would mean doing sick stuff like they did to Ronny Cole. Man, it just wasn't right.

Closing his eyes, he saw Ruger push the knife into the kid's stomach.

"Fuck this," he said, standing.

"Sit down," the piano guard told him.

Brandenburg ignored the command. *Gotta get out of here and get drunk off my ass . . . forget all about David Cole and his son . . .*

He stormed to the three-story soundstage door. As he gripped the handle to slide it open, he felt a hand clap his shoulder. He turned, saw the piano guard and two other guards.

"What do you think you're doing?" the piano guard asked.

"I'm leaving."

"No, you're not."

"Try to fucking stop me."

"I will."

Brandenburg glared. "My uncle pays your salary, dipshit. Now back off."

The piano guard shouldered his assault rifle and drew a .45 pistol, which he stuck in Brandenburg's face. "I'm not going to tell you again."

"Fuck you," Brandenburg spat.

The piano guard smiled, and then his hand disappeared in a red spray. He fell to his knees, screaming.

At first Brandenburg thought the pistol had misfired, but then one of the other guards pointed to the catwalk two hundred feet above them.

He looked up, saw the tiny figure of a man holding a rifle.

Cole!

Body flooding with adrenaline, he gripped the door handle and pulled. The door slid a couple of inches before it halted with a clanking rattle. He yanked the handle again, but the door wouldn't budge. And then he saw the glimmer of polished steel links in the gap between the door and soundstage wall.

They'd been chained inside.

Cole stood on the catwalk, sniper rifle propped on the top rail. He watched through the scope as the sentry he'd shot screamed, blood gushing from what remained of his hand.

With that single gunshot, his plan had gone to shit.

He'd planned on cutting the lights, climbing down the catwalk ladder, and then incapacitating the sentries one by one under the cover of darkness. But it had been obvious the sentry intended to shoot Brandenburg, which meant they'd been given orders to kill the man if he became a flight risk. It was an order that no doubt also applied if Brandenburg were at risk of being captured.

Which meant that he'd have to protect a man who'd helped murder his son. His throat flooded with bile. *I can't . . . I won't!*

Seven sentries were left. Without the element of surprise, there was no way he could take them on, unless . . .

He felt the morass of instincts swirling inside him. Cold. Persistent.

No . . . I promised . . . never again . . .

He saw a Morse code of muzzle flashes from below, then a hail of bullets pinged and sparked along the catwalk.

Seven sentries were too many.

I don't have a choice, not if I want to succeed.

He felt the morass swell and crash against his mental defenses, like a wave against a tide wall.

More bullets sparked the catwalk. Indecisive, he took a step back out of range. The longer he waited, the more time the sentries would have to mount a coordinated counterattack.

He had to act. Now.

Ronny, I'm sorry, but I don't have a choice . . . not if I want to bring the men who killed you to justice . . . just one more time, I swear . . . I swear this is the last time . . .

Hands trembling, he pulled the box of styrettes from his assault vest, as well as the extra in his boot, and pitched them over the rail. He knew he'd be tempted to anesthetize himself if the instincts became too intense, and he couldn't allow that fear to undermine the mission.

He watched the styrettes spill loose from the box and drop end over end until they shattered against the floor.

"Forgive me son," he whispered, and let the morass in.

He felt the icy torrent snuff his burning pain as easily as a candle flame. It felt stronger than it had while battling Watkins . . . much stronger. And colder. It swelled from his waist to his chest and he pushed back, trying to stop it before it could consume him.

Gagging, he thought about sinking irretrievably into the abyss . . . about losing memories of Ronny and Jennifer, about losing himself. The terror helped him focus his will like a missile. He pushed until he finally felt the morass stop, but not before it slithered up into his throat.

Too much . . .

But he had to continue.

His body felt energized by the icy, rancid fuel. He stood as bullets fired from the sentries below continued to spark the catwalk around him, stretching his arms and legs and swiveling his head with complete range of motion.

His actions were fluid now. Measured. Efficient.

Detached.

Like he was watching himself in a movie.

Dropping to a crouch, he pulled four smoke pots from the rucksack, lit the fuses with his Zippo, then tossed them over the rail. They trailed sparks on the way down like comets and exploded into six-foot mushroom clouds of gray smoke when they impacted. Brandenburg and the sentries ducked instinctively as the swirling smoke obscured them and everything else below.

He laid down the sniper rifle and pulled the harness from the rucksack. It was a Jerk Vest, worn by stuntmen when a scene called for a character to be yanked back by a ratchet cable during an explosion. Featuring a mid-spine steel-loop "pick point" where the ratchet cable attached, the vest was also perfect for suspension and highfall-arrest gags.

After double-tightening the leg and waist straps, he fed the wire rope through the pick point and attached it to the catwalk railing with a clamp, shackle and pulley system, making sure the anchor point would stop him five feet from the ground.

Now his hands would be free during descent, allowing him to use the sniper rifle for suppressing fire.

Picking up the rifle, he leaped from the catwalk with effortless precision, and his body immediately flipped face down, parallel to the ground, in freefall. As the wire hissed through pulley above, he fired the sniper rifle repeatedly into the smoke. With suppressing fire, accuracy wasn't important. The thundering report alone was enough to do the job.

The tactic worked. The sentries stopped firing at him, presumably taking cover somewhere in the dense smoke.

Clip empty, he concentrated on his landing as the roiling gray cloud rushed up to greet him. A split-second after he broke its surface, the cable jerked tight, yanking his body upright. He then pressed a button at his waist, releasing the harness, and dropped cat-like the remaining five feet onto the Oriental rug.

Now the smoke was thick as swamp fog. The sentries had resumed firing blind at the catwalk, not realizing that he was among them. He was able to zero them by the red tracer rounds that flashed from their gun barrels like crimson lightning in a thundercloud.

Better to neutralize these men than kill them. Killing would only complicate the mission, giving the police and Ruger more clues to his capabilities and intent.

After switching clips, he leaped at the closest sentry who fired a few feet to his left. He swatted the AK-47 from the man's grasp, then closed an arm around his windpipe from behind. The sentry thrashed but Cole held his grip until the man slumped to the ground, unconscious. Without hesitation, he moved on to another sentry who fired nearby, oblivious to his comrade's fate. Cole struck the man with a forearm across the throat while kicking his feet out from under him. After the man slammed onto his back, Cole punched him in the face, knocking him out. He took down the next sentry by launching a kick into his right leg, and then silenced him with a blow across the jaw.

The firing had stopped. Moving through the dense smoke like a shark through water, he searched for any sign of Brandenburg when he felt a pang of nausea. Relying on the instincts felt natural. Too natural. Even after thirteen years.

Hadn't he changed after all this time? Hadn't he been a good husband and father? Didn't that count for anything?

The crisis of conscience faded quickly, numbed like the pain from his wounds had been.

You have the skills to avenge your son . . . that's all that matters.

Suddenly, he heard a muffled cry to his right. He sprinted

blind for several yards toward the sound until he burst through the smoke. The sound was coming from behind a pair of red doors on a raised platform that looked like the bridge of a starship.

Vaulting a handrail, he landed on a curved walkway and sprinted toward the red doors. When he stepped close, they opened with a squeaking hiss.

Brandenburg was inside, on the floor, knees drawn to his chest. The right side of his abdomen was drenched in blood. "OH MY GOD! PLEASE DON'T KILL ME!"

Cole curled his lip in disgust. The man was hiding like a coward when Ronny had remained brave under torture. "Get on your feet."

"They shot me!" the man whined as if just realizing he was expendable.

"I'll protect you, but we have to leave now," Cole said, grabbing the front of Brandenburg's shirt with both hands and yanking him to his feet.

"YAGGGHHH!"

Now that Brandenburg was standing, Cole could see the wound clearly. Gut-shot inside the left oblique. Painful, he thought with satisfaction. But fatal if not treated.

"Uncle Gary is the one you want!" Brandenburg said, when an egg-shaped object skittered between them into the turbo lift.

Brandenburg shrieked in terror as Cole snatched up the grenade and flung it away. The grenade landed just clear of the bridge before exploding with a WHOOM! and the flaming shockwave incinerated the platform supports causing the bridge to cant violently to one side. Cole went reeling into a computer panel as Brandenburg flipped over the handrail. Bullets strafed the bridge, which shattered instruments and sent sparks flying.

Cole regained his footing and whirled to see Brandenburg huddled beneath the captain's chair. He leaped over the handrail and clutched Brandenburg's shoulder. The man looked up at him with plaintive eyes . . . the expression was similar to Ronny's expression when Ruger was cutting him.

. . . Dad . . . help me . . . Dad . . .

He felt a burning swell of rage. He should let the motherfucker die here at the hands of his uncle's goons. But then he felt the cold inside him surge and numb the emotion as another thought slid into his mind, sharp and focused. *You have a job to do. Keep going.*

Dark terror struck him again at how easily the cold had short-circuited his emotion, but he couldn't worry about it now. There wasn't time.

"Get up!" he ordered, wincing as the huge man laid an arm across the burned flesh on his shoulders for support. With a grunt, he led the way off the bridge and into a graveyard.

Looking over his shoulder, he saw four sentries emerging from the dissipating smoke, AK-47s blazing.

"Faster!" Cole yelled.

Dust swirled around their feet as they shuffled through the graveyard dirt. Cole shouldered Brandenburg forward as bullets stitched around them, tearing holes through plaster trees and blowing apart headstones. He knew it was only a matter of time before a bullet took one or both of them down. They had to make a stand.

He steered Brandenburg toward the edge of a shallow grave. "Jump inside!"

"Are you crazy?" the man screeched. "I ain't gonna make their job easier!"

"I said get in!" he yelled, and slung Brandenburg inside where he landed with a thud and howl of pain.

Cole leaped in after him, the top of the grave coming to his chest. He shrugged the sniper rifle from his shoulder, peered through the scope and saw that three of the four sentries were on the starship bridge.

Sliding the crosshairs over the knee of the lead sentry, Cole pulled the trigger. The joint exploded in a starburst of red, pitching the man forward, howling.

Next, he zeroed the bulletproof vest of the second man, and pulled the trigger again. The round slammed home, pitching the man over the handrail where he hit his head on the edge of the captain's chair and crumpled, unconscious.

Tracking the third sentry who ran along the walkway, Cole fired at his left thigh, but the man suddenly changed direction, and the shot missed wide. The man leaped into the turbolift for cover as Cole's next shot splintered one of the sliding red doors.

Five shots. Change clip.

With fluid motion, he yanked the spent clip from the belly of the rifle and retrieved a fresh clip from the assault vest. He was about to slap in the fresh clip when Brandenburg reared up into him, dizzy with blood loss. The impact sent the clip flying from his grasp, where it landed twenty feet in front of the grave. It might as well have been twenty miles.

Cole knew that he couldn't retrieve the clip without exposing himself to enemy fire.

"That was my last clip," he said.

"Are you shitting me?" Brandenburg exclaimed, scrambling to his feet. "What are we gonna do now?!"

The words rang in his ears as the terrible irony struck him again: He was risking his life to help a man who'd helped kill his son.

This time he felt the icy resolve slide forward effortlessly to numb the pain, like it had been part of his consciousness all along. *Keep going.*

"See that?" Cole said, pointing behind them to a ladder bolted to the soundstage wall. "Run for it while I hold them here."

"I don't think I can," Brandenburg whined, holding his gut. Cole noticed that the man's entire shirt was drenched in blood, and that his face was as white as the headstone marking the grave.

"You don't have a choice! Go!"

With a moan, Brandenburg hefted himself out of the grave and loped away, triggering a flurry of automatic fire from the bridge. Cole knew that once the sentries realized there was no return fire, they would charge.

He looked around for something he could use as a weapon and spotted a skeleton lying half-buried near the foot of the grave. He grabbed it by a rib—the bones were made of hard plastic. Perfect. After snapping off the skull, he pushed the tip of his knife through the crown and emptied a small tin of flash powder from his assault vest into the hole. He then snapped two inches of excess lacing from his combat boot and threaded it into the hole so that one end touched the powder and the other end hung free on the outside. He repeated this procedure with the femur and radius bones before running out of flash powder tins. The entire process had taken less than a minute.

He lit the skull's fuse and tossed it at the turbolift. The skull bounced off the walkway and sailed through the red doors, exploding with a POOM! The man inside was thrown clear and landed facedown on the walkway, unconscious. The remaining man charged, AK-47 blazing.

As bullets kicked up dirt around the edge of the grave, Cole glanced over his shoulder and saw Brandenburg at the ladder. The man slid his right foot into the first rung, tried to boost himself, but slipped and fell to the dirt. He was clearly too weak with blood loss to make it up the ladder.

We're not going to make it.

He refocused on the man charging him, who had crossed into the graveyard twenty-five yards from his position.

He lit and tossed the femur. The bone cartwheeled through the air, clipped the top of a headstone, and exploded. The sentry ran past the destroyed prop full-bore as he switched the clip in his AK, then continued firing.

As Cole lit the radius, a round hammered his assault vest and jerked the bone from his grasp. He scrambled from the grave as the bone exploded behind him with a WHUMP!

He leaped to his feet—when the sentry slammed into him, head-on. The blow sent him reeling into the trunk of a plaster tree. Sliding to the ground, he looked up and saw the sentry rushing him again, assault rifle ready.

He knew he wouldn't be able to find cover before the man fired.

Chapter 16

Brandenburg lumbered to his feet, gritting his teeth as pain lanced the bullet wound in his stomach. He limped toward the guard who stood over Cole, boots digging wide furrows in the dirt.

He had to save Cole. He knew that the sentry had to waste them both for his own protection—they were both liabilities—and he'd be no match for the sentry alone if Cole got wasted, not with this fucking gut-shot. Plus, saving Cole might begin to make up for what he helped to do to his son. It wouldn't make things right, not by a long shot, but it'd be a start. Then maybe, just maybe, the horrible visions might stop.

"Hey!" he called out, trying to distract the sentry. "Hey, asshole!"

The sentry ignored him, and stalked toward Cole who was sitting at the base of a plaster tree, stunned. There was no way Cole could defend himself. Brandenburg shuffled faster, every step sending spikes of pain into his gut. He was a good twenty yards away. He'd never get there in time.

"Hey dipshit, over here!" he screeched.

The sentry made it to where Cole was sitting, and then glanced at Brandenburg.

"Yeah, that's right! Why not pick on somebody who can stand?"

Smirking, the sentry leveled the gun at Cole.

"Hey! HEY!"

But before the sentry could fire, Cole's chest exploded in a flurry of gunshot wounds.

Confused, Brandenburg watched the sentry turn and peer through the smoke that had begun to crawl from the starship bridge. Another guard must have recovered and tagged Cole from a distance!

Brandenburg whirled and shuffled back to the ladder as quickly as he could, pain stabbing his stomach. He had to make it up to the catwalk this time, or the guard would kill him.

Sweat pouring down his face, he grabbed the ladder with both hands, slipped his boot onto the first rung, and slowly, slowly pressed his full body weight forward . . .

Fresh pain speared his stomach, and he fell to his knees, coughing.

I'm fucked!

He grabbed hold of the ladder again, and pulled himself to his feet when he heard footsteps behind him. He turned, and the sentry was there, pointing his AK-47.

Brandenburg raised his hands and stuttered. "C'mon m-man, you were supposed to p-protect me, remember?"

"Unless you became a flight risk or were in danger of being taken prisoner. Then we had orders to kill you."

"You don't have to kill me now! Cole is dead!"

The sentry shot him in the leg. Brandenburg gasped, fell to all fours. *There's no reason for him to kill me! No reason at all!*

"That's for betraying your uncle," the sentry said.

Brandenburg tried to crawl away when the man kicked him in the stomach. The explosion of pain made him gag and roll onto his back. Then the sentry shot him in the stomach.

He didn't feel pain this time, only a strange push-tug sensation as the bullet punched through his body. He coughed something warm onto his chin. He wiped it with his hand. Blood. *Holy shit . . . I'm dying . . .*

"That's for being an asshole," the sentry said.

His vision swam with blood loss. He could barely make out the guard standing over him, but felt when the barrel of the AK pressed against his forehead.

"And this," the sentry said, "is to finish the job."

Brandenburg wondered if the headshot would hurt when he saw a pair of gloved hands slide over the guard's face from behind, and then wrench his neck with a brutal twist.

The guard fell to reveal Cole who was very much alive.

Cole stared down at the sentry's corpse. He'd just killed a man. For the first time since the war.

He closed his eyes as something inside collapsed. His will? His sanity? Some naive ideal of who he thought he was? And then a thought slid into his mind, cold as killing frost: *Killing was the right thing to do.*

He stood above the corpse, still in shock, when the thought came again. Killing was your only option. The mission is all that matters.

Gasping, he tried to push the voice away, to banish it from his body, but it felt like pushing against a glacier. He pushed again, but the cold slithered up past his chin.

"Hey!" Brandenburg's voice barreled into his consciousness. He looked down, and saw that the man was bleeding out. He dropped to his knees.

"Nice gag," Brandenburg rasped, pointing to the squib wires that poked through the bullet holes in Cole's assault vest.

"Tell me where your uncle is hiding," Cole told him.

Brandenburg hitched a clotted breath. "I'm sorry about your kid."

Cole felt a spike of anger. Where was this asshole's compassion when his son was being tortured? It was easy to ask for forgiveness when you didn't have to follow it up with action.

This man was the worst kind of coward. And then his anger was snuffed out, chilled by resolve. "Your uncle. Tell me."

"Uncle Gary . . ." Brandenburg's voice tapered suddenly as blood bubbled from between his lips.

"You can't die." Cole grabbed Brandenburg by the shirt collar and pulled him into a sitting position so that their noses almost touched. The man's breath was weak on his face and smelled like blood and chew tobacco. Cole needed this information to continue. Needed it to succeed. "You can't die, Ned. Not before you tell me."

The man's breathing became shallower, his voice nothing more than a sigh. "I'm sorry . . ."

Cole closed his eyes. "Tell me, Ned. Please."

". . . home . . . Sunday night . . ." Brandenburg said, and then his eyes went wide and his chest stopped moving. Cole knew the man was dead and lay the body down.

Now he had a time and place. Now he and Lawrence could prepare for what had to be done.

As he struggled to his feet, he felt the cold inside rise again.

No . . .

Pulling the tape recorder from the assault vest, he pressed PLAY and closed his eyes as he heard Jennifer's crackling voice . . .

"I love you, David."

But the words fell flat.

He pressed REWIND, then PLAY again.

"I love you, David."

He felt only a glimmer of warmth, and then nothing. He pressed the buttons again, and again *". . . I love you, David . . . I love you . . ."*

But the cold continued to creep up, sliding over his mouth like the smothering hand of a corpse.

Oh God . . .

Lawrence, he thought desperately. His friend would know what to do. He *had* to know what to do.

Trembling, he thrust the mini recorder back into the assault vest and sprinted toward the soundstage door.

A short time later, Cole was speeding down a back road in his truck, racing to make it back to Lawrence's house in the growing darkness.

He'd accomplished another phase of the mission, yes. Gained a valuable piece of intel that might lead to Gary Stanford. But . . .

Gripping the steering wheel, he stared at the truck's headlight beams as they skimmed the dusty road.

He could still feel the guard's head in his hands . . . could still feel the brutal twist and then the sudden, almost gentle slingshot snap as the man's neck gave way before he slumped lifeless to the ground.

You had no choice.

The rationale slithered into his mind again, cold as a snake. But he knew the truth. A buried part of him still untouched by the cold embraced the horrible truth.

He was losing control . . . God . . . losing control . . .

And losing himself.

His reverie was shattered by the screech of rending metal. Gripping the dash for support, he saw the horizon through the windshield rise violently before he was slammed forward into the steering wheel. His vision turned red as lighting stabs of pain arced through his chest.

When his vision finally cleared, he realized that he'd driven off the side of the road into a rain ditch. The truck was canted forward at a wicked angle. The hood had buckled, and steam was rising from underneath it—but the engine hadn't died. Not yet.

Breath rasping in his throat, he cranked the gearshift into reverse and pressed the gas. He listened to the engine rumble and roar as the rear tires churned for purchase. The truck shimmied violently but did not grind free from the ditch. After trying for a few moments longer, he killed the ignition. He would have to get out and push.

Physical and mental exhaustion from the assault had made him lose focus. He needed to get morphine into his system soon or he wouldn't be able to function at all.

Kicking open the door, he tried to ease himself from the cab, but lost his grip on the steering wheel and dumped into the ditch, landing hard on his right knee. The barb of pain that shot up his leg and crashed into his balls caused him to hack violently before it faded away.

Goddammit . . .

And then he heard a sound from behind him. Faint, then growing—wheels crushing dirt, followed by a squeal of breaks and an ignition cutting out. And then a bright light shined on him as a car door opened and slammed closed. A voice boomed from behind the truck: "Hello?" Now the sound of footsteps coming around the long bed. "Excuse me . . . sir?"

Still on his knees, Cole squinted his eyes against the radio car's spot lamp as the highway patrol officer approached with slow measured steps. He stopped a safe distance away, about fifteen feet, with his right hand resting on the gun at his hip. He had a tan uniform with a radio jack clipped to the lapel and a nameplate on his breast pocket that read: Peterson.

Just a kid. Like Ronny.

"Do you need assistance?" the officer said.

Cole turned his head back around to keep the officer from seeing the burns on his face. "I'm fine," he rasped.

"Are you sure?"

"Got the wind knocked out of me is all," Cole said, dragging out the words. He placed a hand against the truck door and leaned against it as pain continued to course through his body.

"I'm going to have to ask you to come out of that ditch so I can make sure you're okay."

Does he know who I am? Cole thought. *Is he trying to confirm my ID without giving away that he's on to me?* With no choice, Cole clambered out of the ditch onto the road.

Now the officer could see him clearly, and his expression registered shock and then involuntary disgust. "Sir . . . you're . . . let me call you an ambulance."

He doesn't recognize me, Cole thought with a relief. "I'm fine, really."

"You may be in shock from the crash," the officer said, giving him the *don't panic* tone that Lawrence had used after finding him in the shower. But his eyes held a distinctly different message: *Man, you are fucked up.*

It was then that Cole realized that the officer's sense of duty would not, in good conscience, let him leave. He felt his breath quicken. If taken to a hospital, it wouldn't be long before the cops were notified and he was arrested.

"I'm going to call an ambulance, don't you worry," the officer said.

"No!" Cole spat in a hoarse voice more loudly than he intended.

"I can't let you drive in your condition, sir," the officer said firmly. "Just sit down and relax while I get help."

"I have to go," Cole said, his chest rising and falling with labored breaths as he took a step forward. "You don't understand."

The officer took a step back, hand gripping the holstered pistol more tightly. "Please don't come any closer, sir."

"You have to let me go."

"I asked you to sit down . . ." the officer began, and then

from the way his eyes flicked to the truck, Cole realized he'd seen the MP5 in the passenger seat. The officer's polite demeanor immediately fell away as he drew the pistol and aimed it with both hands. "Sir, place your hands behind your head."

"Officer—"

"Do as I say!" the man barked.

Cole did, and then the officer used the pistol to gesture him to the radio car, which was parked aslant behind the truck. "Keep your fingers laced behind your head and face the hood."

As he complied, Cole felt his teeth begin to chatter. "No . . . you don't understand . . ."

Before he could finish, the officer grabbed his clasped hands and slammed him roughly onto the hood. Pain gouged his face as he coughed up phlegm that gummed the metal beneath his chin.

"Dispatch, this is Peterson requesting backup," he heard the officer say into his radio jack. The request was followed by a spitting hiss of static and then a woman's voice: "Roger, Officer Peterson. What's your twenty?"

"Off Olden Street in the Santa Susana Mountains."

"Roger, that."

The officer kept the pistol pressed against the base of Cole's skull as his free hand skimmed the assault vest, searching. It didn't take long before the man yanked out the K-bar knife and tossed it onto the hood where it landed with a boom. "Who are you, mister?" he scowled. "Some kind of terrorist?" The officer yanked his head up by the hair and slammed it against the hood again, harder this time. "That's it, isn't it? You're a goddamn terrorist!"

Cole tried to answer, but the tendons in his throat were stretched tight. With a shudder, he tried to control his coldly raging heartbeat, the force of it sending energy crackling through his nervous system. He let out another strangled cough, then gagged as his body was flooded with cold strength.

No! he thought, trying to beat the feeling back. He wanted to escape, but not this way. It was too much . . . too dangerous . . . *I don't want this! Not again!*

But he realized with horror that his pleas had no effect. His arms and legs began to tremble with seismic intensity as they beat against the police car like a drum. He felt like he was holding the tether of some charging beast, unable to do anything but be dragged along behind it.

"Get away from me!" Cole rasped. "While you still can!"

"Jesus . . ." the officer said and pressed his body weight against Cole to keep him steady. He reached over Cole's right shoulder and grabbed his right arm, twisting it around his back before slapping a handcuff around the wrist, ". . . hold still . . ."

"Please . . . get away . . . !"

Ignoring him, the officer reached over Cole's left shoulder next and struggled to grab his flailing left arm so he could cuff that wrist too. "I said hold fucking still!"

"Please . . ." Cole rasped again, then crushed his eyes closed as he tried desperately to conjure Jennifer's voice, but couldn't. Not that it would do any good this time, either. But he had to try.

The officer grabbed his hair again. "You'll do what I fucking tell you—" he began when Cole cut him short with an elbow to the face. The officer staggered back and dropped his gun, nose smashed, gasping for breath.

Cole pushed himself up with both hands, the handcuff around his right wrist clattering against the hood. With all the strength he could muster, he spun away from the radio car and lurched past the officer who was bent over, hands on his knees, spitting up blood. He flung open the truck door. *Gotta get out of here . . .*

He felt a hand clutch his shoulder and spin him around. The

officer, nose and mouth streaked with blood, jammed the pistol in his chest.

"GET AWAY FROM ME!" Cole bellowed and shoved the gun to one side as the officer squeezed the trigger. The shot went through the open door of the cab and shattered the passenger window.

Cole smashed his fist across the officer's jaw with enough force to send him sprawling. Then he leapt into the driver's seat and slammed the door closed, cranked the ignition, jammed the truck into reverse and stomped on the gas. The engine roared as the truck shimmied and the spinning tires ground up the side of the rain ditch for several moments until the tires grabbed enough hold and the truck lurched up and out. Finally, he jammed the truck into drive and sped off. In his rearview mirror, through the dust that the rear tires were kicking up, he could see the officer lying motionless in the cone of light from the spot lamp.

Now that he'd attacked a cop, the police would be out for blood.

He clutched the steering wheel so tightly with his left hand that he thought the bones in his knuckles might snap. With his right, he pulled the cell phone from his assault vest and dialed Lawrence to warn him of his arrival—even more importantly, to warn him of his *condition.* But there was no answer.

I'm losing it . . . I'm losing it . . .

Chapter 17

And then he felt no pain at all. What little emotion remained flickered like a dying flame inside him. He was five miles from Lawrence's house.

I'm not going to make it.

He slid the truck to a halt on the dirt road. Dust swirled around the cab, appearing iridescent in the moonlight.

Pulling off his glove, he smashed his burned fist against the dashboard . . . but still didn't feel any pain. He slammed his fist down again and again, until charred flesh sloughed from the side of his palm, leaving bloody crescents on the plastic. But still he felt nothing.

Desperate to feel something—anything—he rolled up the left sleeve of the jumpsuit, then unsheathed the K-bar knife and sliced his forearm beneath the elbow. As blood welled from the cut, he felt only the slightest static of pain. He concentrated on the sensation, tried to use it as an anchor to force back the cold inside him, but the pain disappeared quickly, like the fading cry of a hawk. He made deeper cuts and watched as blood poured down the sides of his arm, but each time the pain was eclipsed by cold.

He yanked the tape recorder from his vest, pressed PLAY . . .

"I love you, David."

. . . nothing. Jennifer's crackling words felt lifeless now. Trembling, he smashed the tape recorder against the dashboard.

He was losing it.

Still trembling, he yanked the cell phone from his assault vest and dialed. He knew the police would be tapping Jennifer's phone, but he had no choice. He had to hear her voice, not just some recording. He had to talk to her. His humanity depended on it.

He heard several rings, then a click.

"David?" came a whisper.

He closed his eyes as her voice filled him with warmth. He could see her in his mind's eye, sitting on the couch where they'd kissed, brown hair swept back, pressing the phone to her ear.

"Jennifer."

She sighed. A noise like wind through grass. "Where are you, baby? Tell me where you are and I'll come get you."

"I can't."

"Why not? I'll come get you right now."

He closed his eyes. Her voice was edged with such pain. He was hurting her when her only mistake was to get involved with him. And the cold . . . it was still with him. Her voice wasn't chasing it away. "I have to do something first."

"About Gary Stanford? Ted and I are already on the case." Her tone was plaintive, desperate. "We can do this together, David. We can bring the men who killed Ronny to justice together."

Hearing her say Ronny's name lifted a momentary image of his son out of the cold . . . laughing, wearing his blue Dodger cap, the two of them throwing a baseball to one another in the backyard.

"Ted and I believe in you," she continued. "We have from the very beginning. Please let us help you."

He thought again of touching her, holding her. "That night at dinner—"

"Was perfect," she finished.

"I have to do this alone, Jennifer. Please understand that. I can't let you get involved more than you already are."

"Then why the rose?"

"I wanted to let you know I was okay."

"I think it was more than that," she said. "You took the risk that I would catch you. I think you wanted me to catch you, David. I think you want to stop running." Her voice dwindled to a whisper. "It's okay. I'm right here."

He looked at the reflection of his charred face in the windshield. A ruined suggestion of who he used to be. He'd rationalized his visit to her house as a ploy to make her stop searching for him. But there had been another reason. Jennifer was right. Part of him wanted to stop because he knew that he was losing himself.

"I love you, David," she said.

He closed his eyes. Hearing her tell him . . . the words sparkled, shined.

And then faded away like the rest. He felt deep terror, like nothing he'd felt before. It was like an abyss had opened up before him, threatening to swallow him whole.

"I'd hoped to tell you while looking into your eyes, but this will have to do," she continued with a sad little laugh. "I love you. It's important for you to know that. Whatever happens, we can make things right. Please David . . . please come home."

He wanted to tell her that he loved her too, but couldn't form the words. He felt only the cold. Intense. Growing. He couldn't stop it, and realized that neither could she. He let out a soft moan of resignation. Maybe Lawrence could help . . . the big man had an answer for everything . . . please . . .

"David."

He heard scurrying panic in her voice. She obviously sensed that the conversation was ending. "I'm sorry for putting you through this."

"You don't have to be sorry."

"I'm sorry for everything," he said as much to her as to Ronny and himself.

"David—"

He hung up, then lowered the driver's side window and tossed out the cell phone. It was a homing device for the police now, and he had to get rid of it.

He couldn't call her again. If he did and felt nothing next time, he would know that he was truly lost.

The mission is all that matters . . . the words echoed coldly in his mind.

Cranking the truck into gear, he peeled away, hoping that Lawrence would be able to help before he lost himself completely.

Lawrence sat Indian-style on the living room floor, cleaning a dismantled M-16 assault rifle. He pushed a long, oiled brush through the barrel, and then pushed a dry rag through after it to soak up excess oil.

A clean barrel minimized friction for more consistent firing. Cole's mission was tough enough without having to worry about weapon performance.

He watched *Jailhouse Rock* as he worked. Elvis was distorted to funhouse proportions thanks to the crossed wire in the alarm system. It was fucking blasphemy to watch The King like this, but considering how dangerous Ruger was supposed to be, he'd decided to turn the system on for once.

But badass or not, Ruger was in for a surprise if he came calling. The arson investigator had demonstrated how easy it was to track him down, so he'd planted fifty anti-personnel mines among the rolling hills and trees surrounding the cabin. Mean fuckers, too: M-18 claymores and VS-50s "foot poppers."

Enter the kill zone, and the best Ruger could hope for was

debilitating injury. But that was before Lawrence followed the noise and finished the wet work himself. With no small pleasure, either, considering what the motherfucker did to Ronny.

Here I am, he thought, cleaning the bolt assembly with a small brush, *an ex-cop helping my best friend go vigilante.*

He looked at Crystal's photograph on the mantel like he did every time his doubts resurfaced. *No, it ain't that way. You're helping a friend right a terrible fucking wrong.*

He thought that he'd seen it all with NYPD, but Cole was something else. Burned bad, but still moving. He'd felt the same crazy drive after Crystal was murdered—that desperate scrambling inside that kept you going despite the pain.

Cole would crash eventually. It wouldn't be long before his muscles failed from fatigue, infection, or both. When that happened, he'd take the man to the hospital, regardless of how much he argued.

Laying down the bolt assembly, he picked up the stock and wiped it with a rag when a dull *whumpf* shook the house.

A mine. Out back toward the weapons shed.

Heart racing, he crept to the kitchen window and peered into the backyard. Only darkness was visible beyond the circle of light thrown by the security lamp. *Shit,* he thought, gripping the Bulldog at his hip. It was one thing to hunt Ruger in theory, but it was something else to match wits with a Navy SEAL in real life.

He took a step back from the window when another explosion shook the house. Closer this time. He felt another barb of panic.

Take it easy, he told himself.

One explosion might have been Ruger, but two? Unless Ruger could be in two places at once, the detonations were probably deer. One killed by the first mine, and then another, disoriented by the blast, had fled and triggered a second.

He froze, listening for another explosion, but all he heard was the wall clock above him, ticking loudly. After several minutes, he finally relaxed. Fucking nerves.

Sitting again, he realized that his heart was still racing. *What the fuck're you doing?* he chided himself. There was no sign that Ruger was close, and here he was psyching himself out. Two mines didn't mean a thing. All that mattered were the forty-eight other mines between him and the world, and only he could get through them. *Calm the fuck down.*

He refocused on the dismantled M-16. A brass cartridge winked from the end of a clip. He took another breath. Let Ruger try to get in. He was armed, had police training. Let Ruger fucking try.

Elvis was dancing in D Block, his skin a rippling, florescent green. "Fucking alarm," he grumbled. He watched the movie to calm himself down, lip-synching the King's cottonmouth drawl as convicts sung back-up to the title track.

Suddenly, the T.V. reception cleared.

Outstanding! he thought. Now, he could watch The King properly!

And then his spine turned to ice. The alarm was no longer interfering with the reception, which meant . . .

He peered down the hallway toward the garage, where the alarm's power box was, and then the garage door burst open and some demon from the pit of hell emerged, dressed in black combat fatigues, coming in at a low run.

Ruger!

Lawrence looked down at the dismantled M-16. It might as well be a toy for all the good it would do. He looked back at Ruger and felt absolute terror. The man's eyes held a dark savagery even worse than Cole had described.

The Bulldog! He tried to draw the gun, but felt frozen with fear. Ruger had come to waste him. A SEAL assassin. What hope did a fat ex-cop have against someone like that?

He glanced at the mantel and stared deep into his daughter's eyes, furious that whatever had fueled him to avenge his baby years ago was absent now.

Out of the corner of his eye, he saw Ruger swing up his right arm, lightning quick.

Gun!

The realization revved him into overdrive. He bolted through the kitchen and out the back door, then sprinted across the backyard, squinting against the brightness of the security lamp.

Let the bastard follow me, he fumed, hopping over a croquet wicket and veering around a wading pool filled with stagnant water. He'd built an escape route through the mines to the weapons shed, and knew it well enough to run blind. Which is exactly what he'd have to do until his night vision kicked in.

But Ruger . . . the asshole would lose a leg or worse. Either way, Lawrence could score real ordnance from the shed and double back to cap Ruger's ass.

He smiled. Fuckin-A. Nothing boosted your confidence like the promise of a big-ass gun.

Rushing between a waist-high stack of firewood and a rusted Chevy truck chassis, he slowed to step over a low fence, which marked the boundary between his lot and the forest. The crunch of pine needles beneath his feet seemed impossibly loud in the stillness. He threw a glance over his shoulder. The house was about forty yards back with light beaming from the windows into the dark yard. Ruger loomed in the doorway, straining to see through the blackness.

Be right back, asshole, he thought, then holstered the Bulldog and continued into the forest, letting the trees swallow him. He wove through trunks and scrambled over logs in darkness, trusting his memory.

After traveling about half a mile, he stopped to listen. He

heard crickets, the distant cry of a coyote, but nothing else. *Maybe Ruger got smart and gave up.*

Then he heard the faint snap of a branch not too far behind. His breath caught in his throat. Then another snap, then another. Getting closer.

But how . . . ?

Ruger was a SEAL, trained to avoid traps and tripwires. But Lawrence knew he still had the advantage. He knew the path and Ruger, even with his goddamn training, would have to move slowly to keep from blowing himself up.

Lawrence ran. His night vision kicked in, and the tree trunks around him looked like the legs of giants. Another crack behind him, loud as a thunderclap. A thicker branch, which meant Ruger was less concerned with noise, and picking up his pace.

Sweat pouring down his face, Lawrence pushed through a thick cluster of brush when his foot caught an exposed root. He yelped, lurching off the path. Branches snagged his clothing, and then something thin pulled across his chest.

Trip wire!

He froze. Squinting, he saw the trip wire among the confused pattern of leaves and branches around it. And beyond this wire, he could discern more: stretched between fallen logs, hung in loops from low branches. There was no way he could get through them. For every one he could see, there were a dozen he couldn't. He wasn't a SEAL. He'd have to go back to the path.

Behind him, the cracking sounds were getting louder. Ruger was closing.

Lawrence eased back from the trip wire, feeling the razor-thin tension across his chest ease. He retreated with small, smooth steps—slowly, slowly—until he was clear.

Cursing his clumsiness, he lurched back onto the path, and continued to run. He threw a look over his shoulder, scanning the gloomy terrain for signs of movement. He couldn't see anything—he could only hear the cracking of branches.

Pick up the pace . . . pick up the pace . . .

When he turned his head for another look, he felt the ground disappear under his feet. He pitched forward down a shallow slope, and splashed face-first into a creek.

He'd forgotten about the damn creek, and lucky for him, he hadn't been able to set mines in the stony ground. Good thing, or he'd have blown himself up for sure.

He struggled to his feet, panting, wiping mud from his face, then sloshed through the creek a couple dozen yards until it ended, then loped up the slope and out.

Suddenly, a shadow reared in front of him.

"Yaaagghhhh!" He drew the Bulldog and fired. The report sounded like a cannon, and for a frozen instant, his vision went white with the muzzle flash, then crowded with starbursts.

He heard the rush-crunch of branches as something large bolted by. A deer! Jesus!

But the damage had been done. Ruger would know where he was. Sure enough, he heard the hollow knock of stones behind him. The man was moving along the creek.

As blobs of light continued to writhe before his eyes, Lawrence heard more hollow knocks, then a splash. Ruger had misstepped into the creek. The splash was close—too close. Maybe twenty-five yards from his position.

He looked down, straining to see where the path continued. Somehow, even without his night vision, he recognized a fallen log, and bolted in that direction.

As he ran, his legs felt full of concrete. The roar of rushing blood filled his ears. The constant surge of adrenaline and anticipation of death at every step were wearing him down.

Gotta keep going . . .

He remembered when he'd chased the crackhead who'd

killed Crystal. He'd gone into a tenement stairwell alone, afraid the suspect would escape if he waited for backup. Time stood still as he crept up those concrete stairs, leading with his police Glock. He remembered the darkness, the ammonia smell of urine. Remembered how he'd reached the ninth floor landing to find the crackhead cowering and clutching a twisted ankle. He'd shot the fucker on the spot, too late to save his little girl.

But he wasn't too late to save Cole.

He could do this. He could beat Ruger at his own game. He wouldn't let his friend down.

The weapons shed . . . the weapons shed . . .

The words ran through his mind like a mantra. He focused on the assault rifles, carbines, and semi-autos waiting for him.

Finally, he broke through the trees. The shooting range had never looked so sweet. The weapons shed stood on the far side like an oasis in the desert. Since there'd been nowhere to fasten trip wires on the shooting range, he'd seeded these last hundred yards with VS-50s.

He considered making a stand against Ruger rather than run the gauntlet of buried mines, but dismissed the idea. He'd get one shot—in the dark, with his senses scrambled—and if he missed, he was dead.

Visualizing his mine-laying routine, he sidestepped right, then took a tentative step forward, pressing his foot gently into the duff. So far, so good. He took another step forward, foot crunching pine needles, then sidestepped and moved forward again, terrified that he'd remembered incorrectly and would hear the click of a mine's pressure-sensitive trigger.

That's it, nice and easy, take your time . . .

When he was halfway down the range, a mine exploded a few yards to his left.

With a bright yellow flash, a wave of concussion battered him, pitching him onto his right foot. As dirt rained, he yelped and spun his arms to regain balance.

Looking over his shoulder, he saw Ruger, moonlit like a specter against the dark forest, aiming his silenced pistol. The man had inadvertently triggered the mine with his missed shot.

He saw the pistol barrel flash, and then another mine exploded a few yards ahead of him with a thundering burst. Leaning into the concussion, he held his ground, but howled in pain. Blood oozed from a torn hole in his jeans above the knee. Shrapnel.

Lawrence broke into a run, zigzagging. One wrong move would cost him his legs—or his life. Clenching his teeth against the pain in his thigh, he struggled to keep up the pace. He didn't want to make himself any easier of a target for Ruger.

The shed was only twenty yards away. So close, so fucking close. He kept running as more mines flashed, dirt flew, and smoke billowed.

His mouth felt dry. He kept running, the shed becoming larger and larger, and then he was at the door.

A mine exploded behind him, the flash casting his silhouette against the shed's metal wall. He dug a hand into his pocket, fished out the key.

He heard Ruger bellow in frustration behind him. He jammed the key into the lock, flung open the door, lurched inside, and slammed the door closed behind him.

He stood panting in the absolute darkness of the shed, and wiped the sweat from his face with his sleeve. *Got you now, motherfucker. Get ready to say hello to my little friends.*

He flipped on the shed's light, and blinked in disbelief.

Machine guns, assault rifles, pistols, ammo, Kevlar vests—fucking everything—was gone.

Unloaded by Ruger. No doubt well before the chase had begun.

And then came Ruger's barking laugh through the shed wall.

Lawrence felt the blood drain from his face.

Ruger had planned the whole thing—detonating the mines to spark his imagination, chasing him from the house, corralling him through the forest like some sheep. It had all been one big psyche-out, designed to get him out of the house so there wouldn't be signs of a struggle when Cole returned.

He'd been utterly trumped.

Lawrence drew the Bulldog. The familiarity of its grip gave him small comfort. He popped and checked the cylinder before snapping it closed again.

Final thoughts hit him rapid fire: Ronny dead on a morgue slab. Cole crazy with grief. Muzzle flashes in a tenement stair-well.

Crystal . . .

Turning around, he took a deep breath.

Then he opened the shed door.

Chapter 18

Roberts sat in Tiki-Ti, his favorite bar on Sunset Boulevard, nursing a virgin Never-Say-Die at the bar. It was early to visit the dark watering hole, but he'd hoped the wooden tikis and Day-Glo paint would lighten his mood. They didn't. He was still bothered about having to break his deal with Jennifer. But with Ruger involved in the case, the situation was too dangerous for civilians.

His cell phone rang. "I'm sorry, Jennifer, but I haven't changed my mind."

"I just spoke to David."

A million questions flooded through him, but all he could manage was: "Jesus."

"Ted, I'm really worried. He sounded different."

"Different, how?"

"His voice. He's not the same man."

"He's been through a terrible trauma, Jennifer."

"No, it's deeper than that. He sounded distant. Cold." There was a long pause as she tried to articulate her concern. "He sounded *lost.*"

Lost. A word that Roberts would have never used to describe Cole. Until now, that is. On missions, the man knew his capabilities, and brought out the best in those around him, too. That he could change in such a fundamental way, as Commander Burke had described, chilled him to the core. "Jennifer, I promise I'll do everything I can to find him. Did he say where he was?"

"I asked, but he wouldn't answer."

"That's okay. I can track the location of his cell phone."

"Take me with you."

His heart broke with her plaintive tone. "You know I can't. But I'll call you the moment I find him."

There was another pause. "Tell me everything is going to be alright, Ted. Please."

"He called, Jennifer. That means he wants to be found. I'll be in touch."

Hanging up, he paid his bill then hurried from the bar.

Tracking the cell phone location would mean alerting Whittaker, something he could not do, but he'd said it for Jennifer's peace of mind. In reality, he had to continue on his own. But if Cole was desperate enough to break cover and reach out to Jennifer, he had an idea where the man might be headed.

Cole plodded through darkness toward the cabin, feet dragging through the dirt. He needed rest, but there were only twenty hours before Stanford returned home on Sunday. The producer would have plenty of protection, much more than Brandenburg, and he needed a plan of attack—a quick way in and out of the house, with a minimum of hand-to-hand combat.

Otherwise, the instincts might take on a life of their own.

He lumbered up the porch steps slowly, carefully, legs feeling like rubber. He was exhausted. He tried to conjure Jennifer's face and voice, but couldn't, even though he'd spoken to her just minutes earlier.

So tired . . .

He opened the cabin door, and the light from inside blinded him. Squinting, he put a hand in front of his face to shield his eyes.

"Lawrence!" he rasped. "Break out the morphine! I need a shot pronto!"

No answer. The big man was probably in the weapons shed or bathroom. He stepped inside, and felt a light tug against his right boot.

Tripwire! But the realization came too late.

In his peripheral vision, he saw the claymore planted to his left. He spun toward it so the assault vest would take the brunt . . .

With a roaring flash, the concussion slapped him across the room with the force of a wrecking ball. He slammed into the fireplace, crashed to the ground. Nothing hurt. Not yet. Shock had already set in. He hitched a breath. Another. His eyelids fluttered. *Stay conscious!*

In a daze, he looked down. The front of his assault vest was riddled with ball bearings. The fireplace mantel lay in ruins around him, along with the shredded remains of photographs. The head of Lawrence's daughter was on one piece, her tiny face smiling from beneath glass shards and splintered wood. Across the room was Ronny's cap, having been torn from his head.

Ruger was here. And that meant Lawrence was dead.

Cole crushed his eyes closed as bile flooded his mouth. His SEAL Team. His son. Now his best friend. All lost. Tears flowed down his cheeks . . . he knew that he had to find cover . . .

. . . and then the kitchen door banged open and Ruger was there, wielding an M-16. The two of them looked strikingly similar, Cole realized with horror. The black fatigues, the assault vest, the same look of icy determination.

Ruger's entry galvanized him. He scrambled for the couch as Ruger propped the M-16 on the kitchen counter and opened fire. The hardwood floor behind him exploded in a hail of 7.62 bullets. He made it to the couch and lay on his right side, back pressed against the base, to keep out of Ruger's line-of-sight.

Cursing under his breath, he saw no other recourse but

retreat. He was at too much of a disadvantage and needed to counterattack, on his own terms, for any hope of victory.

The front door or the bedroom hallway. Neither option was good, but at least he could use the easy chair as cover if he headed for the hallway.

Bullets stitched the floor in a hail of splinters, then slammed into the back of the couch. *Thup! Thup! Thup! Thup!*

"You're not getting away this time, Commander!" Ruger yelled.

The instincts surged . . . *choked him . . . smothered him . . . chest tight . . . heart ready to burst . . . eyes and nose filling with icy cold . . .*

The firing stopped. Ruger had to be changing magazines.

Time to move.

Roberts pressed himself to the left of the cabin door as automatic fire shook the house. He heard a muffled voice: "You're not getting away this time, Commander!"

Ruger.

He felt a flash of vindication that was replaced by dread. Who was firing the assault rifle? Ruger was unstable, but Cole could have been pushed to the edge by trauma. Was his friend still sane?

He'd called for back up. Could wait. Should. But do that, and he'd be sacrificing Cole's safety in favor of his own.

Whittaker considered Cole guilty, and would likely shoot him given the slightest provocation—and there was nothing slight about the provocation of automatic gunfire. The only way Cole stood a chance was if he were in custody when the cavalry arrived.

Roberts took a calming breath, ready to take the risk to save Cole's life as Cole had saved his . . .

"Frank!" Roberts yells. "We gotta get out of here! Frank!"

But Ruger keeps firing his AR-23 like a condemned man. He grabs Ruger by the shoulder when he notices a bright flash across deck, and then sees a billowing contrail screaming toward him.

He ducks as the RPG sails overhead and strikes the cabin wall behind him. The explosion slams him down. He tries to stand, but pain shoots through his legs.

He gasps, cordite searing his lungs. Closing his eyes, he knows he has no chance now. He'll be cut down like Moscone and Shannon and Bradley and Akmed.

Somebody grabs his wrist, hoists him over a shoulder. He opens his eyes.

"Hold on, son," Cole says, voice steady, face streaked with tears.

And then the world pinwheels again as Cole turns, sprints for the side of the boat, and jumps.

Listening intently to the assault rifle's blast pattern, Roberts judged that it was an M-16. Six hundred fifty rounds per minute. All he had was a semi-auto .40 Smith and Wesson, and one extra clip.

He stepped in front of the door, preparing to use his shoulder as a ram. He could do this.

The firing stopped. Clip change.

He *had* to do this.

Cole turned when he heard the door crash in.

He saw Roberts, aiming his service pistol with both hands—not at him, but at Ruger, in the kitchen.

Plunging upward from the icy cold, he took a saving breath. Now he had a chance to escape . . . a chance to accomplish the mission!

"Put down the gun, Frank," Roberts ordered. "Do it now."

Cole heard a metallic clatter as Ruger put down the M-16.

"Now both of you walk toward me."

Ruger's boots thumped on hardwood, coming closer, and

then he came into view. Cole saw death in the man's eyes, and the single-minded determination that he'd seen earlier.

"The gang's all here," Ruger growled.

Roberts threw a glance at him. "You too, Dave."

Although he knew Roberts was on his side, there was edge in the command. Understandable. The man didn't know the situation and was playing it safe. He stood.

"Oh my God," Roberts whispered.

"I'm fine."

"We've gotta get you to a hospital."

"I said I'm fine."

Roberts regained his composure, pointed the gun at him and Ruger intermittently. "One of you is going to tell me what the fuck is going on."

Ruger smiled mirthlessly, said nothing.

"Ted, this is between Frank and me."

"Hate to say it, Dave, but you involved me when you fled the scene."

"I never wanted it to come to this."

"Well, it has. A lot of people are looking for you. People who care about you, and people out for your blood." When Roberts switched his focus to Ruger, sadness clouded his expression. "What the hell happened to us?" His tone reminded Cole of a younger Ted Roberts, the idealistic recruit. "Why'd you do it, Frank? He was a kid, an innocent boy, and you burned him with phosphorus."

Phosphorus? Cole blinked. The man had burned his son with that hideous chemical? He clenched his teeth, seeing Ronny's body again in his mind. Melted. Misshapen.

Ruger glared. "You have no fucking idea."

"I can get you the help you need."

"The Navy tried, remember, motherfucker?"

"We're in a different time now. A different place."

Cole glared at Ruger, refusing to break his focus. The man stood at military ease, hands clasped in front of his body, looking at Roberts with indignation. But behind he expression, Cole could see the man's mind working. He was biding time to strike. Roberts seemed blind to it all.

"I can't be helped," Ruger said.

"What happened that night on the boat?"

"Ted, enough," Cole warned, keeping his eyes on Ruger. "You don't know the situation here."

"I know all I need to know, Dave," Roberts said, and then to Ruger, "Tell me what happened, Frank. Not what you told the disciplinary board, but what really happened."

"I did what I had to do."

"Something set you off."

So Roberts had wondered about that, too, Cole thought. But whatever it was didn't matter now. Ruger must pay for his crime.

"Yes," Ruger said, playing Roberts. Obviously playing him.

"Tell me."

Ruger appeared almost coy. "Why should it matter? I saved your life. Those fucking ragheads would have killed us all."

Roberts shook his head. "Cole saved my life. You endangered it."

"You look up to Cole when you have no fucking idea who he is," Ruger scoffed. "Or what he's fucking capable of."

Ruger's strategy became clear. The man was baiting him. But the realization didn't help. Ruger's blatant hypocrisy fueled his cold rage nevertheless. He felt his arms and legs tremble with it.

Roberts, on his soapbox, was oblivious to the war of wills. "I wish it didn't have to be this way. Goddammit, I wish I could go back in time and change everything . . ."

Cole couldn't help but stare at Ruger—his son's killer was standing two feet from him! *Two feet away!*—and Ruger stared back, eyes dancing with condescension.

Crushing his eyes closed, Cole tried to force the instincts away. *Stay in control.* He tried to implore Roberts, but couldn't make his lips move.

Instead, he felt his fingers grope for the K-bar knife at his hip.

"The only way we can heal is if we take responsibility for what we've done," Roberts went on. "With one phone call, I can put a stop to this horrible mess. But first, we have to agree to work together like we used to do. As a Team."

"As a Team, I agree," Ruger said.

Cole opened his eyes, and although Ruger had obviously addressed Roberts, the man was still looking at him. Cole gritted his teeth, straining for control, but he felt his hand grip the padded hilt.

No . . .

And then Ruger smirked, the message clear: I'm right here. I killed your son and I'm right here and there's not a goddamn thing you can do about it.

Motherfucker . . . before Cole could stop himself, he drew the K-bar, lightning quick.

Roberts whirled, pointed the gun at his chest. "Drop it, Dave!"

Behind Roberts, Cole saw Ruger produce a pistol—Lawrence's .44 Police Bulldog—from out of nowhere, and open fire.

Roberts reacted without pause, stepping in front of Cole and taking the bullets meant for Cole's heart.

"No!" Cole cried as Roberts slumped forward into his arms.

And then the cabin shook with a whupping roar as light flooded the windows. Police helicopter, Cole knew. Ruger dropped the empty pistol and bolted out the back door.

He guided Roberts gently to the floor. The man's face was pale. "Goddammit, Ted."

"I owed you."

"This isn't a game!"

"You've gotta go, Dave."

For a moment, he was back inside himself, feeling a connection to Roberts—a connection without the distance and like the one they shared on the Team. "No chance," he said, eyes welling with tears. "I'm staying until the medic arrives."

"The cops have it in for you."

"You can tell the cops different."

"I'm not going to . . ."

"Yes, you are."

Roberts arched his back in pain, and then settled uncomfortably. "I tried to earn the second chance you gave me, Dave."

The man was losing it. Giving up. "Hang in there, son. Let me get you a styrette of morphine." But when he started to rise, Roberts clutched his arm.

"Am I a good man, Dave?"

The question shocked him. If anybody should be asking the question, he should be asking Roberts. He'd failed the Team, his son, his best friend. And now here was Roberts, bleeding out on the floor after taking bullets meant for him, honoring him with the question. "You're a good man, Ted," he whispered. "You always were."

A smile crept across Roberts' face as the strain of having to prove himself—the terrible strain that Cole had seen in him since that night in the Gulf—faded slowly away. And then his head lolled.

Cole sat heavily on the floor. With Roberts gone, the feeling of connection wavered, and the cold took over again, numbing his grief. He did nothing to stop it. He didn't have the energy. Not this time.

The light slid away from the windows, and was replaced with cherry-red flashes. When he looked up, SWAT officers armed with MP5s swarmed through the cabin door. They pulled him to his feet, stripped away his assault vest. A detective wearing a raggedy suit jacket entered after them and leveled a .38 pistol at him.

"David Cole, you're under arrest for the murder of Ronny Cole and Levar Watkins," he said, and then added through clenched teeth, "and for the murder of arson investigator Ted Roberts."

As two EMTs flung him onto a gurney and handcuffed him to the rail, he felt mercifully devoid of hope. Numb. Calm. There was no fighting back now.

Forgive me, son.

And then he closed his eyes and let the cold, suffocating darkness envelop him.

Chapter 19

"Jennifer Shrager? This is Detective Whittaker. I'm the officer in charge of the David Cole case."

"Yes, Detective?" she replied, clutching the cell phone in one hand, and pressing an ice pack to her head with the other. Ruger was gone, thank goodness. Her head still throbbed, but that paled with the pain of disappointment from having let David down.

She knew that Ruger would have searched the house and likely found Lawrence's information anyway. But that didn't make her capitulation easier to handle. She'd been weak when she wanted to be strong for David, it was that simple.

"I need you at the Grossman Burn Center immediately," Whittaker told her. "Be prepared to make a statement."

Her stomach dropped. Was David injured? Dying?

"Of course," she said, struggling to maintain her composure. "But you should contact Ted Roberts as well. He and I have information that might exonerate David Cole."

"Ted Roberts is dead," Whittaker said flatly. "And it looks like David Cole killed him."

Jennifer parked her Saab in the Grossman Burn Center's lot, and then ran toward the ambulance, which was stopped at the patient drop-off curb.

Ted was dead. She couldn't believe it. She'd spoken to him *an hour earlier.* Killed by David? No. Another horrible lie in a string of horrible lies.

Tears blurred her vision as she continued across the parking lot. Her mind virtually swam as she thought about the terrible events of the last few days. They just didn't seem real.

She reached the ambulance as the back doors flew open. A pair of EMTs jumped out and pulled out a gurney. *Ted?*

And then she saw the man lying there and gasped. *David . . .*

This can't be him. Please, God, let it not be him.

Clad in black combat fatigues, the right side of his face and both hands were horribly burned. He looked around wildly as he flailed his arms, causing the handcuffs around his wrists to clank against the rails they were attached to. Whatever pain medication he'd been given in the ambulance was obviously causing delirium.

"David!" she cried as the EMTs whisked him toward the entrance ward. She ran alongside the gurney, repeating his name, when Whittaker appeared suddenly, running next to her. Apparently she'd beaten the police to the hospital because now the lot was swarming with officers.

"Detective, I'm Jennifer Shrager," she told him. "I know who may have killed Ted Roberts."

"So do I," he growled, indicating Cole with a jerk of his chin.

"There's somebody else involved. His name is Frank Ruger. He was in my house—"

"I'll take your statement soon enough," the detective said, clearly believing he had his man.

"Please listen to me, Detective. David isn't responsible!"

"I said I'll get to you!" Whittaker barked.

She wasn't going to be intimidated by the detective. Not after had happened with Ruger. She kept running alongside the gurney as the hospital doors hissed open and Cole was barreled into the trauma room.

A burn surgeon and two nurses wearing blue plastic gowns,

masks and latex gloves rushed over, pulling behind them a small metal table covered with instruments. The EMTs gave the surgeon—Dr. Lisa Moore, according to her nametag—the patient rundown: sixty-five percenter, severely hypermetabolic.

"What's his name?" Moore asked.

"David Cole," Jennifer said.

Whittaker shot her a look that said: *Back off.*

She ignored him as the surgeon leaned close to Cole and caught his gaze.

"David, my name is Lisa," Moore said in a quiet voice. "I'm going to help you, okay?"

Cole didn't respond. He continued to pull at the handcuffs, causing the edged steel to peel away the burned flesh at his wrists.

"For God's sake, take off the handcuffs," Jennifer whispered. "He's not going anywhere."

"No way," Whittaker said. "He's too dangerous."

Moore plucked a syringe from the trauma table and injected Cole in the crook of his right arm. His struggling diminished, but didn't stop.

"Why not knock him out?" Whittaker asked.

Moore said, "We don't know what he's taken on his own for the pain. Give him much more than the EMTs already have, and we might trigger cardiac arrest. Now take off the cuffs, Detective, so I can do my job."

After Whittaker grudgingly did as he was told, Moore cut away Cole's fatigues with surgical scissors, starting at the neck and working her way down. The room fell into silence as the blood-sodden fabric halved to reveal a scrimshaw of infected incisions across his chest. The reek of spoiled flesh filled the room.

"Oh my God," Jennifer gasped. She couldn't believe that the man she loved had been so brutalized and battered. Molten rage filled her. Gary Stanford would pay for doing this. So would Frank Ruger.

"These wounds are sewers," Moore said. "Let's get him to the OR, stat!"

"Cole isn't leaving my sight," Whittaker said.

"Fine. But come in dressed like that and I'll put *you* under the knife," Moore called over her shoulder as she and the nurses pushed the gurney through a pair of swinging double doors.

"I'm going with you," Jennifer told Whittaker.

"The hell you are," the detective replied as two orderlies fetched a gown, mask and latex gloves from a nearby closest and helped him hurry into them.

"Then listen to what I have to say!" She knew that she had to make her case to him now, or risk that her side of the story be swept aside in the momentum of events. An investigator—Ted—had been killed. Whittaker and the other police officers understandably wanted payback for the crime, and right now Cole was the only suspect.

"I'm a little goddamn busy in case you hadn't noticed," he said.

"There's someone else involved."

Whittaker glared at her. "Cole was the only one in the cabin, Ms. Shrager. There are witnesses all around you who can testify to that."

Jennifer shook her head emphatically. "You've got the wrong man. You should be after Frank Ruger!"

Whittaker grabbed her arm and pulled her close. "Now you listen to me," he growled. "I will not have you spouting this horseshit in front of my men. Not when they saw what happened at that cabin." He trembled as he spoke, anger and frustration overriding any discretion that he might have had about withholding details of the scene. "Ted Roberts was shot in the back. *In the back,* do you understand? And the owner of the cabin? We found him decapitated and hanging from a tree. That's not to mention the officer who was attacked this afternoon, Levar Watkins, and Cole's own son. There is only one man responsible, Ms. Shrager. One man with opportunity. One man with cause and in possession of the murder weapon. *One man.* Do I make myself clear?"

Without waiting for a reply, Whittaker tied on a surgical mask and then stormed away into the OR. As Jennifer watched him leave, she realized the detective had spoken with a passion that matched her own. Both of them believed they were right. Neither was about to compromise. Still, she had to try.

She ran to the storage closet and hurried into her own gown, mask and gloves, and then strode toward the OR.

When she reached the double doors, an officer stepped in front of her. "Ma'am, I can't let you—"

"Get away from me," she hissed with such force that the man stepped back. She took advantage of his surprise to rush into the OR, knowing that he couldn't follow without suiting up himself. She'd have a few more valuable seconds to press her case with Whittaker.

She stood outside the bustle of activity at the operating table. Everyone was too intent on the proceedings to notice that she had walked in.

Cole had been lifted from the gurney and was lying on the operating table. Moore, now wearing a plastic visor, hurriedly prepared a surgical tray. On it were standard surgical instruments, as well as specialized instruments that she recognized from a documentary on burn victims that she had directed early in her career: a debridement knife, which looked like a small straight razor, an electric dermatome that was used to shave healthy skin for use as grafts, and a skin stapler to attach those grafts.

Cole's IV tethers had been replaced with a three-channel

jugular catheter that was hooked to banana bags labeled "cyclosporine" and "mupirocin," which she knew were antibiotics. There was also a Bard machine catheter inserted into his urethra to monitor body temperature and to determine whether his body was accepting fluids.

Jennifer watched with horrified fascination as Moore used the debridement knife to incise areas on David's stomach and upper thighs that had swollen from under-the-skin build-up of pus, while the second nurse sopped the foul-smelling runoff with gauze. She turned away when Moore directed the blade toward his swollen testicles.

"How could anybody survive this?" Whittaker asked. "How could this guy be running around?"

Moore didn't slow her pace as she answered. "There's no telling how any particular victim will react to being severely burned. Last month, a man who'd scorched his entire body free-basing cocaine, drove himself in here. How do you explain that? The body can withstand a tremendous amount of abuse. If you have incentive to ignore the pain, you can last longer than you might expect. A lot longer."

Jennifer quietly approached Whittaker so as not to disturb the procedure. When she got close, she caught a glimpse of Cole's eyelids. They fluttered, but he was otherwise still. The anesthesia that Moore had administered had been enough to do the job. She clamped her lips together in a conscious effort not to scream. She couldn't bear seeing David like this . . . it was almost too much to handle . . .

After regaining her composure, she whispered in Whittaker's ear, "Detective, we didn't finish our conversation."

He whirled, scowling, and then followed her away from the table.

"I thought I told you to leave," he hissed.

"And I told you that you don't have all the facts. There is

another man involved in this case. A member of David's SEAL Team named Frank Ruger. For God's sake, the man attacked me in my home."

"Look, I don't know what you're trying to pull on Cole's behalf—"

"You don't have to take my word for it. Ted did the research. Search his home, and I'm sure you'll find notes to corroborate what I'm saying."

"Ms. Shrager, we'll give every possibility its equal due. But from now on, you'll leave this case up to us, understand? If you don't, I'll throw you in jail, so help me."

Although the detective paid lip service to impartiality, Jennifer could see that his expression clearly reinforced what he'd stated before: *We have our man.*

He was about to turn away when she grabbed his shoulder in a last ditch effort. "I know David. He's simply not capable of doing this."

"And I know human nature," Whittaker said. "People are capable of a lot more than you think."

"God!" Dr. Moore cried suddenly.

Jennifer whirled to see Moore drop the debridement knife and rear back. The nurses scurried away in terror as Cole sat upright, his eyes snapping open.

Jennifer blinked, unable to comprehend what she was seeing. How could David have fought through the anesthesia—through the pain of debridement—to regain consciousness?

She watched in horror as he clambered off the operating table, causing the pooled blood in his wounds to spatter the white tiled floor. The catheter lines at his neck and groin pulled taut, stretched, then popped free, sending clear liquids spraying.

In Cole's eyes, she saw the same delirium as before, but now it was tempered with something else . . . a look of cold, relentless determination.

"Christ!" Whittaker shouted.

The cry of alarm brought in several police officers from outside. When they saw Cole, their expressions dropped, all saying the same thing: *You've got to be kidding . . .*

"Somebody grab him!" Whittaker ordered.

Nobody moved, and Jennifer understood why. David's body was a mess of exposed muscle and scorched flesh. How were they supposed to hang on to that? She felt her stomach clench as she tried not to vomit. Dr. Moore and the nurses stayed huddled in a corner, too frightened to get involved.

"David," she said, taking a step toward him, not knowing what she intended to do or say, just knowing that she had to help before the police officers shot him.

He snatched the debridement knife from the surgical tray, holding it so the blade angled against his forearm, military style. Whittaker yanked her back by the arm as every other officer drew his sidearm. Seemingly oblivious to the threat, Cole made his way across the operating room floor with slow lumbering steps as a dozen guns were pointed at him.

"David Cole, get down on the floor!" Whittaker ordered, drawing his own gun.

Cole's only answer was his labored breathing and the wet, slapping sound of his feet against the tile as he staggered toward the OR's double doors, leaving a trail of crimson footprints.

"Shit!" Whittaker spat. "Everybody hold their fucking fire. Don't shoot, I repeat, don't shoot!"

Jennifer knew that Whittaker did not want to kill their only suspect, but she also knew that he couldn't let an armed man leave the room and put the hospital staff at risk. The officers converged on Cole, but kept a respectful distance from the knife he wielded. It was like some slow-speed chase on television . . . Cole couldn't escape, but the police were also powerless to halt his progress.

Jennifer looked around the OR for some way—any way—to slow Cole's advance when she spotted a syringe on the surgical tray. There was a risk that mixing more sedative with the amount he'd already been given could kill him, but she didn't have any choice.

"Cole, this is your final warning!" Whittaker bellowed.

Cole ignored the command and continued to hobble forward, his bloody feet streaking the tiles. He was ten feet from the doors. Jennifer knew that if he reached them, he would be killed.

Before Whittaker could stop her, she snatched the needle from the tray, closed in behind Cole, and then stabbed the needle into his shoulder and jammed down the plunger. Cole screeched in frustration, and the sound pierced her heart.

"I'm sorry, baby," she whispered as she backed away, tears flowing down her cheeks.

He turned to follow her, but tottered on his feet. The knife slipped from his grasp and clattered onto the floor.

When he began to slump, the group of officers rushed forward and caught him, then loaded him back onto the operating table.

"This time we make sure that motherfucker stays under," Whittaker said.

Without argument, Dr. Moore prepared the anesthesia tanks. The detective motioned to an officer, then pointed at Jennifer. "Get her the hell out of here."

Tears still flowing down her cheeks, Jennifer walked out of the room before being escorted and fell into a chair across the hall.

Her thoughts collided in a confused jumble. David should be dead. Something was keeping him alive. Something beyond his love for his son. Something that she couldn't begin to understand. Whatever it was had driven him to get up from the operating table and grab the knife . . .

She moaned in desperate protest as she followed the thought to its logical conclusion: Had the same motivation pushed him to kill Ted?

Placing her head in her hands, she wept as her belief in him—which, up to this moment, had been strong and without question—began to slip away.

Cole woke up swathed in fresh bandages. He tried to raise his arms, couldn't. Looking down, he saw that soft restraints bound him. He was lying on a spongy mattress inside a transparent cylinder that looked like a cross between a test tube and space capsule. Judging by the sealed metal door at his feet, he guessed that the cylinder was vacuum-sealed.

Hyperbaric chamber, he realized as the cobwebs in his head cleared. The chambers were standard issue for Navy SEAL teams in case a diver came up too quickly and had to be treated for the bends. The chamber was used to treat burns, too.

And then memory came flooding back: Ruger killing Roberts and Lawrence at the cabin. The police arresting him. Debridement surgery. His failed escape attempt.

Shook his head in disgust. Delirious with pain drugs and fatigue, his judgment had been severely impaired. Once he'd felt the handcuffs come off, he'd acted rashly. He wouldn't make the same mistake twice.

Jennifer had been there, too, he remembered. He felt a glimmer of warmth for her that was quickly numbed by icy, emotionless resolve. Whatever he'd felt for her in the past was gone.

His feelings for her—and hers for him—had proved to be a liability. She'd been the one who'd ultimately doomed his escape attempt by stabbing him with the syringe. She didn't understand what needed to be done, and he wouldn't allow anybody to stand in his way.

"Good morning, Mr. Cole." The male voice crackled through

a speaker at the top of the chamber.

Cole craned his neck and saw a young, sandy-haired technician sitting at a control panel across the room.

"You may be feeling disoriented from the general anesthesia, but there's nothing to be afraid of. You're in a hyperbaric chamber. The HBO unit will keep the skin we've grafted to your face and body fresh with concentrated doses of oxygen."

The technician was talking to him like he was a civilian who had no idea of his situation or surroundings. He tried to set the man straight, but the grafted skin on his face restricted movement of his jaw. Looking at his reflection in the metal door at his feet, he saw a brown patchwork of mottled, leathery skin grafts on his cheek and throat. Frankenstein had had better days.

"The grafts will help the damaged areas of your body retain fluids and fight infection. We'll keep applying them until your skin cells are healthy enough to grow on their own," the technician continued. "Okay, we're ready to start the procedure. I'm going to take you to three atmospheres absolute."

He watched the technician's hands play over the control panel, then heard a hiss and felt fullness in his ears, like he was descending in an airplane. The moisture saturating the bandages wrapping his chest began to steam, and then he felt pressure, as though a child were sitting on his chest.

As he took slow, measured breaths, he noticed that the sluggishness from the general anesthesia was fading. He closed his eyes, feeling the mask of grafted flesh shift with his facial muscles.

He thought about Ronny.

. . . rigging squibs on the Iraqi guard . . . wearing his blue Dodgers baseball cap . . . lying dead in the charred ruins of the stronghold . . .

The images flipped through his head like photographs in a dossier.

He knew what he had to do. Justice demanded that Stanford and Ruger die.

That was the mission.

When he accomplished this mission, he would move onto the next one. There would always be another mission to accomplish. There would always be other another enemy to vanquish.

The mission is all that matters.

And a new realization . . .

The enemy was everywhere.

Mobility would return soon enough. Until then, he would keep himself in check, and wait.

Jennifer kept vigil in the hallway, not knowing what she should do—or could do—for Cole. But a part deep inside would not let her give up on him. Not yet. Not until she saw him one more time.

"I know you're innocent, David," she whispered to no one, doing everything she could to ignore the fact that her confidence in him had been shaken.

He's experienced multiple traumas, she rationalized, both physical and emotional. Any one of which could drive a person mad. In the operating room, he could have been delirious, acting out.

Biting her lip, she gripped the sides of the chair. She wanted to help him. She did. But she needed reassurance that he was still the man she fell in love with. She felt ashamed at her lack of faith, but there it was. She had to know that she wasn't crazy to believe in him.

She looked up at a wall clock. There wasn't much time. Over objections from Moore, Whittaker planned to transfer Cole to a more secure facility tonight after the hyperbaric treatment. The premature move would put Cole at risk, but after what had happened in the operating room, the detective wasn't taking any chances.

What could she do? She spent the next hour considering options. Could she bribe the officers guarding the room? Put on another gown and mask and pretend she was a doctor? She came up with a few other possibilities, each more ridiculous than the last, when she heard a click and turned to see the sandy-haired technician, who had gone into the hyperbaric room down the hall, reappear from a different door close to where she was sitting. A door that wasn't guarded by police officers.

An adjoining room, she realized. She waited until the technician disappeared around a corner, then slipped through the door into what looked like a storage area for medical files, then continued through another door into the hyperbaric room.

Running to the side of the chamber, she saw Cole inside, his body appearing hazy through the condensation that had formed on the thick glass. He lay on his back with his eyes closed.

She placed her hands on the warm glass, and then brought her lips close to it. She knew there had to be an intercom system within the chamber, but she couldn't afford the time to figure it out. No doubt the technician would return soon to check on his patient.

"David, can you hear me?" she said as loud as she dared without alerting the officers outside.

He remained motionless, his breathing constant and even.

"They plan to move you tonight. After that, I won't be able to see you or talk to you or . . ." her voice choked, ". . . help you."

Still, he didn't move.

"I need a reason to believe in you," she continued. "A sign that the man I fell in love with is still in there somewhere. I need—"

His eyes snapped open. Met hers.

They were bottomless, she realized with horror, taking an involuntary step back. Filled with the icy, emotionless resolve that she'd seen earlier. Utterly devoid of soul or recognition.

And then he lunged up as far as the restraints would allow and slammed his forehead against the glass of the chamber. WHAM!

In that terrifying instant, she felt her confidence in him, and in herself for believing in him, threaten to collapse into ruin.

No, she thought. *I refuse to give up on you. Not after all we've been through.*

She steeled herself and walked back to the chamber. Pressed her hands against the glass.

He slammed his head against the glass again and again—WHAM! WHAM! WHAM! WHAM!—causing it to reverberate under her palm.

She threw a glance at the door, petrified that the officers would rush in at any moment—why they hadn't already, she had no idea—and then looked back down at him.

WHAM! WHAM! He kept slamming his head with such force that the skin graft on his cheek tore away, exposing raw flesh and leaving gory smears on the glass.

Her stomach lurched, not at the gore, but because she realized that her presence was causing him such pain. She said nothing, kept her eyes locked onto his. *I need a sign from you.*

And then for the briefest moment, his eyes cleared.

Was it the light playing through the condensation? Wishful thinking?

She retreated as he continued to slam his head against the glass, and then ran back through the adjoining room before the noise attracted attention.

Upon returning to the hallway, she had to admit that she was so desperate for communication that she would have interpreted anything as a sign. But a feeling tugged at her heart. She'd seen something real, it said. Seen *him.*

What if she was wrong? What if she sacrificed everything to help him and he was, in fact, a murderer?

Despite her fears, she knew deep down that she couldn't risk losing him. She had to believe that he'd communicated with her, as much as he could, in his own way.

She would continue to help, she decided. Her life meant nothing without David. Not anymore.

Thank you for trusting me, baby, she intoned, and then hurried out the front doors.

Chapter 20

Fluorescent lights buzzed, casting a green pall in the windowless room, which was empty except for the bed he was lying on. Isolation ward.

Although his hands and ankles were bound to the mattress with soft restraints, he knew the situation could be worse. He could be in a jail cell. But his fortune wouldn't last. Now that he'd undergone treatment, the police would move him soon. Likely tonight.

His thoughts turned to Jennifer standing over the hyperbaric chamber. She'd hoped to communicate with him. Persuade him to abandon his mission. She was persistent, but misguided, and had allied herself with the wrong side.

The mission was all that mattered. And she—like the police officers and hospital staff—was the enemy.

And then more thoughts of Jennifer emerged . . . sitting next to her on the couch . . . the gentle weight of her head on his shoulder . . . the soft warmth of her hand . . .

As the memories sank away, he searched his mind to eliminate the sentiment that had triggered them, but found nothing. Whatever the source, it had disappeared into the dark morass of his mind, like an evasive guerrilla soldier.

He strained his arms against the restraints, but they were too strong to tear through. He looked down at his hands. They'd been wrapped in bandages to protect new skin grafts.

That was the key to escape, he realized.

He clenched his left hand into a tight fist, then opened it again as wide as he could, hyper-extending the fingers. Feeling the bandage loosen slightly, he repeated the movement several times until the bandage loosened even more. Taking advantage of the give, he wormed his wrist back against the restraint. When the swell of his palm halted the advance, he rotated his wrist back and forth while continuing to pull. The bandage began to bunch, millimeter by millimeter, as he made progress.

When the edge of the restraint was below the first bone in his thumb, he yanked his hand violently back, tearing it free and leaving behind the bandages and a glove of grafted flesh.

He winced as molten pain shot through his bloody hand, but the sensation quickly faded. The instincts continued to mitigate his pain. Good. After freeing his other hand and legs, he sat up, tore a strip from his cloth hospital gown, and wrapped it around his bleeding hand so he wouldn't leave a trail for the police to follow.

Slipping out of bed, he padded quietly to the door. To his surprise it cracked open. He saw a single cop in a chair to his right, reading the latest issue of *Star Power.*

He felt insulted that the police had posted only one man to guard him, but then again, who would expect a bound burn victim to escape?

Looking past the officer, he saw an empty hallway, beckoning like a pipeline to freedom. But first things first. He threw open the door and lunged.

"Hey!" the man yelped, managing to draw his gun, but Cole batted the weapon down the hallway where it slid underneath a scrub hamper. Then he grabbed the officer by the lapels, yanked him off the chair and whisked him into the room, where he whirled the man toward the bed and kicked his feet out from under him. The officer fell, striking his forehead against the metal bed frame with a reverberating WHANG!

After hefting the unconscious body onto the mattress and covering it with the blanket, Cole exited the room. He crept down the hall, bare feet squeaking against the tiles, ready to leap into another room if someone happened by.

He soon reached the receiving area, adjacent to the trauma room. There were several uniformed police officers milling around, including a man wearing a ratty suit jacket that he assumed was the detective in charge. The detective was arguing with the woman who had performed the debridement procedure. He couldn't hear what they were saying, but assumed the conflict was about how and when to move him from the hospital.

Suddenly, the detective whirled with an angry flourish and headed toward the hallway. Cole ducked into a nearby room, searching for another way out of the hospital.

He moved past an empty bed to the window, opened it and climbed out, grateful that the ward occupied the first floor. He loped around the building to the parking lot and hid behind a row of shrubs until foot traffic into and out of the hospital subsided, then sprinted for a blue Toyota pickup parked on the street. After smashing the driver's side window with his elbow, he opened the door and slid behind the wheel.

He knew that Stanford and Ruger wouldn't be alone at Stanford's house. The producer would hire more bodyguards than he had for his nephew—many more who were better armed. The man had too much at stake to leave anything to chance.

It took him only seconds to hotwire the ignition, and then he peeled away, heading home to prepare himself for the coming war.

Jennifer pounded on the cabin door. "Gary! I know you're in there!"

In fact, she didn't know that he was there at all—his BMW wasn't in the driveway, nor were there any lights on that she could see. But given the evidence she'd found in his office, if Gary were hiding out, it would be here. And she knew from countless auditions that it was better to project confidence than undermine your goal with timidity. And she felt anything but timid at the moment.

Anger coursed through her body, driving her like an engine. It wasn't right that a good man like David suffer while a man like Gary Stanford benefit.

She'd seen the look in David's eyes while he was in the hyperbaric chamber, glimpsed the humanity buried there. But his actions were no longer his own, that much was obvious. He was being driven by severe physical, emotional, and psychological trauma.

The closest she'd come to feeling that out of control was when she was a struggling actress. Her blind and overwhelming desire to achieve the Hollywood Dream had felt like an addiction—and had driven her to other addictions, as well. Sex. Drugs. At the time, it felt like she'd be trapped forever in that cycle of self-degradation and degeneration.

And that suffering paled to what David was enduring now.

Goddamn you, Gary!

A direct confrontation with Stanford wasn't the subtlest way to go about getting answers, but she'd passed the point of being subtle a long time ago. Stanford *would* confess to his role in Ronny's murder, or she'd do everything in her power to destroy him. Her career be damned.

She continued to pound on the door when it opened suddenly. Gary was there, his brow furrowed. "Jennifer, what are you doing here? Is everything alright?"

Before she could stop herself, she pushed past him into a small foyer decorated with deer antlers and antique furniture. "I know you had something to do with this!"

Stanford turned to face her, brow still furrowed. "Jennifer—"

"Right now David Cole is in intensive care at the Sherman Oaks Burn Center fighting for his life. You had a hand in putting him there, Gary. I know you did. *I know it.*"

"Jennifer, please, calm down."

She glared at him. "Don't play dumb with me."

"It's true that David and I had our differences, but . . ." Stanford's voice trailed off as he continued to look perplexed. "You said that he's in police custody? Last I heard, he was missing."

"You changed your name after moving here from New York," she said abruptly. She wanted him to know that she was in control, that his past was no longer secret, and that his salvation went through her and only her. "You wanted to hide your connection to your father's crime family, which continues to be active on both coasts."

Stanford slowly closed the door. "Come sit on the couch, Jennifer. Let's talk this through."

His calm demeanor only fueled her anger. Clenching her fists, she took a menacing step forward. "Tell me exactly how you were involved in Ronny Cole's death, or I'll go to the police, so help me."

He reached out and gently gripped her elbow. "Jennifer, please. Let's sit down."

"Don't touch me."

He removed his hand, took a long slow breath. "Yes, I changed my name after moving to Los Angeles, you're absolutely right about that. But it was so I could make a fresh start. I didn't want the stigma of my father's business to hurt my chances here. A fresh start, Jennifer. I know you know what that's like. You told me how you struggled to become a director. That's exactly the type of fresh start I was creating for myself."

She blinked, feeling her anger undermined by his explanation. Yes, she had craved a fresh start after moving to Hollywood from the Midwest. Had Gary simply craved the same thing? *No,* she countered. His explanation was too convenient. He was lying to her. Wasn't he?

She watched his expression shift from confusion to empathy. *Sincere* empathy, it seemed. He reached out and touched her elbow again, and she shrank away. His sincerity did not excuse Steven Huxley's hostility in the office, which was a clear indication of guilt.

"Steven told me about the incident at the office," he said as though reading her mind. "You'll have to excuse him. He gets a little protective at times. Don't worry, your standing with Loki Productions is sound, as is your reputation in this town." He smiled. "Now come have a seat."

She followed him to a brown leather couch. Despite her suspicion, what he said about his background, even Huxley's behavior, seemed logical. She sat on silk cushions as he sat across from her in a matching armchair.

"I don't understand," she said. "Why would you leave town after Ronny Cole's death?"

"I'm not proud of my actions, Jennifer," Stanford said, looking at the floor. "You see, I have a major production deal in the works. I left because I was afraid the tabloids would make a circus out of this whole affair, and ruin what my company worked so hard to achieve." He met her gaze again. "It's not the best way to handle the situation, I admit. I don't usually run from a fight, you of all people know that. If you think talking to the police would help, I'll gladly do it, though I don't know what I could tell them. But please understand that I left town to protect my company and employees from harm."

Not only had he confirmed what she knew about his deal with Devereaux, but his explanation made perfect sense. What had she hoped to gain by coming here? She felt ashamed of her rashness. Had she really expected Stanford to confess because she wanted him to? Yes, it would have made things easier. Gary, guilty. David, innocent. Case closed. As much as she believed that David was innocent, she realized that Stanford could be, too.

Frank Ruger, the man who had attacked her in her apartment, and who had no doubt killed Lawrence Fuchs and Ted Roberts, could be acting on his own. He had motive, opportunity. Cole could have linked Stanford to Ronny's death in his delirium because Stanford was the last person he'd argued with. It was possible.

"David thinks you're responsible for his son's death, Gary," she said.

Stanford rested his elbows on his knees. "How would any of us react after losing a family member and friends? We might lash out at those around us. Fortunately, David has you to help him distinguish fiction from reality. I'm not involved, Jennifer. Neither are you, for that matter, even though there might come a time where he believes that, too. It's important that he knows the truth, not only for our sakes, but for the sake of finding the true perpetrator." He smiled gently, took her hands in his. "David Cole is lucky to have a woman like you on his side. He needs you, and you're gracious enough to be there for him. Now go back to Los Angeles and give him the support he needs."

She nodded, feeling tremendous fatigue. So much had happened in the past few days. It was no wonder that her judgment was flagging.

They stood, and she walked with him toward the door. Although she'd been wrong about Gary Stanford, now she could focus her energies on tracking down Frank Ruger. At least there was that.

"I'm sorry, Gary," she said. "I don't know what else to say."

"There's no need to apologize. You obviously care for David Cole very much."

She was about to reply when a word that Stanford had said suddenly flashed in her head like a neon sign.

Friends.

He'd been talking about how Cole might react after losing a family member and friends. Ronny's death had been covered extensively in the press over the last couple of days, but there was no way he could know that Ted and Lawrence had been killed. The police hadn't released the information to the public. No way, unless . . .

Her stomach turned to ice. She fought to keep from showing a reaction, but he lashed out suddenly and grabbed her wrists. Struggling, she broke free, then bolted for the door when a man appeared out of nowhere and blocked her way.

Frank Ruger.

She felt a burning wave of terror, but didn't let it slow her down. She slammed into Ruger at full speed in an attempt to push him out of the way, but it was like running into a brick wall. He grabbed her shoulders and spun her around roughly so that she faced Stanford.

"You should have left while you had the chance," Stanford said. "I know you used to have a taste for needles. This should bring you back."

Before she could respond, she felt a pinprick in the hollow of her right arm before familiar heat rushed from that spot to flood her body.

Heroin!

She tried to scream, but could only mewl in resignation as the drug short-circuited her vocal cords and turned her muscles to rubber. She wilted to the floor.

"We should waste this bitch," she heard Ruger say as he loomed over her. "She's a fucking liability."

"No," Stanford told him. "Our meeting tonight with Anne Devereaux takes priority. Now contact Ned and tell him to be ready to move after the meeting is over. Cole will have more trouble finding a moving target."

"Too late," Ruger said. "Cole assaulted the soundstage. The men had to take out Ned, as you ordered."

There were a few moments of silence before Stanford continued. Even though her head was swimming, Jennifer could hear the tremor of grief in the producer's voice. "A necessary sacrifice."

"So what about her?"

"After the meeting, we'll find out what she knows and who she's told," Stanford said. "And then we'll take appropriate steps to keep her quiet."

Cole parked the stolen pickup in the driveway of his house, climbed out and went to the front door, which was locked and sealed with yellow police tape. He kicked it in.

He continued into the living room, knowing that Ruger had likely unearthed his buried cache of weapons, even before he walked out into the backyard and saw the hole. It had to have been Ruger. The cops wouldn't have known that SEALs buried extra weapons in case their position was overrun, so they could double back, retrieve the stash, and attack the enemy from behind.

The crate lay open and empty outside the hole. Inside had been an MP-5 SD3 semi-automatic, four fragmentation grenades, a K-bar knife, a packet of flexicuffs, a Kevlar vest and a few bricks of C-4 and Semtex. He had a special state film permit to keep the high explosives on hand in case a movie needed a destructive blast instead of a cosmetic one. And now Ruger had it all.

He entered the shed; it too had been raided. Ruger was trained in high explosives—and it was that training that had caused him to leave behind the wire, squibs, electric matches, blank cartridges, and tins of pyrotechnic powders stored in the explosives locker. No doubt he'd thought the supplies were good only for mock explosions.

"Big mistake, Frank," Cole said. "You just gave me a fighting chance."

He was also thankful that the police hadn't collected this evidence. Lucky, but understandable. The cops had enough to deal with as it was.

Assaulting Stanford's house would not be easy. The man would take defensive measures with Ruger acting as adviser. Cole knew he'd have the element of surprise, but once the attack was underway, he'd need appropriate firepower.

After slipping into a gray jumpsuit that hung on a hook, he collected two hundred blank 7.62-millimeter assault rifle cartridges from the explosives locker and dumped them onto his worktable.

Using bolt cutters, he snipped off the crimped head where the bullet would be in a live round, and poured the black powder into a heaping pile. To this pile he added more tins of black powder from the locker, and then distributed the powder among a dozen one-gallon food storage bags, which he wrapped tight with electrical tape. He used more tape to strap each powder bag to a plastic, half-gallon milk container filled with rubber cement before loading them all into a waterproof sack.

He saw a shotgun mortar propped in a corner. The tube was five feet long and six inches in diameter, similar to the one that he and Ronny had used the day before he was murdered.

His son's face appeared vivid in his memory—smiling, wearing his blue Dodger baseball cap. But Cole felt nothing for him. He regarded the memory objectively, like he was looking at a missing photo of someone else's child. But emotion didn't matter, he knew. Only the mission mattered. Justice dictated that Ruger and Stanford pay for killing his son, and pay they would.

With their lives.

He drained gasoline from a lawnmower into a shallow metal tub, and then mixed in black powder and naphthalene to make the concoction burn hotter and brighter. He rummaged through the storage locker for liquid detergent to act as a gelling agent so that the fireball would stick to a target's surface, but couldn't find any. And then a more appropriate solution occurred to him.

"Bloody perfect," he grunted.

Unwrapping his injured hand, he dipped it into the metal tub. He watched the mixture cloud, knowing that the fat cells in his blood would act as a gelling agent instead. After a few moments, he pulled out his hand, poured the slurry into the mortar tube, and then plugged the end with wadding to keep the mixture in place. The mortar went into a second waterproof sack.

He looked at his hand. Realizing he couldn't allow the dripping blood to give away his location during the attack, he pulled a Zippo from the tool drawer that dated back to his service in the SEALs. On the silver plating was engraved a black skull dancing with red flames, below which read: BURNED IS JUST THE BEGINNING. The Team left lighters like this behind for the enemy to find whenever they torched a target. They were signatures of death. And promises of future reprisal.

Flipping open the Zippo with a click-hiss, he touched the flame to his gasoline soaked hand. He grimaced as tongues of orange flame danced on his palm and fingers and cauterized the wound, but the pain quickly faded. The instincts had done their job again.

After the fire burned itself out, he pulled a long coil of det cord from a hidden drawer in the locker and slipped it over his head and under his left arm like a bandoleer, then loaded a mini air ram, large smoke pot, pack of 9-volt batteries along with several SD-100 squibs and tins of pyrotechnic powder into the second sack. Finally, he slung both sacks over his right shoulder.

A surge of adrenaline washed through him as his muscles strained under the weight. He grinned. It was like being in the SEALs again, humping two hundred pound rucksacks over shitty terrain.

Walking outside, he loaded the sacks into the bed of the pickup, and then returned and checked for one more piece of gear—a couch-sized crate with the word ZODIAC stenciled across it in white letters. Using a dolly, he wheeled the crate outside and loaded it into the truck as well. Satisfied that he had everything to accomplish the mission, he drove away, heading west.

The night was warm. A luminous red moon hung above the ocean, highlighting the crashing waves with its crimson glow.

Using a crowbar, Cole pried open the crate and pulled out a large cube of black rubber, which he let fall into the powdery sand. With a tiny electric pump, he inflated the ten-foot Zodiac raft in mere minutes, the black rubber unfurling like the wings of some giant bat.

As the raft inflated, he clenched his fists in cold anticipation. The men who murdered his son would be brought to justice soon. Nothing could stop him from accomplishing his mission. Nothing.

Pulling a small outboard motor from the crate, he attached it to the back of the raft, and then tossed the waterproof sacks inside. Finally, he pushed the raft into the surf, jumping inside when the water threatened to wash over his boots.

He pressed the motor's ignition switch and it hummed quietly to life. It was insulated, designed for stealth, and barely audible. Revving the motor, he sped toward a building wave, hoping to breach it before it crested. If the wave upended him, the salty ocean would burn his wounds like acid and drown him.

He kept the engine full throttle as the wave grew and grew—and then suddenly, it loomed over him. Crouching as the water slammed down, he screamed in pain as the raft shot into the air and then slapped down beyond the breaker with a shuddering splash. He was still afloat. And alive.

He headed out to sea for a quarter mile until he reached calmer water, and then turned right, parallel to shore, and headed for Stanford's private beach.

Chapter 21

It was dark before Stanford's house came into view. From the street, the place had looked like some ancient temple with its white walls and geometric shapes, but from the water it looked like some crystal cocoon, with every outfacing wall on the first floor made of glass to provide an unobstructed ocean view.

Of course, it also provided him an unobstructed view of who was inside.

Inside, Cole saw several men in matching red waistcoats preparing bottles of wine and trays of food. Their movements were efficient and precise—too precise, Cole thought. Members of a security force, doubling as help. With so many men on the first floor, the second floor would be a softer target. That would be where he breached the house.

Scanning the lit rooms, he saw no sign of Stanford or Ruger, but they had to be inside. Stanford wouldn't miss this meeting when the future of his company depended on the outcome. And Ruger would be tasked with protecting him.

As Cole motored forward, he turned his attention to the private beach, which he judged to be two hundred yards wide and twenty yards deep. Thanks to light spilling from the house, he could distinguish a guard at either end, positioned near rocky outcroppings that walled in the area. There was a third man just outside the house, and no doubt more in sniping hides on the roof. Half a dozen more patrolled a pier that rose five feet from the water, and stretched a quarter mile into the black ocean.

Cole could see the MP5s slung over their shoulders and the soft lines of black life jackets that covered their Kevlar vests.

Their placement denoted Ruger's influence. The man favored a Y-shaped defensive perimeter with flanking forces to reinforce the middle. It would have been a good strategy had the men not clustered at the end of the pier in boredom, leaving the area behind them unmonitored.

Cole cut the motor and paddled to the pier's midpoint, knowing the black raft would blend seamlessly with the dark water. After angling the raft alongside a support piling, he secured the sack filled with the black powder–rubber cement bombs to his belt, then hefted himself underneath the pier. Hanging upside-down from a slick crossbeam, he looked at the water. Slip, and not only would the salt water burn him, but the heavy sack would drag him to the bottom.

Pulling a bomb from the sack, he planted it on the right side where the piling met the thinner upper plank, then planted a complementary charge on the left side and connected them both with a length of det cord from the coil wrapped across his chest.

Finished with the first pair, he spidered forward, letting the det cord unravel behind him like a strand of yellow webbing, and planted two more bombs in the same configuration on the next pilings. Continuing the pattern, he planted the final two bombs ten feet from where the sentries stood talking. As Cole worked, he could see the cherry-red glow of their cigarettes through the weathered planks above him, and hear bits of conversation over the crashing surf.

". . . producers always think somebody's out to get 'em . . ."

". . . easiest fucking money we'll make this year . . ."

After spidering back to the raft, Cole rowed away until he was clear of the blast radius, letting the det cord trail behind from the spool. He then cut the det cord from the spool and attached the end to a blasting cap.

He took in the scene one last time: the glowing glass house, sand sparkling in artificial light, the dark pier, the dark water.

How the calm would change. Abruptly. Violently. Just as his life had.

I love you, David . . .

He felt a spark of warmth as Jennifer's voice echoed softly in his ears, then faded.

"The enemy is everywhere. The mission is all that matters," he said defiantly, and then touched wire to battery.

The first pair of charges exploded with a bone-rattling BOOM! as the black powder and flaming rubber cement incinerated the planks in whitelight fury. The second pair of charges detonated a split second after, and then the third pair—BOOMBOOM—and then every pair to the end, each blast building off the preceding one to create a rolling wall of flaming concussion that careened toward the men at the end of the pier.

Cole watched with icy satisfaction as the orange glow illuminated the expression of terror on their faces. They had barely time to scream when the concussion slapped them from the pier with grand-slam force a moment before it was incinerated.

"Not so easy after all," he whispered to the men as they bobbed unconscious in their lifejackets like harmless bath toys.

Stanford's men were merely pawns, Cole knew. And although he would do his best to spare their lives—the higher the body count, the higher the probability the police could track him after—it didn't mean he would go easy on them.

The beach sentries scrambled like ants around a destroyed nest, helpless to do anything but watch the flaming pier send gouts of black smoke into the night sky . . . just as the Kuwaiti oil fires had done those many years ago when they transformed the Iraqi marshland into a parody of hell.

Cranking the raft motor into high gear, he veered inland toward the north outcropping of rock. He landed thirty yards west of the sentry who was gaping in shock at the flaming pier.

Cole jumped from the raft into ankle-deep water and sloshed ashore, towing the Zodiac behind him. After hiding the raft in the shadows, he pulled a handful of SD-100 charges from the second waterproof sack, which he wrapped together like a bouquet of deadly flowers.

After securing the rubber sack across his back, he wedged himself into a rock crevice and tossed the cluster toward the sentry where it thudded softly in the sand. The sentry turned and spotted the bouquet's bright yellow casing, which attracted him like a trout to a colorful fly. When the man bent down for a closer look, Cole touched the lead wire to the 9-volt battery, which detonated the bouquet with a sharp *flashbang* that knocked the man unconscious.

Cole sprinted toward the prone figure to grab his gun when he noticed movement in his peripheral vision. He whirled and the stock of an M-16 smashed into his jaw, pitching him back into the surf.

Salt water frothed over him, scalding the raw flesh beneath the skin grafts. "Ggghhhgggghhgggg!"

He struggled to his feet when another wave clipped him at the knees, and he went down again. He flailed, body awash in burning agony.

Hands gripped his collar. The sentry who jumped him.

The man lifted him from the water and tossed him onto the sand. He landed hard on his stomach, the sand scraping away the graft on his cheek.

Get up . . .

Rolling onto his back, he saw through swollen eyelids the sentry scrabbling across the sand toward him. He tried to move, but his muscles were still paralyzed. The crippling pain was fading, but nowhere near fast enough.

Blood pounding in his ears, he prepared for another beating—when he realized the sound wasn't his pulse at all, but the rotor blades of a helicopter.

Jennifer saw murky, muted shapes. Felt cold hard tile against the back of her head and shoulder blades. Dim light was coming from somewhere.

She mewled weakly as memory returned.

Gary. Frank Ruger. The pin-prick in her right shoulder, and the warm, terrible rush . . .

She sat up slowly, head spinning. And then she vomited, thick and warm, down the front of her blouse.

Moaning, she struggled to her knees, and grabbed the doorknob. Locked. She ran her hand along the wall adjacent to the door, felt a light switch, flipped it on.

A bathroom. From the *I Married a Zombie* production poster on the wall, she knew she was at Gary's beach house.

I've got to contact Detective Whittaker . . . tell him about Gary . . .

Grabbing the edge of the sink, she pulled herself up. She looked at herself in the mirror. The woman who stared back was pallid with deep bags under her eyes.

She recognized the face from thirteen years ago, when she was desperate. Vulnerable.

No.

She wasn't that person anymore. No matter what Gary did to her, she would never become that person again. She wouldn't let the man win.

Her stomach lurched again, and then she felt a deep itch, like her skin was crawling with bugs.

A shower . . . she thought, craving the cleansing spray. Lurching to the tub, she grasped the hot and cold knobs and cranked them full blast. The roar of water pounded into her head. She tore open her blouse, yanked her bra over her head, wormed out of her jeans.

I can handle this, she told herself, but felt a pang of fear. If Gary injected her one more time . . .

She didn't know how she would react. What she might become.

When she stepped into the tub, her foot slipped and she slammed down on one knee.

"Ow!" she cried in frustration. How could she hope to escape when she couldn't even climb into a bathtub?

For a few minutes, she tried to kick-start her rubbery muscles, but remained frozen—left hand pressed against the tiled wall, right hand gripping the rounded edge of the tub not far from her right leg which was still planted on the dry bath mat, left knee tickled by the rising tepid water from the booming spigot.

Finally, she managed to crawl inside the tub, and exhaled in relief as the cascading water chased away the itching sensation. She pressed her temple against the warm tile wall and heard voices from the next room.

"We could be under attack from a competing syndicate," Stanford said. "Are you certain it's Cole?"

"I'm sure."

"What the hell do you plan to do about it?"

David is here? she thought as the men moved out of earshot. But how? It didn't matter. All that mattered was that she help him somehow.

Pressing her back against the wall of the tub for leverage, she tried to stand, but after a few inches of progress, slid back down.

Helplessness flooded her. She took several deep breaths to marshal her strength, tried again to stand, and failed . . .

Cole looked up and saw a large black helicopter buzzing the

house. Blackhawk. Flying so low he could feel the vibration caused by the main rotor, and read the white ATF emblazoned across its belly. The roof sentries fired at the helicopter as it streaked toward the pier, but their bullets sparked off its armored hull.

The cops weren't reinforcements. They were just another enemy that stood between him and his goal.

He refocused on the sentry who had attacked him. The distraction gave Cole the opening he needed.

He kicked the sentry hard in the crotch, and when the man dropped to his knees, Cole sat up and slammed a fist into his face. With a moan, the sentry slumped over and lay still.

Panting, Cole clambered to his feet. *Storm the beach. Enter the house. Neutralize anyone who gets in your way.*

As the roof sentries were busy firing at the retreating Blackhawk, he bolted up the beach toward another armed sentry who stood underneath a second floor balcony. Instead of dodging side-to-side as the man might expect, he went straight for him. The man was so shocked by the direct assault that he panicked and fired wide. Closing, Cole jammed the fingertips of his right hand into the man's throat, which dropped him to the sand, gagging.

Through the first-floor windows, Cole saw Stanford's men take defensive positions at the foot of the staircase and near the kitchen, which meant he could flank them if he breached the house on the second floor.

He pulled the stuntman's mini air ram from the waterproof sack, placed it below the balcony, then primed it. The balcony was high, about twenty feet up. It would be a close jump. Fastening the bag to his back, he retreated to the water line to get a running start when he heard a growing roar behind him.

Turning, he saw the Blackhawk hurtling back toward the beach as the searchlight on its nose roved the sand. The Blackhawk crew had already given its equivalent of a warning shot—the flyby. This time, the M-60 door gunner would target anything that moved.

With the helicopter coming in fast, Cole scurried toward the air ram. When his boots hit the platform, his body weight triggered the hydraulics, and with a sharp hiss, he was flung fifteen feet through the air—high enough to grab hold of the frieze along the bottom of the balcony.

In his peripheral vision, he saw the searchlight slide toward him—and then it turned his world blazing white. The sound of the rotor blades behind him was deafening. He scrambled over the ledge just as bullets shrieked around him, punching fist-size chunks from the balcony and filling the air with concrete dust. The barrage stopped when the helicopter flew by slowly, presumably to check if he was dead.

Pulling the remainder of the det cord from around his chest, Cole tossed it with all his strength at the passing helicopter while holding onto one end—and when the unraveling coil looped over the tail boom, he ignited it. The high-grain cord severed the boom as neatly as a hot knife through butter, causing the helicopter to immediately spiral out of control and disappear from view behind a nearby hill, where it crashed with a loud roar, but no explosion. The crew had gotten lucky.

You'll have to do better than that to kill me.

Sliding open the balcony door, Cole moved through a guest bedroom and continued down an L-shaped hallway. At the end was the master bedroom, which meant the staircase was around the corner.

Suddenly, the thunderous flyby of a second Blackhawk shook the house and triggered a flurry of activity from the master bedroom. *So not everyone was downstairs,* he thought, counting four voices.

Pulling the portable mortar from the sack, he propped the

barrel on his hip and strode into the room. Three of the four men were peering through the floor-to-ceiling windows, trying to monitor the helicopter, as a fourth man spoke into a cell phone to his ear. When the men saw him enter, they drew their M-16s. But he had them dead-to-rights.

"Don't forget to drop and roll," he growled, and pressed the mortar's ignition switch. With a hollow cough, the barrel spewed a six-foot tongue of flame that fried their weapons and ignited their waistcoats.

Screaming, the men at the window crashed through the glass and fell two stories to the sand below. If they took his advice and rolled, they'd extinguish the flames before sustaining serious burns. The fourth man dropped the cell phone and flailed at his waistcoat as the flames leaped around his face.

Cole dropped the expended mortar, shoved the man onto the bed, and wrapped him in a white comforter to smother the flames. When Cole unwrapped the man a moment later, his body was smoking, but he was alive, and smiled gratefully. Cole answered with a jab across the jaw, which knocked the man out. He then stripped off the man's bulletproof vest and put it on.

"What . . . hell is going . . . up there? Give . . . a report!" The broken voice came from the man's dropped cell phone.

Stanford.

Face twisting into a snarl, Cole snatched up the phone and said into it, "You're dead."

He heard a click as the line disconnected. The broken reception could mean only one thing: Stanford was in the downstairs screening room.

Cole bolted from the room to the staircase where he was met with automatic gunfire. Bullets stitched up the wall, sent plaster dust flying. Opening the rubber sack, he pulled out a smoke pot, lit the fuse with the SEAL Zippo, and flung it at the bottom stair where it burst with a *fwoosh!* The men retreated as white smoke filled the staircase.

Using the smoke as cover, Cole sprinted down the stairs—and discovered that not all of the men had retreated. One remained, waiting for him in a firing position across the living room.

The man's M-16 flashed. Cole felt hammer blows on his bulletproof vest, which pitched him crashing back through a plate glass window and onto a wooden deck. Without missing a beat, he rolled from the deck into the sand as bullets splintered the wood behind him.

Lying on his stomach, Cole looked up as the second Blackhawk whupped past overhead.

From one enemy to another . . .

As the helicopter veered around, he spotted a crawlspace grille about twenty yards away and scrambled toward it on all fours. Reaching it, he wedged his fingers under the metal lip to pop it free when a white-haired man wearing a charcoal suit leaped from the smoky deck and rushed at him.

Cole recognized him from Stanford's office: Steven Huxley.

The man drew a silver-plated Desert Eagle Magnum, and fired. The .44 bullet kicked up a fountain of sand an inch from his left knee.

Gun's too heavy for him, he thought. *But that won't matter if he gets closer.*

He couldn't strike at Huxley without leaving himself open to attack from the Blackhawk—and if he entered the tight crawlspace to evade the Blackhawk, he'd be a sitting duck for Huxley.

He tried again to pop the grille as the Blackhawk's approaching rotor blade thunder grew to a deafening roar. He managed to get a couple of fingers under the grille when another bullet stung his left forearm, tearing the sleeve and drawing blood.

He clenched his teeth in grim determination, and yanked

harder on the grille . . . felt the metal bend back . . .

And then wash from the Blackhawk's rotor blade whipped the sand into an opaque cloud around him. The swirling grit would spoil Huxley's aim, but it also meant the Blackhawk door gunner was close enough to draw a bead.

Squinting against the flying sand, he kept pulling on the grille. He looked over his shoulder and saw the hazy silhouette of Huxley approaching, waving the mammoth pistol, and then he looked up and saw the Blackhawk's door gunner swinging the M-60 around at him . . .

Suddenly, the grille popped free.

He dove headfirst into the crawlspace as Huxley reached his position and the Blackhawk opened fire. The patch of sand erupted in chaotic fury.

When the fusillade stopped, all that was left of Huxley was a heap of gore and tattered charcoal suit.

The man deserved his fate, Cole thought. He'd aided and abetted the enemy.

As the helicopter thundered away, he pulled the Zippo from his pocket and flipped it open, releasing its tiny flame.

He could see his ruined features reflected in the Zippo's silver plating and wrapped around the flaming skull design and ominous engraving: BURNED IS JUST THE BEGINNING.

When he found Stanford and Ruger, he would burn them, yes. And much, much more.

Worming deeper into the crawlspace, Cole searched for a second grille that might lead into the house. The sputtering flame caused shadows to dance. He turned corner after corner, until the crawlspace widened like the center of a labyrinth.

Suddenly, he realized that the advantage was no longer his, and never really had been.

Adhered to the supports were blocks of C-4 and Semtex . . . the supply that Ruger had stolen from his shed. They were primed with pencil-sized detonators and booby-trapped to prevent disarming.

Ruger was in control here. And if the man sensed the battle was lost, Cole knew he would obliterate the house.

Chapter 22

Otto Anderson stood a quarter mile away from Stanford's house in a makeshift staging area. Fellow ATF agents wearing military camouflage and bulletproof vests scurried through the scrub around him, hurriedly erecting tents, unloading equipment from pickup trucks, and seeking firing positions.

"Blackhawk One, this is Anderson!" he said into a walkie-talkie. "Please respond!"

"Blackhawk One, here," came the crackling reply. "We went down, but everyone is okay."

"Roger, Blackhawk One. Glad you're safe. Hunker down until this plays out."

He breathed a sigh of relief for the crew, but hoped they hadn't taken out David Cole in the firefight. He'd heard over the agency band that Cole had killed Roberts, but dismissed it. From what Roberts had said about Cole, the man wasn't capable of murder—much less murdering his son and now his friend. As such, Cole deserved his day in court. It was that simple.

I'll do what I can to bring your friend in safely, Ted, he thought. Mobilizing this ATF response team was the least he could do to honor Roberts' memory. If Whittaker had a problem with that, he could go to hell.

As if on cue, half a dozen radio cars and a blue SWAT van sped into the staging area. Police officers leaped from the vehicles, Whittaker among them.

"Agent Anderson!" Whittaker barked as he approached. "I thought I restricted you to your fucking desk!"

"With respect, sir, you should be thanking me for the back-up."

Whittaker surveyed the scene. The distant *pop-pop-pop* of gunfire proved the point, and kept the detective at bay. For now. "Why haven't you assaulted the house?"

"Not enough intel," Anderson said.

"They're firing on us, agent. How much more intel do you need?"

"They might have hostages."

"All the more reason. Break out the CS gas and prepare to assault."

Anderson looked back at the house. Muzzle flashes were everywhere. "Sir, I'm sure you know CS gas is highly flammable."

"Cole and his ilk are special forces, agent, and no doubt resilient to the civilian tear gas used by my department. Now do as I say before I relieve you of your job along with your command."

Whittaker was being more than an asshole. He was being reckless. Any open flame—even a candle—could ignite the CS gas and set the house ablaze, which would endanger bad guys and good guys alike.

"Detective, I strongly suggest you reconsider."

Whittaker stormed past him and relayed the order to a young agent nearby who ran off and returned a few moments later with two other agents who wielded tear-gas guns. They stood side-by-side, aiming the weapons at the house.

"I'll deal with you after we're done here," Whittaker told Anderson, and then ordered the agents to fire.

Cole punched out another grille and crawled into the kitchen.

Standing, he crept to the door leading to the living room, cracked it open and was immediately greeted by a rush of gray smoke and heat. Everything, it seemed, was burning. The air was thick with smoke, but not yet so thick that breathing was impossible. Flame licked Stanford's paintings, sculptures, film posters, and furniture—everything scorching, burning, melting.

The smoke pot should not have ignited the carpet, he thought. And then he smelled a chemical tinge. CS gas. That would explain it. The ATF must have fired it when he was in the crawlspace.

He had fifteen minutes, maybe twenty, to find Stanford and Ruger before the house was consumed.

Covering his mouth with his hand, he pushed through the door when he saw a pair of guards trying to fight the fire with cooking pots filled with water. They turned, spotted him.

"There he is!" one yelled, and opened fire with his M-16.

Cole dived back into the kitchen as bullets punched into the doorframe. He wedged a chair under the doorknob, but knew it wouldn't keep the guards out for long. Opening the sack, he saw only wire, pyrotechnic powders, and squibs. *Shit.* Yanking open drawer after drawer, he looked for a knife—even a fork would do—but there were none. The guards had removed any potential weapon in case the house was breached.

Pounding on the door drew his attention. A moment later, the door exploded with gunfire that sprayed the kitchen with splinters.

An idea flashed. He grabbed a two-gallon pot from the kitchen island, threw it into the sink, and turned on the taps full force. By the time the door was blown off its hinges, the pot was half-filled with warm water.

He reached into the sack for a tin of calcium turnings—a powder used to mimic boiling water when there was no heat source—and poured it into the water, causing the water to bubble wildly. Dry, the powder was harmless. But wet, it burned like acid.

As the guards charged into the kitchen, he splashed them with the roiling water. They fell onto their knees, screaming, as their hands, assault rifles and bulletproof vests sizzled. Vaulting over them, Cole sprinted into the living room, which was almost fully engulfed in flame.

When he felt the heat on his face, he stopped, unable to move. Memories hit him rapid-fire . . . *the special effects mortar exploding . . . Ronny screaming as the concussion tore him away . . . the raging fire and scorching heat . . . burning . . . Dad, help me! . . . please, Dad, help me! . . .*

And then as quickly as the thoughts came, they faded away. Numbed by the cold inside him.

"The mission is all that matters," he hissed, and then leaped into the flames.

Heat blasted him from all direction, singeing the grafts on his hands and face. He couldn't see through the churning flames, but icy determination drove him forward . . . *the mission is all that matters . . . the mission . . .* He kept running as the swirling flames cooked his body, the smoke choked the air from his lungs. He coughed violently and hitched breaths, but kept moving, and then finally broke through.

Flesh and jumpsuit smoking, he leaped down the staircase and kicked open the screening room door. Inside were a dozen rows of red, theater-style seats.

And behind them, underneath the projection booth window, was Gary Stanford.

They locked eyes, and then the producer leveled an M-16 and opened fire. Cole zigzagged forward, evading the thundering fusillade of bullets as it punched holes through seats and sent yellow foam flying. As he closed the distance, Stanford became frantic, firing haphazardly until the clip ran dry with a *click!* He hurried to load another clip.

Leaping over the last row of seats, Cole kicked Stanford in the knee, driving him down, and snatched the M-16 from his grasp.

He felt cold surge through his body, filling his heart with icy rage. Stanford had ordered the death of his son. And now he would die.

"Please don't hurt me," Stanford croaked.

He'd hoped to relish Stanford's fear as Ruger had relished Ronny's, but the producer looked up at him calmly. Almost with confidence.

"I'll give you anything . . . anything you want," the bastard said like he was reciting lines from a script.

Cole spun. Too late.

Ruger was beside him, growling like an animal—like he had been on the Iraqi boat before opening fire. The man's fist slammed into his cheek with such force that it cracked the bone underneath the socket. Cole pitched into the wall of the projection booth, and slid to the floor.

"This time you'll stay down for good," Ruger told him.

"Agent Anderson, some lady wants to talk to the man in charge."

Anderson looked up at the young agent from the driver's seat of his ATF Chrysler. The young agent had seen Whittaker commandeer the ATF unit, but here he was, addressing him like he was boss.

"Over there," the young agent said, pointing to a white limousine that had pulled behind an ATF van parked in the street.

"I'll take care of it," Anderson told the agent. "And thanks for your support."

"No problem, sir."

Anderson walked to the limo. Apparently in the commotion,

no one had set up a roadblock. When he got close, the rear window hummed open to reveal an attractive blonde. He recognized her from a billboard on Sunset Boulevard, but couldn't remember her name.

"This is a law enforcement emergency, ma'am," he said, stooping so they were eye-to-eye. "I'm going to have to ask you to leave this area immediately."

"My name is Anne Devereaux," the woman said. Next to her sat a pair of anxious-looking men in dark suits. "I'm on my way to Gary Stanford's house for a dinner party."

"I'm sorry, Ms. Devereaux, but—"

"I'm an *actress,*" she interrupted. "I have a very important meeting with Gary Stanford, *the producer.*"

He gritted his teeth in an effort to stay polite. "Ma'am, please, it's for your own safety. My men would be happy to escort you back to the main road."

Devereaux looked past him. "Oh, I understand what's happening now. You tell Gary Stanford that I refuse to work with a producer who tries to curry favor with cheap-looking stunts. The deal is off. My people will be in touch tomorrow morning." And with that, the window hummed closed and the limo pulled away.

Anderson turned. Black smoke poured from every window in the house as a wave of ATF and SWAT agents swarmed toward it.

Hardly a stunt, he thought grimly. The CS gas had ignited, and Whittaker had ordered a full breach, no doubt ordering the officers to take no chances, and shoot anything that moved.

Gearing up, he followed them in.

Ruger grabbed Cole by the jumpsuit, yanked him to his feet, and then delivered a savage right cross that sent him reeling.

The blow reawakened Cole's burns, and it felt like every

exposed nerve was being scraped by razor wire. He managed to scrabble onto his hands and knees when Ruger pulled him up again, and launched a vicious upper cut to his solar plexus while holding him in place. Breath exploded from his lungs in a searing rush as his vision went white, then red. Ruger punched him again, letting him go this time. He reeled across the room and slammed ass-backward into a seat.

Cole felt the strength drain from his body as barbs of pain tore at his arms, legs and chest. He was tired. So tired. Barely able to move much less save himself from Ruger's next attack.

"David!" The clotted voice behind him sounded muted, far away. "David!"

With massive effort, he turned and saw Jennifer in the doorway of an adjoining bathroom. She was wet and loosely wrapped in a towel. Her face contorted with pain, and it was obvious she could barely move, herself. But still, she stood with the same dignity that he'd always seen in her.

Even though the cold morass still gripped him, he felt a warm smile cross his face.

"Jennifer . . ." Just saying her name felt so good.

"I'm right here, baby," she rasped. "I'm right here and always will be . . . don't give up . . . I'm right here . . ."

As she looked deep into his eyes, Cole felt a hidden part of himself—a far recess of his soul that had remained untouched by the cold—suddenly spark to life. It wasn't much, not enough to save him completely, but it was enough to rev his muscles with energy.

"Jennifer . . ."

Struggling to hold onto the warmth as it flickered inside him, Cole stood as Ruger drew a K-bar knife and drove it toward his sternum. Cole sidestepped the strike, and chopped Ruger's wrist with the edge of his hand, causing him to drop the blade.

They grabbed each other's throats, but Ruger's grip was

stronger. Cole gagged, finally letting go to claw the man's hands and face.

As Cole's vision fogged, he looked up and met Ruger's gaze. There, deep within the black of Ruger's pupils, he found reflected visions of the botched mission in Iraq . . .

. . . Ruger firing, suicidal . . . Akmed and Moscone and Shannon getting wasted . . .

The scene repeated in grisly detail as Ruger's hands tightened around his throat. Cole tried to breathe, growled like an animal . . .

Like Ruger had done that night a lifetime ago when the Team went down.

Like he'd done himself two nights ago when he found Ronny's melted, mutilated corpse. Mutilated and sliced to ribbons.

Just as Bradley's body had been at the hands of the Iraqi soldiers.

Oh Jesus.

The truth hit Cole with the force of a sledgehammer as he realized for the first time that Ruger's loss of control wasn't a result of carelessness or recklessness—but of witnessing Bradley's torture. The man had opened fire after being overwhelmed by the horrible spectacle . . . after watching Bradley get cut to pieces, after hearing Bradley's screams of pain for mercy.

That night, Ruger hadn't acted, but *reacted.*

Just as Cole had been doing this whole time on Ronny's behalf.

Cole opened his mouth in silent scream as anger and pity and horror collided. After the botched mission that night, he'd been so consumed by rage and frustration at losing his SEAL Team that he'd refused to listen to Ruger's explanation, wanting a scapegoat. If only he'd listened. If only he'd made sure that Ruger got the help he needed, instead of doing everything he could to lock him away.

Ruger was responsible for the terrible things he'd done, for the choices he'd made, but Cole could have done more to help him years ago. It might have made a difference.

With this understanding—this final truth—Cole felt the part of himself that Jennifer had sparked to life suddenly catch fire and spread, filling his body, and with it a message: *enough.* There had been enough pain, enough death.

Enough.

The cycle of violence had to end here. Now.

ENOUGH.

Cole felt like he'd broken the surface after being trapped underneath a flood of grief and guilt and denial for an eternity. He moved his arms, his legs. Control. He had it again. For good, this time. He could feel it deep in his soul. The instincts were gone. The mission was finally, forever over.

"Frank," he rasped.

He felt the pressure on his throat ease. Ruger kept his hands in place, but there was a connection between them.

You understand, Ruger's expression told him. *Finally, you understand.*

And then Cole discerned something else in Ruger's eyes . . . the man's own understanding . . . of who he'd become . . . of what he'd done since . . . of his own responsibility and terrible remorse . . .

And then suddenly, Cole saw Stanford behind Ruger, at the foot of the staircase, aiming an M-16.

"Frank!" Cole yelled.

Ruger turned, and then covered Cole's body with his own as Stanford opened fire. Ruger convulsed before slumping to the floor beside him.

As Stanford fled upstairs, Ruger slumped to the floor beside Cole. Cole struggled to his knees and looked down at his old teammate—the man had been struck by a bullet in the back of the neck above the Kevlar vest. His arms and legs twitched as the carpet around him turned red.

First Roberts, then Ruger. Each had taken bullets meant for him. Roberts to prove to himself that he was worthy. And now Ruger, clearly as some sort of penance.

"Jesus, Frank," Cole said, not knowing what to say or how to begin.

The man opened his mouth, but was unable to speak past the blood that filled it. Instead, he moved his lips to shape the words: *I'm sorry . . . I'm sorry.*

The sentiment knifed into Cole's soul. His vision blurred as tears began to cascade down his cheeks. He could not forgive Ruger for all he'd done. But with those words, the past between them could finally be just that.

Ruger pulled a detonator from his assault vest. A red digital timer counted down from five minutes, signified when the C4 and Semtex would demolish the house. No doubt Stanford had engaged the countdown sequence from a second detonator.

"You still with me, baby?" Cole called over his shoulder to Jennifer.

"Don't worry about me." Her voice was still clotted, but strong with resolve. He wished he had half her strength and integrity.

"Let's get you out of here, Frank," Cole said.

Ruger shook his head.

"We don't have time to argue. Take my hand."

Ruger shook his head again.

Cole looked at Ruger steadily. "We can put this shit behind us if we try."

He searched Ruger's eyes for any indication that the man would change his mind—and for a moment it felt like old times, with him placing unequivocal trust in Ruger and Ruger always coming through. But he saw no indication the man wanted anything else.

A riot of sound erupted from overhead: splintering wood followed by bursts of automatic fire, screams, multiple yells of "All clear!" and finally footsteps thundering down the stairs. An ATF agent and two SWAT officers burst through the door, leveling their MP5s at them.

"Whatever you've got, drop it!" the ATF agent yelled at Ruger.

"The entire house is wired," Cole told him. "Come closer, and he may set it off."

The men stopped immediately. And then the ATF agent took a careful step forward. "Are you David Cole?"

"Yes."

"I'm Agent Otto Anderson. Ted Roberts was a friend of mine, too. I'm here to get you out of here. For him."

Cole felt a pang of grief at the mention of his friend. "Not yet, agent. I have unfinished business."

Anderson shook his head. "I can't let you stay."

"I need you to trust me like Ted trusted me."

Anderson paused, looked at him evenly. "Ted believed in you, and died for that belief. Does his leap of faith justify mine?"

Cole could hear a tremor in the man's voice. Obviously, the two had been close. "Only you can answer that."

Anderson paused another moment, then nodded. "You sure you know what you're doing?"

"I'm sure."

"Then make sure you're close behind." Anderson looked past him to Jennifer. "Ma'am, you're coming with us."

"Touch me, and you'll be sorry you ever came down here," she growled.

Cole wanted Jennifer away and safe, but knew it would be pointless to insist that she leave. Besides, she'd earned the right to stay. The least he could do was honor her wish. "You'd better get your men out of the house, agent," Cole said.

Anderson threw one last look at Jennifer, and then turned and led the officers back up the stairs.

Cole looked back down at Ruger. In reply, the man held up his right hand in a victory sign: *Two minutes till show time.*

Cole turned to leave when a wave of grief for everyone he'd lost washed over him suddenly. Without the instincts to dull the terrible feeling, it threatened to consume him. He slumped to his knees as the terrible gravity smothered his heart, his soul.

He knew that Stanford needed to be brought to justice, but the pain was too much. Simply too much. He could end it right here, with Ruger . . .

Suddenly, Jennifer was by his side, as though she'd read his mind. "I know what you're thinking," she said. "But this isn't the way. We can get through this together. Trust me. Please."

She touched his face, and it galvanized him. He thought he'd lost her when he'd lost himself, but now here she was with him, warm and loving and alive. He gently pushed her back so he could look into her brimming green eyes that were so full of love. They could survive this together. Only together.

He glanced back at Ruger. His expression said, *GO!*

The command detonator read a minute-thirty.

Cole grabbed Jennifer around the waist. She'd just saved his life, as she had throughout this ordeal. He never wanted to stop touching her. She was his life now. His home.

"Can you make it up the stairs?" he asked.

She wavered on her feet. "I can try."

Not wanting to take the chance, he hoisted her in his arms.

Jennifer pressed her face into his neck. She didn't seem to care that the flesh there was burned and bloody. "Don't let me go."

"Not for the world," he said.

★ ★ ★ ★ ★

Ruger struggled to stay conscious. He could smell how much blood he'd lost, could feel the sodden carpet beneath him, as he counted the remaining time in his head.

So the enemy hadn't been around him, but within him. An enemy he'd allowed inside for reasons he didn't understand, and now, was too well entrenched to expel.

Voice bubbling with blood, he said, "I'm sorry." He said it for Cole, for Ronny, for himself.

God, I'm so sorry . . .

He'd always wondered how it'd feel to give his life for something more than the abstract notions of God and country.

A second later, he found out.

Stanford watched the explosion from beyond the burning remains of the pier in what he assumed was Cole's raft.

He sat rocking in the waves, outboard motor idling softly, unable to tear his gaze away from the massive cumulonimbus that sent the flaming remains of his house high into the night sky.

I'm sorry for failing you, father, he thought, but refused to allow the night's events to dampen his resolve. His enemies were dead. He was not. That was the most important thing. If he'd learned anything, it was that there were always opportunities. He made a mental note to write the script of this ordeal as soon as things blew over.

As he continued to stare at the flaming shoreline, he noticed a tiny figure waving to him from the beach. A woman with long brown hair, seemingly wrapped in a towel.

Jennifer?

He blinked, but the hallucination remained. There she was. Still waving.

He considered going back. She was a living witness, after all. But then he remembered that the evidence pointed overwhelmingly at Cole. Even if the police questioned him, it would be his word against hers: An ex-actress with heroin in her blood.

He was safe.

And then he saw a figure approach from behind her. Staggering, seemingly disoriented from the blast, but very much alive.

"No," he growled, feeling a surge of rage. Cole. The bastard who had taken everything from him had survived. Every breath the man took was an insult to him and to his father. He gripped the engine handle, seething.

Cole continued to stagger forward. When he got close to Jennifer, she turned. Stanford expected a joyful reunion—but instead Jennifer snatched the holstered pistol from his hip, stepped back, and opened fire.

Stanford watched in stunned disbelief as Cole convulsed with each bullet strike, then collapsed.

"Yes!" he cried out in triumph, and knew immediately what had happened. Jennifer was a junkie, and junkies never changed. She was proving that she'd do anything for her next rush.

And then he felt even greater joy as Cole crawled away from her.

Stanford steered the raft toward shore. This was an opportunity he could not pass up. Cole was wounded, but conscious. He would deliver the killing shot himself.

Landing on the beach, he pulled the raft behind him with a towrope. He would need the raft to escape the police.

Jennifer fell to her knees in front of him, the towel wrapped around her matted with sand, the pistol hanging loosely from her right hand.

"Good girl," he said, snatching the pistol from her.

He strode after Cole who was crawling away in a pathetic attempt to escape. He circled around so that his feet blocked the man's path, then aimed the pistol down at his head. "Look at me."

Cole froze, kept his head down.

"I said look at me," he repeated, cocking the hammer with his thumb.

Hearing the click, Cole did as he was told. Stanford noted with satisfaction that the man's eyes were wide and desperate.

"You cost me everything," he said. "But I want you to know something before I kill you."

Cole shook his head, obviously trying to deny this horrible turn of events.

He said, "I want you to know that I ordered the hit on your son. I also want you to know that Jennifer is mine now."

Cole closed his eyes, the defeat apparently too much to handle. Then he opened his eyes and slowly, painfully raised an arm to gesture Stanford close.

Keeping the pistol trained, Stanford stepped forward. He was seconds from ending the man's life, so why shouldn't he relish his pitiful pleas?

"I want you to know something, too," Cole rasped weakly.

"What's that?"

Cole climbed strongly to his feet. "These are squibs, asshole," he said, pointing to his chest.

Stanford blinked and fired the pistol. But Cole remained standing.

"And that," Cole said, pointing at the pistol, "is loaded with blanks."

Stanford looked down incredulously at the pistol, and when he looked up, Cole punched him hard in the jaw.

After Stanford collapsed, Cole stripped off the man's suit jacket, rushed to Jennifer's side and covered her with it. They sat on the sand quietly holding each other for several minutes.

When the house fire died down, he hugged Jennifer more tightly, knowing that he might not get another chance for some time as they sorted things out with the police.

Presently, they were surrounded by SWAT officers.

"David Cole, you're under arrest," said an unkempt man in a shaggy blazer. Cole recognized him from Lawrence's cabin.

Cole held out his hands. "I'm all yours, Detective."

A SWAT officer slapped handcuffs around his wrists and led him up the beach. For the first time, he noticed the scale of response: ATF agents, police, ambulances, fire trucks. News vans as well were starting to appear.

As they passed the smoldering ruins of Stanford's house, Agent Anderson approached. "I see you got out okay."

"Thanks for what you did back there."

Anderson nodded. "Like I said, Ted Roberts was a good friend. I'll do what I can to make sure you get a fair trial."

"Thanks again."

The agent walked away as SWAT officers continued to escort Cole up the beach.

"I still can't believe that worked against Stanford," Jennifer said, arms around his waist.

"Fifteen years and I've never blown a cue," he said smiling.

She titled her head back. "Is that so?"

"Yep."

"And what about me?"

He kissed her forehead. "You gave the performance of a lifetime."

Epilogue
ONE YEAR LATER

Cole sat in the upper deck of Dodger Stadium with a small box of popcorn in his right hand and Ronny's baseball cap clutched in his left, watching the infield grooming machine drive slowly around the diamond as a family of squirrels frolicked in left field.

It was late afternoon on Saturday, Ronny's favorite time to watch the stadium gardeners do their work. Ronny had liked the way the low sun glimmered off the scoreboard to give the stadium an unearthly, almost heavenly feel, like Jackie Robinson himself could emerge from the dugout.

Jennifer arrived, as he'd known she would, and sat in the seat to his left. When he "disappeared" there were only a few places he liked to go. Lately, Dodger Stadium topped the list.

"Who's winning?" she asked.

"I think the squirrels are about to rally."

"How was therapy today?"

"Okay. Yours?"

"Great, actually."

"That's wonderful, babe," he said, and held the box of popcorn out to her, still acutely aware of the purple scar tissue on his fingers. Sometimes, he didn't know how Jennifer could stomach his full-body disfigurement, but apparently, she didn't seem to mind. In fact, whenever he brought it up, she winked and told him to stop being shallow.

He watched her delicate fingers dip inside the popcorn box

and retrieve a few pieces. "What's wrong?" she asked, placing them into her mouth.

Taking back the box, he kept quiet. How many times could he voice the same concerns before she grew tired of him? She hadn't so far—she was wonderful, loving and understanding beyond his expectations. But that didn't mean it would last. His psychological scars were deep, and would take a long time to heal. This when she'd made extraordinary progress in fighting the addiction reawakened by the heroin Stanford had given her. He was thrilled for her, but feared that she would consider his slower progress as a failure.

"Hey, just because we're living together doesn't mean you get to ignore me like we're married," she teased, pressing an elbow into his ribs.

He smiled wanly. "I feel . . ." he began, and then stopped, afraid to continue.

"You feel like you got away with something," she said, finishing for him.

He nodded. She always knew what was bothering him, he thought. It was a quality he found attractive and, frankly, a little frightening. Around her, there was no hiding from himself. Not anymore.

"Well, the Grand Jury thought otherwise," she said. "They compared your ordeal to being at war because you *were* at war, David. Even Whittaker concurred after reviewing the evidence Ted and I dug up on Gary Stanford."

"A lot of good that does Ronny," he whispered. "Or Ted and Lawrence."

"Ted was committed to proving your innocence. Nothing could have kept him from doing otherwise. Lawrence risked his life because he loved you. And Ronny . . ." She placed a warm hand on his leg. "You couldn't have known how Ruger would react to his circumstances."

Cole placed a piece of popcorn on his tongue, felt it break apart into tasteless bits. "I was looking for a scapegoat," he said.

"You felt regret about your command *after* you reported Ruger. I'm not putting words into your mouth, David. I'm simply repeating what you've told me, and what the Navy tribunal concluded."

"I helped make him what he was."

"Just as you're taking responsibility for your choices, you have to let him take responsibilities for his. It was his choice to descend as far as he did."

He looked at her. "You missed your calling as a lawyer."

"Ronny would be proud of the progress you've made," she continued. "I know I am."

He glanced at the field again. The grooming machine and the squirrels were gone, replaced by lengthening shadows as the sun continued to set. "I still feel guilty as hell."

"I know. I felt guilty for disappointing people when I was younger, and for disappointing myself. Heck, I feel guilty now for how easy it was for Stanford to put me back into rehab. Though I have to admit, his life sentence is making it a bit easier to deal with."

"Finally getting what he deserved," he said flatly.

"And you deserve a fresh start, which is what you're earning every day."

He turned back to her. "Thanks again for believing in me."

She kissed him lightly on the lips, and then nestled close. With the simple contact, any lingering doubts he had about his progress melted away. Jennifer had helped him reconnect with himself, which in turn had freed him to connect with her—and Ronny's memory—in the best way he knew how.

One day, he would feel ready to give up Ronny's baseball cap, but not today. And for now, that was good enough.

ABOUT THE AUTHOR

After fourteen years as an award-winning copywriter in the advertising industry, **Marc Paoletti** decided to focus his energy and passion on fiction (of a different sort, anyway).

Scorch draws upon his experiences as a special effects pyrotechnician in Hollywood, when he blew things up for movies, television shows, and commercials.

His short fiction, which has been published alongside such authors as Stephen King, Irvine Welsh, and Jeffrey Ford, has been listed in Ellen Datlow's *The Year's Best Fantasy and Horror* and nominated for a Pushcart Prize.

His next two novels, installments of a dark fantasy series co-authored with Patricia Rosemoor, are forthcoming from Random House/Del Rey.

A native of Detroit, Paoletti now lives in Chicago.